Elusive Passion

"Miss Varya," he began in his smooth, deep voice, "I am honored to make your acquaintance." He took her offered hand and raised it to his mouth. The feel of his lips through the thin silk of her gloves was shamefully erotic.

"Thank you, my lord. It is indeed a pleasure to meet you."

"Lord Wynter's been honored to meet many ladies in this room, haven't you, Miles?" Lord James announced jocularly, elbowing the marquess in the side.

Lord Wynter winced as if the jab hurt more than it should have.

"Do you require any assistance, my lord?" she asked, her brow furrowed with concern.

Too late she realized her folly and knew that he had realized it as well. By repeating almost word for word the taunt they had exchanged two nights before in the alley, she had revealed herself to him.

She watched, frozen as his eyes hardened into cold green-gold stones and his face stiffened. His mouth flattened into a hard, grim line and he caught her outstretched hand in a grip that made her flinch.

"Yes, madam," he ground out between clenched teeth, "I believe I do."

Other AVON ROMANCES

A Belated Bride *by Karen Hawkins*
Highland Rogues: The Fraser Bride *by Lois Greiman*
His Forbidden Kiss *by Margaret Moore*
The Lawman's Surrender *by Debra Mullins*
Master of Desire *by Kinley MacGregor*
Outlaw's Bride *by Maureen McKade*
The Wicked One *by Danelle Harmon*

Coming Soon

The MacKenzies: Zach *by Ana Leigh*
The Warrior's Damsel *by Denise Hampton*

And Don't Miss These
ROMANTIC TREASURES
from Avon Books

A Breath of Scandal *by Connie Mason*
Never Marry a Cowboy *by Lorraine Heath*
One Man's Love: Book One of
The Highland Lords
by Karen Ranney

KATHRYN SMITH

Elusive Passion

AVON BOOKS
An Imprint of HarperCollinsPublishers

AVON BOOKS
An Imprint of HarperCollins*Publishers*
10 East 53rd Street
New York, New York 10022-5299

To my grandmother, Mildred Berry, whose constant devotion to the memory of my grandfather taught me what true love really is.

To my family and friends, most notably Nicola, Lisa, Danelle, and the ladies of *The Romance Journal*. Without your support, I never would have been able to do this.

And finally to my husband, Steve, for being a better man than any I could invent, and for giving me the freedom to pursue my dream. To simply say, "I love you" would be an understatement.

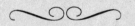

Chapter 1

London, England
June 1814

Come on, you bastards. Come and get me.

Miles Edward Thomas Christian, Marquess of Wynter, staggered down the dimly lit London street not far from Covent Garden. Weaving exaggeratedly and reeking of gin, he gave the appearance of being hopelessly drunk.

Which he wasn't. Not in the slightest.

His keen eyes watched the shadows, searching out his quarry. He clutched an open bottle of cheap gin in one hand and sang at the top of his lungs in a rusty baritone.

"Oh, it's the size of her melons that be the cause of

1

me swellin' and makin' me trousers so tight. But the face that I seen, shriveled me beannnnnn . . ."

As his deep voice cracked on the sour high note, a dog howled in the distance.

". . . I wish I had snuffed out the light!"

They were there, watching him. He could feel their canine stares; he could almost feel their breath on his neck. The ennui he had been suffering from these past few months faded before his mounting anticipation.

He had been studying these thieves—he knew their tastes and their habits. At this moment, they were no doubt salivating over the plumpness of his purse, which did not contain the gold they hoped for. Instead it contained thin slices of tin—worthless, but it made a lovely tinkling sound as he walked.

Miles's prey were also cautious. Taking down a gentleman of his stature would be a daunting task, but not if the thieves believed he was as jug-bitten as he pretended to be.

C'mon, boys. Easy pickings.

Miles searched his memory for another naughty lyric. He knew only a handful, and he hoped his repertoire didn't deplete itself before he lured the thieves out of their hiding spot.

He tightened his grip on the bottle and began to sway. He knew from experience that fallen quarry was practically irresistible to predators. With any luck, the thieves would pounce and he would turn their own trap against them.

He could see them. Edging out of the shadows like rats, the thieves were moving in for the attack. Adrenaline coursed through Miles's veins. Soon, he would have them.

Toppling into a forgotten cart that smelled suspiciously of manure, he fell heavily onto the rotting boards, smashing his hip on what felt like a pair of boots.

"Oof!" The contents of the bottle emptied all over his clothing and splattered on his face. He sputtered as gin splashed up his nose. Damnation, but the Home Office had better appreciate what he was doing!

He sneezed.

"Bloody hell!" yelled a voice near his ear.

Miles winced as the boots he had landed on—or rather, the person *wearing* the boots—kicked him in the small of his back. Above his own muffled curse he heard muted voices and the sounds of several pairs of feet running away. The thieves were escaping!

He tried to give chase, but he was hopelessly entangled with the drunk, who smelled as if he had just fallen off a fish wagon.

"Get yer own bloody cart!" the man shoving at him yelled, his breath strong enough to knock out a bull.

"Apologies, my good man." Miles groaned, wiping his wet face with his sleeve as he hauled himself to his feet. His back and left side hurt like the devil, and it would only be worse in the morning.

He passed the half-empty bottle to the man. "Here. You need this more than I."

"Thankee, guv'nor." The drunk accepted the bottle as if it were made of gold.

Grimacing, Miles bowed stiffly. "Think nothing of it." Slowly, he turned to walk away.

Wouldn't Carny have a good laugh at this. Despite their friendship, Carny liked nothing better than to see Miles make a fool of himself. He claimed it made up for the fact that Miles was better-looking, was taller, and possessed a richer title. Miles was more inclined to believe that his friend just liked to have a chuckle at his expense.

One thing Carny wouldn't find amusing, however, was that the thieves had eluded capture once again. The gang was becoming increasingly brazen with their attacks, even violent. They had to be stopped before someone was seriously injured or, God forbid, killed.

Miles had agreed to be used as a decoy for the thieves after one of his friends had fallen victim to their greed. Fitz was still laid up from the attack, his left leg having been seriously sprained. The regent was terrified the violence would worsen, and Miles felt compelled by his position as a peer of the realm to help put a stop to it. Since returning from the war, Miles had plunged himself into a dangerous variety of new duties.

Wiping at the gin-soaked wool of his coat with a damp glove, Miles wrinkled his nose and started off in the direction of his hired coach. He smelled like a drunken sheep with poor sanitary habits.

He hadn't even made it three steps when he heard it—the subtle click of a pistol being cocked. Ever so slowly, he turned his head to glance over his right shoulder.

Standing in the pale light from a street lamp was a slender, hooded figure clad entirely in black.

Now what? "Who the bloody hell are you?" he demanded. Could this night possibly get any worse?

A pistol glinted in the flickering light and Miles caught his breath, cursing himself silently for not having the good sense to reach for his own weapon first.

"I shall assume that you weren't so stupid as to wander into this part of London without a weapon," the stranger said silkily. "I would ask that you hand it over to me now, my lord."

Whoever his attacker was, it wasn't an Englishman. However, it was definitely a female who held the pistol trained at his throat.

"Listen, love . . ." He paused, turning to fully face her. Her features were completely concealed by the mask she wore, giving not even a hint of the face beneath. "If it's blunt you're after, you've come to the wrong man. I haven't a shilling on me."

"It's not your money I'm interested in, Lord Wynter," she replied, leveling the gun at his broad chest.

Even in the murky glow of the streetlights, Miles could see the barrel tremble. Whoever she was, she obviously didn't make a habit of accosting men at gunpoint. The knowledge did little to ease the feeling of dread that rendered him frozen at her use of his title.

"I'm impressed." He willed himself to remain outwardly calm. "You know my name."

"It was not meant to flatter you."

Miles listened carefully. Her English was good, almost perfect, but the hint of an accent lent her words a sensual quality. He had never heard anything quite like it. She was also nervous—her voice vibrated with tension.

"So what are you going to do, pet? Shoot me in cold blood and make it look like a robbery?" He smirked. "Or are you going to force yourself upon me and rob me of my virtue?" Perhaps he might distract her enough to wrestle the weapon from her. He would have to be careful—there was nothing more dangerous than a woman holding a pistol.

She held out her hand. "I believe someone has already relieved you of that particular burden, my lord. No doubt close to twenty years ago."

He raised a brow, reluctantly placing the pistol he had taken from his coat pocket in her open palm. "Twenty years ago would have put me at thirteen. As much as I appreciate your confidence in my prowess, I'm afraid you've overestimated my allure." He tried his most charming smile. "Suffice to say it has been less than twenty years but more than fifteen."

He took a step closer, his long stride narrowing the distance between them. "Why don't you tell me what this is all about?"

She stiffened and tightened her grip on the pistol. Miles's mouth flattened into a grim line. Evidently charm and flirtation was not the tack to take with her.

"I'll tell you in my own good time, my lord," she replied coldly, gesturing with the barrel. "Start walking."

He did as he was told, convinced that he'd not get to the bottom of this bizarre turn of events unless he did. He could probably overpower her if he tried, but one of them might end up injured or dead, and *another* woman's blood on his hands was a stain his conscience couldn't take.

One thing was certain—no one was going to rescue him. The only time a crowd gathered in Covent Garden was to watch something that didn't require their involvement. At the first sign of danger those interested parties would fade back into shadows or peer around dusty curtains, careful not to get too close. Careful not to get involved unless a profit was to be made.

The coachman he had hired had orders to send for Carny should Miles not return at the agreed time, but God only knew if Miles would even still be in the vicinity, let alone alive by the time his friend came looking for him.

"Where are we going?" he asked over his shoulder as she pressed the pistol against his back, nudging him through an alley.

"You'll find out soon enough."

Miles raised his eyebrows but kept walking. He heard her stumble behind him and smiled. No doubt it was hard for his captor to see through her hood, especially when his immense height deprived her of what light the street lamps provided.

"Do you require some assistance?" he inquired, his voice mockingly polite.

A sharp jabbing pain struck him in the tender flesh behind his left knee, buckling it. He stumbled to the ground with a surprised grunt, hissing in pain as the already smarting joint struck the hard cobblestones.

"Do *you* require some assistance?"

Miles cursed as he hauled himself to his feet. He could hear the laughter in her throaty voice. She had kicked him!

Barely able to contain his fury, he whirled around to face her, a muscle ticking in his jaw.

"You're on very thin ice, my lady," he warned before allowing a sneer to curve his lips. "I've never struck a woman before, but you're making the prospect very tempting."

He was rewarded with a sharp gasp. He couldn't see her eyes through the narrow slits in the shapeless hood, but he didn't doubt that they snapped with indignation.

She raised the pistol to his chest. The barrel wasn't trembling anymore.

"I could kill you right now and no one would ever know who did it." Hostility deepened her voice, adding a huskiness that Miles found both threatening and sensual.

He leaned down so that his nose was almost touching her hood. "What makes you think I've got anything to live for?" he snarled, his question surprising even himself.

He didn't give her a chance to reply, but spun on his heel and resumed walking. His anger and disgust with himself quickened his pace, and his long legs quickly ate up the length of the alley despite the pain in his knee.

She practically had to run to keep up.

"Stop!"

He continued walking as though he hadn't heard her.

"I said stop!"

Miles slowed, bracing himself for the shot. It struck him hard between his shoulder blades, knocking the breath from him. He stumbled, gasping and tripping as something bounced to the ground by his feet. In the dim lamplight he could see it as it skidded to a stop not even a foot away from him. She hadn't shot him. She had hit him with a large chunk of cobblestone!

Cursing yet again, he straightened and turned on her, only to find himself staring down the barrel of the pistol.

"Very soon," he promised her from between clenched teeth, "I'm going to take that pistol and your mask and then I'm going to see you jailed. But not before I have a chance to strangle you with my bare hands!" He watched with satisfaction as the muzzle wavered slightly.

She pushed out to her left with her free hand. A door swung open with a belligerent squeak. How she had ever seen it he didn't know, for it was indistinguishable from the rest of the building in the dark.

"We're here." She handed him a lamp and tinderbox that she pulled out of her cloak. "Light this."

Cursing both her and her forebears under his breath, Miles lit the lamp and held it up.

The gun poked him between the shoulder blades.

He grumbled all the way up the narrow stairs. He could just barely squeeze his shoulders between the confines of the walls that lined either side.

Her shuffling footsteps were hesitant behind him, and he knew that she was next to blind in this darkness. Her hood and the wall of his body eliminated much of the lamplight. Surely she must realize that he sensed her difficulty, but she said nothing.

She was a proud one, he thought. Too proud. Did

she not understand how easy it would be for him to overpower her when she could not see? He could turn on her now, and she wouldn't be able to defend herself.

But if he turned on her now, he would never know what this was all about. For all he knew, she could be a French spy sent to coerce information from him. Just because they dumped Napoleon on Elba didn't mean he would stay there. He would discover what this woman was up to, and then he would deal with her.

But he wasn't about to underestimate her.

He didn't understand why he did it, but he lifted the lamp higher so that some of its brilliance slipped over his shoulder and lit her path.

The footsteps behind him halted, and he turned.

She was staring at him, her head tilted to one side, the pistol aimed cavalierly at his belly. For one dry-mouthed moment Miles thought she intended to shoot him there on the narrow steps.

"Thank you."

He nodded curtly, turned his back on her, and resumed climbing.

The stairs led to a small, sparsely furnished room. The floors were dirty and the air smelled of mildew. At least two rats scurried into darkened corners and stared with hostile, beady eyes as the yellow glow of the lamp trespassed into their territory. The amount of dust and cobwebs was proof that no one had been there in quite some time. The thought wasn't exactly comforting.

"Move over there," she commanded, gesturing to the rickety table in the far corner.

He did as he was told, wondering if she had deliberately contrived to put as much distance as possible between him and the only route of escape.

He seated himself on one of the dilapidated chairs by the table. One leg was shorter than the other three, and the chair lurched as he shifted his weight. Perspiring under the growing heat of his frustration, Miles leaned back, forcing himself to sit as still as possible.

"Have we come to the part in this Drury Lane tragedy where you tell me just what the devil you want?" he asked softly with just a touch of malice. His lips curved slightly, without humor. It was a smile meant to intimidate.

"Yes," she admitted, standing over him as if she enjoyed being able to stare down at him. She seemed completely unperturbed by his demeanor. Miles's ire rose another notch. Pistol or no, he was sorely tempted to teach this arrogant witch a lesson.

"And?"

"I want to know why you killed Isabella Mancini."

Miles jerked upright so quickly that the wobbly chair almost bucked him to the floor.

Surely he had heard her wrong. She couldn't have said what he thought. Hot disbelief coursed like grains of sand through his veins.

"Bella's dead?" There had to be some kind of mistake. His stomach churned. *Please, let there be some kind of mistake.*

A picture flashed through his mind—a beautiful, olive-hued face with wide, obsidian eyes and a lush mouth parted in laughter. Ebony hair spread out across a down-filled pillow, reflecting glimmers of blue in the morning sun. Nobody had been more alive than Bella.

"She was your mistress," his captor jeered. "Do you expect me to believe you knew nothing of her death? That you didn't kill her in a fit of jealousy?"

Miles stared at his abductor as if she had suddenly announced she was the queen of Persia. The tears in his eyes quickly evaporated.

"You think *I* killed Bella?"

"Are you telling me you didn't?"

He nodded vigorously. "You're bloody right that's what I'm telling you. I haven't seen Bella in months. We parted company a few weeks before she was to leave for Paris. I assure you she was very much alive the last time I saw her." *And heartbroken*. He had seen to that.

"You parted on bad terms," she reminded him coldly.

Again he nodded—absently, taken with his thoughts of Bella. The smile that curved his lips was a sad one.

"Yes." He shook off his melancholy and raised his gaze to his captor. His jaw was set. "What happened between Bella and me is none of your damned business."

"You killed her!" There was conviction and anger in the cry.

"She wanted more than I was prepared to give!" he shouted in return, then, lowering his voice, "We said goodbye and I left her there. A sad but wealthy woman."

She snorted. "A likely story. She did not need your money. She wasn't one of your English whores!"

He glanced at her and felt himself turning almost sympathetic. Crazy or no, this woman had obviously cared about Bella. "No, she wasn't." He looked away. "Bella didn't want my money. She wanted my heart."

Another snort.

He smiled bitterly. He doubted she would ever believe his innocence. Whether she intended to kill him remained to be seen.

"I couldn't give it to her and she would settle for nothing less." He shrugged. "It's true that our ... arrangement came to an unsatisfactory end, but I was not the injured party. I didn't enjoy hurting Bella emotionally. I certainly wouldn't harm her physically. Whether you believe me is your business."

He was lost in thought for a moment, remembering the sad smile Bella had given him when she had asked him to leave. She had her pride, she had told him.

His captor started when he turned his attention back to her, as if she too had been lost in her own thoughts.

"How did Bella die?"

"She was strangled," she replied quietly.

Icy fingers gripped his heart as his mind conjured up an image of Bella's lifeless body. He almost could see her laid out on the bed in a lacy peignoir, her sightless eyes wide with terror. He shivered.

"When?"

"The twenty-sixth of April."

At least he had an alibi. "I was in the country with a friend on the twenty-sixth. Ask anyone, they'll tell you."

"You lie." The pistol was pointed right at his head.

He shrugged, trying to appear nonchalant even as his heart twisted in his chest. "It's true. Unless you want to kill an innocent man, I suggest you ask. Everyone can tell you that both the Earl of Carnover and I missed a party in honor of Lord Byron due to our visit to my country seat." It was a lie. He'd rather cut out his own tongue than spend an evening with Byron and his cronies.

He had raised a doubt in her mind; he could tell by the hesitancy of her movements. Her grip on the pistol loosened.

Miles acted swiftly, knocking the chair to the dirty floor as he leaped at her. She cried out and raised the gun. His fingers wrapped around her wrist, effectively cutting off the circulation to her hand and causing her grip to slip.

She swore at him, a torrent of words that would have made a sailor swoon coming out in her crisp, perfect English as she fought him wildly. Even as her stiff fingers lost their hold on the weapon, her long, strong limbs twisted and struck out at him, searching for an area of vulnerability.

"Stop squirming, damn you!" He tightened his grip on her wrist. Most men would have yielded to him by now, but this woman fought as though her life depended on it.

"I'm . . . not . . . going . . . to hurt you!" he cried as he fought to subdue her. "I just want some answers!"

"Let go of me!" She struck out at his head and shoulders with her free arm, her booted feet kicking mercilessly at his shins.

"Damn it, stop that!" He grabbed her other wrist and bent both arms behind her back, securing them with one hand. He set the pistol on the table with his other. As she continued to struggle like a trapped animal, he took advantage of her lack of concentration. With one deft movement, he forced her legs apart and stepped between them. She could no longer kick, and her balance was thrown off.

Still she thrashed against him. He could only imagine the pain she was causing to her shoulders as she fought to pull free of his grasp. He tightened his hold, pulling her backward so that she was bent over the table and unable to squirm so much.

Unfortunately, it made him all too aware of the soft, feminine warmth now pressed tightly against his groin and of the full breasts straining against her twisted cloak.

"Now," he said somewhat breathlessly. "Why don't you explain yourself?"

Her eyes blazed through the slits in the hood. It was too dark to discern their color, but not their brilliance. "Go to hell."

Miles grinned. If nothing else, she certainly had spunk. "That doesn't answer my question. Let's try another—who are you?"

She muttered something under her breath.

"How do you ever expect to offend me if I don't understand what you are saying?"

Her body was rigid with anger, but other than that, it felt good beneath his. She was softer, rounder than he had first thought. Obviously there was *one* part of his body that *didn't* take exception to the fact that she had kidnapped him at gunpoint.

"I said," she growled, "that you are a son of a bitch and that you should have intercourse with yourself!"

Miles was so stunned by her admission that he couldn't help the laughter that bubbled up in his throat. If it weren't for the grim reality that had brought her here, this entire situation would be one of the most exhilarating things that had ever happened to him. He had to be going mad.

"This has gone on long enough," he announced. "I'm going to take your hood off now and put an end to this charade. Then I expect you to tell me how you came to suspect me of killing Bella."

It was a mistake to announce his intention to her. He thought he had her secure until he saw her head coming at him alarmingly fast. With little time for him to react, the top of her head connected with his forehead with all the force of a large hammer. Dazed, he released her, staggering back a step.

Damn.

She reached for the gun, wrapping her fingers around it just seconds before he caught her.

"I've had just about enough of you!" He grappled for the weapon. "Stop this nonsense!" With that, he seized her wrist and slammed it down on the table with enough violence to force her fingers open. She hissed.

The pistol clattered to the floor, discharging its ball into the opposite wall with a loud *crack*. His abductor shrieked as several trinkets and an old plate tumbled off shelves to smash on the floor.

The crashing cacophony was over in seconds, but it rang in Miles's ears, transporting him back to Spain and all the death and destruction he had seen there. More than half a year had passed since a wound had sent him home. Napoleon had abdicated that spring, but Miles still woke up some mornings with the smell of gunpowder and decaying flesh in his nostrils.

Varya was suddenly aware that the marquess's attention was elsewhere. The throbbing pain in her forehead and arm dulled with the realization that she was free! Her limbs trembled with adrenaline. She could practically smell the fear emanating from her own body—her sweat was ripe with it.

Frantically, she looked around for some other weapon, but the hood made it impossible to see anywhere other than directly in front of her. And standing directly in front of her, finally fully highlighted by the glow of the lamp, was the most incredible-looking man she had ever seen—despite the fact that he smelled like a dockside tavern and his catlike eyes were strangely glazed.

A pallor had fallen over his chiseled features, as though he had just seen a ghost . . . Yes, Bella's ghost! Until she discovered otherwise, she had to remember that he was her prime suspect—her only suspect. She had no business finding him attractive. He very well could be the man who had murdered her dearest—her only—friend.

She forced herself to remember Bella, not only in life but also in death. Varya had been the one to find her body, and she would not let Miles Christian's pretty face make her forget!

He had her backed against the table; its sharp edge cut into her legs through the worn fabric of her breeches. The only route of escape was past him, which meant she would have to overpower him in order to flee. She could not risk his unmasking her. If he did, all her years of freedom would be for naught.

She brought her knee up, thrusting it into his groin with enough force to stun him without doing serious injury. She felt the air rush out of him as he sagged against her, his handsome face white with pain and shock. She shoved him away as though he were contagious, and he stumbled to the floor.

Panting, she scooped up the pistol with her good hand—she had lost feeling in the other—and fled toward the door. Her heart was hammering wildly in her chest. If he caught her this time, there was no telling what he might do to her. Her fear was almost feral in its intensity. *Run from him*, it told her. *Run as fast as you can.*

She was only inches from the stairs when he caught her by the hood. Panicked, she struggled, frantically shaking her head. The hood twisted over her face, partially obscuring her vision and taking some of her hair with it as it slid up over her jaw. His fingers closed around her arm. He was speaking to her, trying to calm her. She couldn't make out the words, only the soft sound of his voice. She didn't want to be calm. She wanted to be *free*!

Blindly, violently, she struck out with her arm. The butt of the pistol connected with the side of his head just as her hood came off in his hand. She watched in stunned horror as he crumpled to the floor with a loud crash. His head struck the crude wooden boards and then he was still.

"Dear God," she whispered. "What have I done?"

Something very close to hysteria washed over her. She had killed him. She had killed a peer of the realm!

No, she hadn't killed him, she realized, willing herself to remain calm. She could see his chest rise and fall with every breath. She had only rendered him unconscious.

For a moment she could only stand and stare at the large form at her feet. Even unconscious, there was a raw kind of power that surrounded him. He looked like a lion she had once seen in a menagerie in Moscow.

Against her better judgment she knelt beside him, her gaze feasting on his pure male beauty. A part of her now wished that she was wrong—that he hadn't killed Bella. He looked so young, so angelic with his eyes closed, that it was easy to forget just how feline he appeared with them open.

There was nothing innocent about him. That was evident from the way her body had reacted when he had thrust himself between her splayed legs. She had been caught between the hardness of his body and the unyielding wood of the table. The table had only cut into her flesh, while it felt as though the pressure of his hips against hers had branded her, sending a shocking current of sensual pleasure through her even though she feared him. No, any man who could inspire lust over panic was certainly no innocent.

Still, something about the way his russet hair fell over his forehead and the laughter that had softened his features moved her. Tentatively, she reached out and touched his cheek. The skin above the shadow of his beard was golden and soft . . .

"Idiot!" She leaped to her feet as though his flesh had scorched her and cursed herself thoroughly for allowing herself to be affected by him. That was his charm. And it was this that had attracted Bella and had gotten her killed. Varya would do well to remember just what a monster this man was.

And she had plenty of experience with monsters.

Imagine Bella's reaction if she could see what Varya had done. She had brought the Marquess of Wynter to his knees.

She carried that thought with her as she hurried through the shadows and down the rickety stairs on legs that shook faster than they ran.

Chapter 2

With the bump on his temple skillfully hidden behind a lock of hair, Miles gingerly set his beaver hat on his head and exited the carriage. Although the spot was still tender to the touch, it was no longer throbbing. He was fortunate that the only serious injury he had sustained was that to his pride.

Two days ago he had woken up on the rough-hewn floor of the abandoned storeroom where his demoness abductor had left him, with Carny hovering over him, clucking like a mother hen.

Miles's tiger had disobeyed orders to stay with the carriage and had watched the scene unfold from the shadows. He followed Miles and his abductor to the warehouse and then ran for Carny. Miles didn't know whether to reward the boy or throttle him.

21

Once his friend had determined that he wasn't seriously injured, and had managed to pull almost every detail of the humiliating affair from him, Carny's clucking turned to chuckles. Miles hadn't the strength to shut him up.

Every inch of him had been bruised or battered, and he smelled of cheap gin and manure. If fate ever delivered the harpy back into his hands he would make certain she did not escape him so easily. And he would make sure she answered all his questions about Bella's death.

So far, his own investigation had turned up little information that he hadn't already possessed. From the one report in the newspaper and conversations with both the doctor who had examined the body and the Bow Street Runner assigned to the case, Miles had discovered that Bella had indeed been murdered, most likely by a man.

A jealous lover was the likeliest suspect. After answering his questions, Bow Street had a few of their own, leaving Miles no choice but to confess being out-of-town at the time of Bella's death.

One of his housemaids had become pregnant by a local man caught up in a smuggling ring. Because she was fearful that she was going to be turned out without a reference and that her beau would be hunted by the authorities, Miles had little choice but to return to his estate for a few days.

It seemed that no matter how much the rest of the staff assured the girl she wouldn't be turned out, she would only believe it from Miles. Of course, once he was there he could hardly refuse her tearful plea to help her young man.

Miles had found the scared youth in a cave, where he had hidden to escape capture. Miles sent the boy home with enough money to marry the maid and start working his own small homestead on Christian land. He had also warned the young man that if he wasn't prepared to accept the consequences of his actions, he was better off not getting himself into such predicaments.

After that, he and Carny had a word or two with the smuggling gang about doing their recruiting somewhere other than the village Miles's estate protected. Miles would buy their brandy, but he would not pay them with the blood of his people. That bit of information he did not reveal to Bow Street.

"Are you coming?" Rowan Carmichael, Earl of Carnover, asked, sticking his blond head through the open carriage door. "I'd like to get inside before the music starts."

Practically folding himself in two, Miles rose and stepped down to the street. "Apologies, my friend. I was thinking of other things."

Carny nodded in understanding, his usually jovial countenance grave. He had liked Bella, and understood how deeply news of her death had affected Miles.

The King's Theater had been the very stage where Miles and Carny had first heard Madame Isabella Mancini sing. Her voice had been lovely, but Miles had been more taken with Bella's body than her talent.

They had shared many months together, but he hadn't set foot in the theater since ending their liaison six months ago. It felt almost eerie to be entering it now, knowing that Bella would never grace its stage again.

Outside the theater, the night was alive with voices mingled with raucous laughter, and the glow of the street lamps caused many a jewel to sparkle like stardust. Why, on this night, in this part of town, it was hard to believe that anyone in London could possibly be a murderer.

Or an insane foreign woman with a gun.

"Explain to me once more why I agreed to come here with you," he demanded of his companion as they were suddenly caught in the middle of the swarm of patrons clamoring to get inside the theater. Like a herd of sheep trying to get through the opening in the fence all at once, he thought.

"You are here," Carny humored him as he narrowly escaped stepping in a pungent pile of horse droppings, "to celebrate *my* brilliant apprehension of the band of thieves you failed to capture and to see the Elusive Varya perform." This was said with such reverence that Miles forgave his friend's ribbing to wonder at Carny's regard for the woman. That Carny had caught the thieves bothered him not at all.

He was becoming less and less enamored of playing the hero and rounding up villains. His life needed a different kind of excitement, though he had no idea where or how to find it. The rich man's disease—after gout—was boredom.

Miles nodded a polite greeting to an acquaintance.

Carny hadn't said a word about Miles's decision to give up spy work for good.

Calling himself back to the conversation, he smiled sardonically. "Ah yes, your little piano player."

Carny rolled his eyes as they walked through the doors of the King's Theater. "She's a *pianist*, Miles," he drawled, "and exquisite."

"Mm." Miles's disinterest was apparent as he took in the glittering minions of the ton surrounding him.

Society both fascinated and repulsed him. On the surface, everything seemed placid and calm, but he wondered what seethed just below the surface of even the starchiest lord. How could any man be content with such a mundane existence? Not much wonder the regent ate too much and spent too much—what else had he to do? Parties, recitals, and soirées were all he had to look forward to. If war with the French had taught Miles anything, it was not to live his life as though he were already dead. Although, sometimes, he wondered why he wasn't.

"Oh, Lord Wynter, there you are!"

Miles turned toward the voice. His eyes scanned his immediate vicinity and saw nothing. Then a slight tugging at his sleeve made him glance down.

Standing before him, their heads just reaching the middle of his chest, were Lady Fenton and a pretty young chit that he supposed to be her daughter. Just how many daughters did the old hag have? Over the past three years she had thrust as many female offspring in his face, hoping he'd take a fancy to one.

"I wonder if I might present my daughter Harriet to

you, my lord?" Lady Fenton inquired, a smug smile on her cherubic face.

Miles smiled graciously, seeing the distress on the poor girl's pretty features. It was quite obvious that she found his size—a throwback to his father's Norse ancestors—intimidating, and no doubt thought him far too *old*.

"She's just had her eighteenth birthday!" Lady Fenton gushed as if the girl were a mare ripe for breeding. Miles chuckled inwardly at the comparison. Lady Harriet was far too young, her bloodlines too pure for his stable. On the other hand, she did have fine teeth and a large chest.

He bowed over Harriet's hand, pressing a light kiss on the gloved knuckles. "How do you do, Lady Harriet?"

"Very well, thank you, Lord Wynter." Blushing furiously, she sank into a deep curtsy.

"Oh my, there's Lady Esterbrook!" Lady Fenton exclaimed, cooling her florid face vigorously with a hand-painted silk fan. "I simply must discover whether or not she will be attending my dinner party Thursday evening. My lord, would you please stay with Harriet for a few moments? Oh, thank you."

Miles watched in wry amusement as Lady Fenton's considerable girth barreled across the foyer toward the unsuspecting Lady Esterbrook. The woman had no shame. It was bad manners, not to mention scandalous, to leave her young daughter unchaperoned with a gentleman.

"I'm surprised she didn't invite you to dinner," Harriet muttered under her breath.

Miles laughed out loud, causing the girl's blush to deepen to a dark crimson.

"You've a sharp tongue, Lady Harriet!" He chuckled.

"Forgive me, my lord," she mumbled to his chest.

"Do not apologize. Personally, I find it refreshing."

She stared at him, a hopeful light in her brown eyes. "Do you mean that, Lord Wynter?"

He nodded, his lips curved into an easy grin. "I do. I'm sure you are aware that your mama has introduced me to every one of your sisters for the past three seasons?"

Harriet nodded, her cheeks pink.

"Yes, well, so far you've been my favorite."

She beamed at him. She really was a pretty little thing. It was unfortunate really, that she was the daughter of such an odious woman, otherwise he might be tempted . . .

But instead, he'd introduce her to some young bucks her own age. Such a vibrant young girl deserved better than an embittered ex-soldier like himself. She deserved love and a family—two things he could never give.

"Tell me, Harriet," he began, defying propriety by using her Christian name. "Have you seen any young men here tonight who've caught your eye?" He asked because he had noticed the Marquess of Standhope's son Marcus watching them very closely.

Harriet managed to raise her rosy face long enough to quickly scan the bustling foyer. Her eyes settled on the handsome young Marcus, who tipped his hat to them both and sauntered toward them at Miles's beckoning wave.

"Good evening, Wynter." But his eyes were on Harriet.

"Evening, Marcus," Miles replied jovially, trying to suppress a grin. "May I present Lady Harriet Fenton, Lord and Lady Fenton's youngest"—Miles raised a questioning brow, hoping that Harriet was indeed the last. When she nodded, he almost sighed out loud in relief—"daughter."

Miles pointedly ignored the two young people as they awkwardly entered into conversation. He might be a matchmaker, but he wasn't an eavesdropper. Instead, he contented himself with watching Carny attempt to work his wiles on an unsuspecting miss—and fail when the girl's chaperone intervened. The smile with which he greeted the returning Lady Fenton was a self-satisfied one. One more ambitious mama's machinations ruined.

Carny came up beside him as the happy trio strolled away. Lady Fenton's disgruntled expression had changed to joy when she realized that Marcus would be a powerful marquess someday.

"How many narrowly escaped betrothals does that make this season?" his friend demanded with a chuckle.

"Six. I'm thinking about going into business. I've introduced them all to other eligible gentlemen. Four have already announced engagements."

Carny clapped him on the back. "You're amazing."

Miles grimaced. "It would seem so. I'm tired of standing here like a stallion at Tattersall's. Let us go inside."

"There are many gentlemen of our set who would

be more than happy to see you put out to pasture, my friend, and leave all the fillies to the rest of us."

A grin parted Miles's lips at his friend's dry tone. "I'm not ready to spend the remainder of my days grazing just yet, Carny. And I've witnessed your pathetic attempts at seduction." He tapped his friend's shoulder with his gloves. "Now, shall we go inside and wait for the entrance of your little pianist?"

Miles was glad for the seclusion of Carny's private box. There he was finally safe from the intrusions many society matrons attempted to make into his private life. He had not taken a mistress since he and Bella had parted company, and many took that as an indication that he was looking for a wife. Consequently, all of London was looking for one for him as well.

He removed his hat and raked his hands through his thick, shaggy hair, careful to avoid the lump on his temple.

It was vanity and not indifference that made Miles wear his hair longer than what was truly fashionable. He realized that it only stood to reason that a large man have large ears, but he was determined to keep his hidden.

He leaned back in the cushioned chair that was too short for his large frame and stretched his long legs out in front of him. With any luck he'd fall asleep within a few minutes, as he was in desperate need of some rest.

Much to Miles's astonishment, the noise level inside the theater dropped almost to a complete hush as the time to begin arrived. Even the bucks and bruisers down front, who usually used an evening at the theater to make complete asses of themselves, fell quiet.

Carny punched him in the shoulder. "See what I mean?" He cackled softly. "She's mesmerized the entire city!"

Miles jokingly rubbed the spot where Carny had hit him. "She" wasn't even on stage yet. "Your exuberance is overwhelming."

But despite his cynicism, Miles found himself sitting upright and lifting the opera glasses to his eyes to get a better look at the mysterious musician who seemed to have charmed all of London and had earned herself the title of "Elusive" from the lust-struck gentleman she had rejected.

She stepped onto the stage to thundering applause. Through the glasses, Miles could see that she was tall for a woman, but still a great deal shorter than his six feet, three inches. His gaze traveled up the bodice of her dark blue satin gown, and he was somewhat surprised to find that the scalloped neckline revealed very little of the swell of her impressive bosom. Under the lights, her skin appeared the color of alabaster, a stark contrast to the gown and inky black hair. Her face seemed bare of the cosmetics he had known many female entertainers to use when on stage. While he couldn't make out the color of her eyes, they were large, and the rest of her features fine. Her lips curved into an appreciative smile at the warm reception, and Miles was struck by her simple loveliness.

He turned to Carny. "She's lovely, I grant you," he commented in a loud whisper, "but I still don't understand what all the fuss is—"

"Shhh!" Carny hissed, waving his hand frantically in Miles's face.

Miles raised his eyebrows at his friend's rudeness. He turned back to the stage with his opera glasses, feeling like a scolded child.

And then she began to play.

Never before had Miles experienced such music. Until then he had thought Beethoven to be the most gifted musician he had ever heard, but that was before he heard . . . What was her name? Vanya, Verushka? Damn, after Carny's rude dismissal he knew better than to ask him until after the concert.

The entire hall seemed enthralled as her nimble fingers caressed the keys of the piano. The melody was almost mournful in its tone, but somehow she managed to make it sound sweet and full of hope.

It was over all too soon and Miles surprised himself by jumping up from the edge of his chair where he had been perched for the last hour and seizing Carny by the coat.

"We're going backstage," he announced, steering him toward the backstage entrance. He propelled his slow-moving friend down the crowded, humming corridor.

"What did you think?" Carny asked excitedly, seeming not to notice that he was being used as a kind of battering ram through the jostling bodies filling the narrow arcade. "Did I not tell you she was magnificent?"

"I think you grossly understated her abilities, my friend." Miles scowled at a smaller man who tried to push in front of them, giving him a not-so-friendly shove.

Carny shrugged, too caught up in the beauty of the

music he had heard to take offense at his sarcastic friend.

They were not the only gentlemen who had pushed their way backstage in hope of begging an audience with the lovely pianist. Miles was surprised that a few of the gentlemen even had ladies with them. It meant that they actually intended to tell Victoria ... Vivica ... whatever her name was that they enjoyed her performance, not proposition her.

Miles's great height and muscular build made it easy for the two of them to push their way through the crowded backstage area. A few of the gentlemen were above him in rank, but he was a well-recognized war hero, not just a lord, and this fact intimidated many into moving out of his way.

"I do so enjoy going out into society with you, Miles," Carny commented brightly as they stepped up to the green room door long before Carny could have made it there by himself.

Miles grinned. "Remember you said that the next time I'm so foxed you have to carry me home." He knocked on the door.

A burly man, almost as wide across the shoulders as he was tall, greeted them. He did not speak—he just gazed at them questioningly.

Miles smiled his most charming smile. "The Marquess of Wynter and the Earl of Carnover to see Miss . . ." He faltered, her name still escaping him.

"Varya," Carny chirped.

"Varya," Miles repeated, willing himself to remember.

The man stepped aside and Miles wondered why

he had allowed them to enter and no one else. Then he saw a few other guests milling about inside.

"Apparently, he's very picky as to who he allows in to meet his employer," Carny informed him sotto voce.

Miles nodded as if he understood the ugly guard's reasoning, but he didn't. What did he base his judgment on? Looks? Title? Neither was very conducive to determining who could be trusted and who couldn't.

He spotted Varya surrounded by a small group of admirers, both male and female. She was smiling and laughing with them as if they were old friends. Miles watched, entranced by the animation on her lovely face, and was ridiculously pleased to see—even from that distance—that her eyes were blue. Sapphire blue.

As she spoke, she gestured wildly with her hands. Miles found the fluttering motions of her long, slender fingers almost mesmerizing. What would the rest of her look like beneath that silk evening gown? Was the flesh of her body as smooth and white as that of her unblemished cheek? If he pulled all the pins from her raven tresses, how far would they fall down her voluptuous form?

Lord, but he was beginning to sound like that fool Byron! It was foolish to wax poetic about a woman—even if the woman in question was *the* most enchanting creature he had ever seen.

He would be the first to admit that he had had more than his fill of women of the stage. And even though he could almost picture Bella sadly shaking her head at him, Miles still found himself wondering if Miss Varya was in want of the protection of a man such as himself.

* * *

Varya loved meeting people after each performance. Though sometimes she worried that some well-traveled lord or lady would recognize her. She knew it was unlikely, however, as the only people she had seen so far in London who were even familiar with Russia were Count Lieven and his wife, Dorothea, one of the patronesses at the exclusive Almack's. Varya had never been invited to Almack's, nor did she have any desire to attend. No doubt if the countess ever found out who she was, she would be more than welcome inside those hallowed walls. For now, Varya was content with her haughty distance—they had never even been introduced.

The hypocrisy of London society did not bother Varya. She'd much rather drink vodka and dance around the music room with Piotr and Katya, the maid and footman she had brought with her when she fled from St. Petersburg. She glanced over at Piotr, who was acting as doorman, and smiled warmly at the stocky Russian.

Her smile froze when she saw the men Piotr had allowed to enter the room. She was already acquainted with the Earl of Carnover, but it was his companion who captured her attention. Her heart raced at the sight of him, not just from fear but from stark awareness. Miles Christian was the kind of man a woman had no choice but to notice. What if he recognized her?

No, she told herself, trying to quell the nausea rolling through her stomach. She had kept herself disguised and it had been very dark. Even after he pulled off her hood she had kept to the shadows, and only seconds had passed before she hit him. There was no way he could recognize her. Still, she found herself holding her breath and only half listening to the conversation around her as he approached. Blood pounded in her ears with his every step until she was fairly certain she would suffer an apoplectic fit before he even reached her.

Instinctively, she cradled the arm he had smashed onto the table against her waist. It was still tender and bruised.

In the few days that had passed since her dreadful abduction of the marquess—why couldn't he have been a shopkeeper, or a baronet? Someone with a little less *importance!*—she had investigated his claim to have been out of town when Bella was killed. A few gentlemen had remarked on his absence from the clubs, but no one could say for certain where he had disappeared to.

His grief at the news hadn't been feigned, and as much as she despised herself for it, Varya wanted to believe him incapable of such a crime—and not because of her own bizarre attraction to him, but because Bella had loved him.

His innocence was unlikely, but not impossible.

But if he didn't kill Bella, who did? And how was she ever going to prove it?

Lady Milton complimented her on her gown; she smiled and nodded. Lord James asked if he might take her for a ride in Hyde Park the following afternoon; she smiled and shook her head. Somehow, she managed to maintain her composure even though the

Grim Reaper was surely approaching, lifting his gleaming scythe . . .

Suddenly, she was staring at a very stiff, impeccably tied cravat. She forced her gaze up even though her lungs threatened to collapse at the sight of the breathtaking face above her.

Blessed Mary, but he was a beautiful man! Never before had she seen a face so harsh and yet so handsome. His catlike eyes were large for a man's and set beneath arched brows. Even his eyelashes were darker and thicker than any man had the right to claim. His nose was long and straight—perfectly patrician—and his mouth was wide and full, followed by a jaw that wasn't quite square, but was still very strong. It was a face that should have been arrogant in its beauty, but smiled warmly at her instead.

Oh Bella, I think I must envy you.

Lord James introduced them. The Marquess of Wynter bowed.

"Miss Varya," he began in his smooth, deep voice, "I am honored to make your acquaintance." He took her offered hand and raised it to his lips.

She forced herself to speak, despite the fact that her heart was hammering in her throat. Whether it was from fear of being found out or from his touch, she had no idea. The feel of his lips through the thin silk of her gloves was shamefully erotic. Odd how he was now so gentle when just nights before he had smashed that same arm onto a rickety table.

"Thank you, my lord. It is indeed a pleasure to meet you."

Something flickered briefly in his unusual eyes. She

watched in horror as he frowned slightly, but then it was gone and the good humor was back in his countenance. Varya had to bite her lip to keep from sighing in relief. She could feel tiny beads of perspiration forming along her hairline.

"Lord Wynter's been honored to meet many ladies in this room, haven't you, Miles?" Lord James announced jocularly, elbowing the marquess in the side.

Lord Wynter winced as if the jab hurt more than it should have. Varya wondered if he also carried wounds from their struggle, or if he had been injured while fighting the French in Portugal. She stepped forward.

"Do you require any assistance, my lord?" she asked, her brow furrowed with concern.

Too late she realized her folly and knew that he had realized it as well. By repeating almost word for word the taunt they had exchanged two nights before in the alley, she had revealed herself to him.

She watched, frozen as his eyes hardened into cold green-gold stones and his face stiffened. His mouth flattened into a hard, grim line and he caught her outstretched hand in a grip that made her flinch.

"Yes, madam," he ground out between clenched teeth, "I believe I do."

Chapter 3

Varya did the only thing she could in such a situation.

She feigned a swoon.

She pitched herself right into the arms of the Marquess of Wynter, who tensed and swore under his breath. Had they not been in company, she had no doubt he would have gladly dropped her.

Or worse.

He carried her to the chaise and draped her along its length as though she were the heroine in a tragedy. If she weren't so aware of what the marquess could do to her, she would have smiled at the irony. She rather felt like an actress in a bad play.

As with most public swoonings, there was a collective gasp and immediately the crowd closed in. Piotr and the Earl of Carnover ordered them all back while Miles made a great show of chafing her wrists.

Varya was conscious of the eyes upon her. She was also conscious of the pain in her arm caused by the marquess's savage rubbing. She winced and slowly opened her eyes, although what she really wanted to do was club him over the head.

The chafing ceased, but he did not release her. His fingers had a death grip on hers. Avoiding his piercing gaze, she glanced around at the faces of her guests.

"Did I faint?" she inquired in a small, confused voice. Lord, could anyone else hear the deception in her tone?

"Yes," Wynter replied, sending shivers of dread down her spine. He leaned close and whispered in her ear, "I think it would be best if everyone left now. Obviously, the night has already been too taxing for you."

Varya forced herself to meet his cold stare and was surprised to find that it wasn't cold at all. It was hard, yes, but seemed to radiate the heat of his anger.

With a slight nod she raised her gaze to the crowd gathered around her. A strange warmth flooded her veins, flushing her chest and neck. Despite the anxious faces, the worried murmurs, she wasn't aware of any presence in the room other than the man sitting beside her, his hard thigh close enough for her to touch.

"Please forgive me, everyone." How firm her voice sounded. The anxiety that bound her insides had yet to reach her tongue. "I fear the night has exhausted me and I must cut our visit short. Please come back after my next performance."

A low murmur of disappointment followed the crowd as Piotr began ushering people out. A torrent of farewells and felicitations rushed at Varya in a gentle buzz. She couldn't distinguish one voice from another. Smiling at her adoring public, she waved and prayed silently for them to be gone. If they knew what she had done to their precious Marquess of Wynter, they would turn on her in a minute.

Those who still waited outside loudly voiced their discontent when they realized they would not be seeing Varya in person that evening, but left with the satisfaction of at least catching a glimpse of the elusive performer. Some of them called out to her, others tried to fight their way inside. Piotr closed the door in their faces.

Varya frowned. She found the male attention disarming. She didn't know what kind of fantasies they had built around her, but she was certain she didn't want to find out.

"Are you coming, Miles?" Carny asked on his way out. Varya frowned at the blatant disapproval in the man's pale eyes. Her life was none of his business.

"No." Miles glanced over his shoulder at his friend. "I'm going to stay and make certain that Miss Varya is set to rights."

The young earl raised a dubious brow. "Of course. I shall see you tomorrow, then. Good luck."

His meaning was obvious, Varya realized angrily. Many of her male admirers visited in hopes that she would take one of them as her lover. She'd heard they even made wagers over her at their clubs. She wondered how much money Lord Carnover had already won at her expense.

"Good evening, Lord Carnover," she called coolly.

He met her gaze with no hint of mockery whatsoever. "And to you as well, Miss Varya." He bowed smartly, placed his hat on his fair head, and strode from the room.

With a sigh Varya briefly closed her eyes and leaned back against the chaise.

"How much do you have riding on your charm and good looks, my lord?"

Silence met her question. Looking up, she found the marquess watching her with a curious expression on his face. A half smile curved his lips, as though he had read her thoughts and found them terribly amusing.

With more hauteur than she felt, she stared imperiously down her nose at him. "If you are going to have me arrested, my lord, please do so quickly. I am very tired."

Meanwhile, her heart hammered furiously in her chest. If he turned her over to the authorities, they would certainly discover who she was. Then they would send her back to Russia. Back to the monster waiting there.

"I'm not certain what I'm going to do with you." Propping his elbow against the back of the chaise, he pinned her to the cushions without even touching her. "However, I can assure you that I'm not going to have you arrested—not yet."

Uneasiness began to churn in her stomach. If he

wasn't going to have her carted away to Newgate, what was he going to do?

"Then why are you still here?" she demanded. She glanced toward the door to make certain Piotr was there in case she needed him.

The marquess followed her gaze, and one corner of his mouth quirked as he turned back to her. Leaning closer, he brought his face down to hers. She could feel his breath against her cheek, smell the spicy sweetness of his skin.

"Why do you think?"

Varya's cheeks—and other parts of her anatomy—flamed as his voice slid over her like silk. Surely he didn't mean . . . not after all she had said and done to him!

His harsh laugh as he straightened was like a bucket of ice water in her face. Of course he didn't want her. He hated her. And she him.

"At the risk of offending your delicate sensibilities, Miss Varya, I must assure you that I have no desire to force myself upon you. My last encounter of a physical nature with you is still rather—fresh." His fingers went to the bruise on his temple.

Shamed that he had read her thoughts, Varya clenched her jaw. "I too remember our last meeting, my lord." Deftly she removed her glove and unbuttoned the cuff of her sleeve. She pushed the delicate silk up her arm, revealing to his gaze a large yellow and purple bruise followed by a similarly colored—and rather large—handprint.

He winced at the sight of his handiwork, but the

gaze that met hers was devoid of any regret. "You were waving a pistol in my face, madam. I believed you were trying to kill me."

"I was simply trying to escape." It was true. She didn't believe for a minute that she could have actually pulled the trigger—no matter how much she wanted to avenge Bella's death.

"A fine job you did of it too. It was morning before I awoke."

She lowered her sleeve and concentrated on buttoning the cuff in an effort to keep her voice steady. "If you are looking for an apology, I cannot give you one. More than I regret hurting you, I regret allowing you to hurt me." Lifting her chin, she bit the inside of her lip to keep it from quivering.

He nodded in concession. "Then it appears that we are even on one account."

She raised a brow. "And the other?"

He stood. "On that account, we are not even. Now, why don't you fetch your wrap and allow me to escort you home?"

Her brow jumped even higher.

Much to her chagrin, the handsome marquess burst out laughing.

"You didn't think I was going to let you off that easy, did you?"

Varya flushed hotly. For one moment she had thought he was just going to let her go. She should have known that as a man, he would have another agenda.

"I want some answers," he informed her as he offered her his hand. She placed her much smaller one in his palm and rose to her feet. "You appear to be the only one who can give them to me."

"I suppose I owe you that much," she allowed, lifting her gaze to his. She tried to appear calm, but inside a tiny voice was screaming for her to run before he killed her as he had killed Bella.

She could not run. And she now had some doubts that he could have murdered her friend. *Doubts*—not convictions.

He smiled down at her, but the curl of his lips held little humor. Her heart skipped a beat. Few men frightened her, and it did not comfort her to add Bella's former lover to the list of those who did.

"It would seem we're finally in agreement, madam," he replied silkily. "But you'll forgive me if I'd rather have you at my mercy than place my own throat at yours."

Meeting an enemy on his—or in this case *her*—own territory, Miles had long ago learned, often gave that enemy a false sense of security.

Not that he planned to attack the exquisite creature sitting on the sofa opposite him, but he would rather be the one on guard in unfamiliar surroundings than the one feeling safe and comfortable in her own home. There was nothing more detrimental to one's defenses than the sensation of being safe and comfortable.

He had expected something different from the Elusive Varya's townhouse. He hadn't expected it to be situated in an area as exclusive as the West End. He hadn't expected her to have such taste and elegance in her decor. Walls painted in soft colors were accented with delicate plaster work in the Adam style. Everywhere he looked—at a carpet, a painting—there was evidence of wealth and good taste.

Miss Varya obviously came from a different background than most women who graced the stage. She had the kind of grace, poise, and hauteur that could only come from having been raised with money and power. Interesting.

Dragging his gaze away from a Wedgwood vase, he turned his attention to the woman who had held him at gunpoint only a few nights ago. Her face was pale, but she kept her expression perfectly blank. She would not intimidate easily. He felt an odd respect for her that annoyed him.

He had almost laughed out loud when she feigned an attack of the vapors at the theater. In fact, the only thing that had kept his temper at bay was her audacity. Her skill at deception should have enraged him further, but instead he found her quest for self-preservation admirable.

And then there had been something in the swirling indigo depths of her eyes that had snuffed out his anger. Defiance. Anxiety. And a vulnerability he hadn't expected to see.

She had been afraid of him. She was afraid of him even now, and it wasn't just because she feared he might be a murderer. He couldn't quite fathom why he sensed this about her, but something told him that she saw him as a threat in more ways than one. He decided not to hand her over to the authorities just yet—this could prove to be a very enjoyable mystery.

Besides, she claimed to be Bella's friend. She might

be the only person able to give him clues to the identity of his former mistress's murderer.

And it would be a sin to send a woman so beautiful to Newgate. Not when he could think of much more pleasurable uses for her.

How could he even consider it? The very thought of bedding such a harridan should chill his blood. Instead, he wondered if she would be as passionate in bed as she was in battle.

"You have a lovely home," he remarked casually, forcing himself back to the matter at hand.

She frowned at the compliment. "Thank you."

"Your landlord must be a patron of the arts."

Varya's only reply was to tilt her head to one side and stare at him intently. Miles was vaguely uncomfortable with the fact that his question had been so transparent.

He took a sip of his vodka. "Have you lived in London long?"

"Not quite half a year."

"And why here? Why not Paris or Rome?"

She tilted her head again, contemplating the question as if he had just asked for the secrets of the universe. It immediately put his guard up.

"I grew tired of always traveling. I told Bella how I felt. She said, 'Come to London,' so I did."

Six months would have been right around the time he and Bella had parted company.

"Bella never spoke of you. If you were such good friends, why is that?"

"Did you talk to her about your family, Lord Wynter?"

Miles's brows drew together at the ridiculous notion. He made it a point never to discuss family with his mistresses—such intimacies only led the women to believe there was more than sexual attraction on his side.

"No. I did not."

Again that mocking tilt of her head. Did the woman have a nervous tic?

"Then why would you expect Bella to discuss hers with you?"

"You were related?"

Varya shook her head, a slight smiling playing about her lips. "No, my lord. We weren't. I meant that figuratively. I was the closest thing Bella had to family and vice versa. We've known each other since we were schoolgirls." She arched a brow as her smile grew. "You may never have heard about me, but believe me—I heard *much* about you."

Miles's cheeks warmed. If she was telling the truth, he could only guess at the kinds of things Bella had discussed with this friend she had held too dear even to speak of.

Time to get back to the matter at hand. "So, you went to Bella's townhouse because she failed to show up for a breakfast meeting the two of you had planned?"

She didn't stop to think of her reply, which pleased him. So far she appeared to have been perfectly candid, but he would not let his guard down. If she was hiding anything about Bella's death, he would discover it.

"Yes. The servants didn't find it strange that Bella was still abed, but she never missed an appointment."

Her features clouded. "I found her as soon as I entered her chamber."

"She had been strangled?" He schooled his voice to remain level and impersonal, but inside his guts were tied up tighter than rigging in a ship. How could anyone ever harm Bella?

Varya nodded. There were tears in her eyes, he noted, and she clenched her jaw to keep them from falling. He wondered if she fought to hide her emotions only from him or if she loathed showing weakness of any kind.

"She looked so peaceful. Her eyes were closed . . ." She swallowed. "I almost believed she was sleeping until I saw the marks around her throat. Handprints." She nodded toward his free hand. "A man's hands—big."

That surprised him. Most women he knew would have been too hysterical to remember anything. "You actually remember the size of the marks?"

"It's not the kind of thing one forgets."

If abducting him at gunpoint had cast any doubts as to her intellect, the matter was now put to rest. She had an eye and memory for detail.

"And you immediately concluded the marks were left by my hands?"

Her cool veneer cracked for a second, revealing a flicker of discomfort before snapping back into place. "You were her last lover. I knew how hurt she was—how she made a fool of herself begging you to come back to her . . ."

Miles's throat constricted painfully. Bella had sent him letters—many letters. His proud Italian beauty promised to do—and be—whatever he wanted if only he'd come back. He had finally stopped reading anything she sent him; he couldn't stand the guilt.

"Bella never made a fool of herself," he informed her, his voice hoarse.

The expression on Varya's face told him she disagreed, but there was a glimmer of admiration in her eyes. Miles did not want her admiration.

"How did you know to find me in Covent Garden?"

Her chin rose a notch. "When I began to suspect you I had men watch your house. When I received word that you were in residence—"

"So you believe that I was truly out of town until last week?"

Cold blue eyes met his. "I believe no such thing, Lord Wynter. I know nothing of your whereabouts when Bella was killed—*yet*. All I know is that for the past week, you've been keeping very strange hours, hanging about the seedier parts of town. The night I found you, my man had overheard you giving directions to your hired coachman. He reported back to me and I followed."

"And ruined a very important investigation I was working on, mind you!" Anger tingled along Miles's skin, shivered in his rising voice.

She shrugged. It mattered nothing to her that the thieves had been given an extra day to brutalize their victims. The only thing the chit cared about was her completely erroneous conclusion.

"I wanted to catch you off guard, force you to confess."

"That's all very well and good," Miles drawled, unable to curb his caustic tone. "But why would I confess to something I didn't do? And what did you plan to do? Shoot me if I did confess? Good Lord, woman! Do you know nothing of gathering evidence, of building a case? You have nothing but your own anger and need for vengeance against me. Give me one reason why I could have killed Bella."

"Because she was hounding you and you were afraid your precious family and friends would find out how horribly you treated her!"

Miles was shocked. He'd never treated a woman badly in his life—except for Charlotte . . . But now wasn't the time to think of his long-dead wife.

"I'm sorry to tell you this, Miss Varya, but my *precious* family and friends knew about my relationship with Bella. I certainly never discussed her with them, but there are no secrets in London."

Her face fell and Miles was sorry for her. Her loyalty to Bella, her determination to avenge her friend were touching and downright admirable.

"I didn't kill her."

The softness of her countenance disappeared, hardening once again into a cold mask.

"A man killed my dearest friend, Lord Wynter. And until you can prove your innocence, you are still a suspect."

Prove his innocence? Did this lunatic know whom she was speaking to? He was a marquess, a peer of the realm. He didn't have to *prove* anything!

"And I suppose that it never crossed your mind that a woman might have killed her?" he asked. Certainly a jealous wife could have done the deed, or hired someone else to do it. Since he hadn't seen the marks on Bella's neck himself, he refused to believe Varya's conviction that the murderer had been one of Bella's lovers.

Varya shook her head. The movement loosened a lock of hair from her delicate coiffure and sent it tumbling down around her shoulder like an ebony ribbon. Miles wondered what her reaction might be if he were suddenly to reach out and touch it.

Touching her would be as wise as stroking a lion.

"No. It was a man."

"And what makes you so certain?" He tore his gaze away from that shining lock of hair and met her determined gaze.

"Because she was dressed to receive a gentleman caller. She was wearing one of her negligées—a silver one with pearl buttons."

He waved away her deduction with a flick of his wrist. "She wore that often." At least for *him* she had. He had given it to her. The idea that Bella might have worn it for someone else was oddly provoking. "It means nothing."

Varya smiled ruefully, with a hint of smugness. "Perhaps it means little to *you*, Lord Wynter, as you were her lover and no doubt saw her in many peignoirs—and less—but I was her friend and I know better."

She paused and Miles jumped at her bait. "And just *what* do you know, Miss Varya?"

Again, she fixed him with a knowing smile. "I know that Bella only wore those flimsy gowns when a gentleman was coming to call. Every other night she wore an old linen nightrail that her grandmother had made for her. A hideous thing, but Bella loved it." Her smiled faded. "*That* is how I know a woman did not kill Bella."

"And no doubt you are correct," he allowed, strangely envious that he had not known such a small detail of Bella's life.

His path was clear. Regardless of his animosity toward her friend, he owed it to Bella's memory to avenge her death.

"Rest assured I will discover the guilty party, Miss Varya. Just leave everything to me."

And find the killer he would, even if it meant disrupting Varya's own plans. For now, he was content with her appearance of innocence, but the last thing he wanted was a woman underfoot when there was work to be done.

"I beg your pardon?" She was staring at him with such a look of incredulity that he thought he must have said the words out loud.

"I will most certainly *not* leave everything to you, my lord." Her voice trembled slightly, betraying her anger. "A few minutes of conversation does not put you above suspicion. Do you think that just because you are a charming man I'll believe you innocent and better equipped to find Bella's killer?"

Miles frowned. He didn't like her tone. "I think, madam, that as a gentleman, I am able to enter into certain spheres in which you would not be permitted."

The color drained from the rest of her face and

pooled into angry red splotches on her cheeks. Her nostrils flared with indignation. Obviously he had struck a chord.

"I'll have you know that I am welcome in society's finest homes, Lord Wynter."

He gave her what he knew was a patronizing smile. "No doubt you are, madam. I spoke merely of those clubs whose doors are open to gentlemen *only*."

Varya tilted her head. "And are these *gentlemen* in the habit of discussing murders they may or may not have had a part in at these clubs?"

Miles felt his cheeks warm at her sweetly spoken sarcasm.

"Not as a general rule," he replied with forced lightness. "But I may be able to discern where some of Bella's former lovers were on the night of her death. Have you even bothered to investigate the others, or have you played judge, jury, and executioner with me alone?"

She rose abruptly to her feet, leaving Miles little choice but to stand also. Her face was flushed with rage, her eyes as bright as moonlight on the ocean. Whatever else he thought of her, she was one magnificent-looking woman.

"I'll tell you what, my lord." She gave the bell cord on the wall a healthy tug. "You go right ahead and spend as much time as you wish at these clubs. You'll find nothing there except partners in your depravity. I shall continue on as I have been—trying to unveil Bella's murderer. Ah, Piotr. Please show Lord Wynter out."

A muscle twitched in his jaw at her insults and blatant dismissal. His spine was straight as a poker as he turned to meet her glittering gaze.

"One word of advice, madam," he offered between clenched teeth. "You should be most careful when playing detective. The next person you accuse of murder might actually be guilty of it, and you won't be so fortunate to escape with merely a bruised arm."

She paled at his words, and he was pleased to crack her composure. Damn her insufferable arrogance!

"Thank you for your advice, Lord Wynter. I hope you will also take a care during your endeavors—that is quite a nasty bruise on your temple."

"Oh, 'tis not so bad. Much preferable to a bullet in the heart." He smiled mockingly. "Aren't you glad that I prevented you from spilling my blood, madam? Why, you might have been a murderer yourself."

At this point all pretense of politeness on her side disappeared.

"Then I would see you in hell, Lord Wynter. Now I'll thank you to get out of my house."

The burly servant came to take his arm, but Miles shrugged off his meaty paw. He wasn't about to give his harridan hostess the satisfaction of having him tossed out into the street.

He paused at the door to face her once again, a mocking grin on his face.

"Good evening, Miss Varya. I wish you luck in your endeavors and sincerely hope that you manage to keep from killing anyone before *I* solve the puzzle."

* * *

Ivan was coming for her. He knew that she had been watching from his bedchamber door. She had seen everything.

Varya ran, but her legs were heavy and stiff. Each step was like pulling her foot out of soft mud. Ivan caught her without difficulty, his strong hands grabbing her by the hair. Tears of pain sprang to her eyes as he threw her to the ground.

She rolled into a sitting position, her scalp stinging and tears blurring her vision. Using her hands and feet to propel herself backward, she scooted away from him.

He stalked her like a cat with a mouse. His shirt was stained crimson. His face and hands were covered with blood. He reeked of death, and he was coming for her.

Varya's back hit the wall. There was nowhere left to go. He was practically on top of her, blood slicked his hair like a gory pomade. She kicked out, catching his shin with her heel. He stumbled and almost fell.

She staggered to her feet, hunting frantically for some kind of weapon. A heavy pewter candlestick on a table caught her eye. She dodged to the right and grabbed it. Brandishing it like a club, she slowly circled toward the center of the room and began to back away.

Ivan advanced toward her, his bloody face twisted into a demonic grin. She swung her weapon. She missed.

"Put it down, Varya," he commanded softly. "Put it down and I won't hurt you."

It was a lie and they both knew it. She swung again.

This time she did not miss. The heavy base collided with the side of his head with a dull thud.

He stumbled, shook his head, and advanced on her again, a low growl crawling up from his throat. Blood that was actually his own trickled down his temple.

She struck out again. He narrowly avoided the blow. He staggered again as blood trickled into his eye, and Varya seized the opportunity his weakness afforded her.

Her arm vibrated with the force of the blow, this time to his shoulder. She didn't give him time to recover; she struck again and again, until finally he fell to the floor and was still.

Stunned by what she had done, she dropped the candlestick and raised her hands to her face; they came away smeared with blood. A wave of revulsion swept over her.

She woke up screaming as she realized it was his blood that dappled her face . . .

Chapter 4

"**O**h, don't you look handsome!"

Miles rolled his eyes heavenward as he stepped into the drawing room in his stark black evening attire. As he had expected, his mother and sister were already assembled.

"Thank you, Mama," he replied, kissing her smooth cheek. "You look lovely as always."

The dowager marchioness smiled absently as she ran her thin hand down her son's cheek. She didn't have to speak for Miles to know that she was thinking of his father. The man had been dead for eight years and she still thought of him daily—especially when she looked upon the son who was almost a mirror image of his sire.

"Mama tells me you're attending the Pennington

musicale," Blythe piped up from across the room. "I have to wonder who she is."

"Who?" he demanded, then realized he should know better than to step into his younger sister's traps.

"The woman who has captured your interest so avidly that you would sit through one of Pennington's dull affairs for her."

Damn. Damn. Damn.

Miles merely shrugged and flicked a tiny speck of lint from his lapel. Let his sister think what she would. A chance to annoy the lovely Varya was only the icing on the proverbial cake. Her recital gave him ample opportunity to search Pennington's personal correspondence.

"If such a woman existed, brat, she would not be any acquaintance of yours."

Blythe rose to her full height of six feet and strode lazily toward him. Her height and striking beauty intimidated most men, but not one who remembered when she had knobby knees and spots.

"I can think of only one whom I know will be at Pennington's tonight that has never crossed or been thrown into your path." Her catlike eyes narrowed. "Would the attraction be *tonight's* attraction—the Elusive Varya?"

Damn again.

He tugged at his cuff. "I have made the lady's acquaintance, yes. She is charming, no doubt—if you like that sort of thing—but there is nothing between us." *Except for Bella*, he added silently.

His sister smiled. "She's beautiful, elegant, and very

ladylike. Don't tell me she hasn't fallen victim to your charms?"

Miles was peculiarly insulted by her teasing. Was he truly that much of a tomcat?

"Varya was a friend of Isabella Mancini's," he said softly. "It was she who informed me of Bella's death."

Blythe's grin faded and was replaced with an expression of uncomfortable contrition. "Oh."

He felt guilty for discussing such delicate matters. A mistress was something a man never spoke of with his maiden sister.

"Forgive me, Miles. I only meant to tease you." Blythe's gaze was sincere. "Obviously you and Varya share nothing but grief."

Miles's guilt deepened as a pink flush spread across his sister's cheeks. Why had he said anything? Blythe had sought only to play matchmaker. He had ruined her fun and no doubt ruined her impression of Varya, who would be tainted by her association with his former mistress. Despite all the trouble the woman had heaped upon him, Miles had no wish to soil her reputation—which, he had ascertained, was above dispute.

"Do not berate yourself, brat," he said with a soft smile, his tone teasing. "I doubt you need to worry about Varya falling victim to my charm."

That much was true. He realized that Varya could very easily befriend Blythe to get at Miles, but he couldn't imagine her stooping so low. She was not without a sense of honor.

Why was he even thinking of her in a positive light? Yes, Varya had been a friend of Bella's, but she had also abducted him at gunpoint with the intention of forcing a confession out of him. She had single-handedly held him at her mercy, had stood up to him when others would have cowered . . .

God help him, but he was attracted to her. And everything Blythe had said about her was correct. She was beautiful and elegant, and had all the appearance of being a lady.

He had lain awake half the night replaying the scene in her sitting room over and over in his head. By the time sleep had finally claimed him, he had rewritten the event so completely that instead of kicking him out, Varya had begged him to stay, trembling with passion rather than rage. The fantasy had evoked contrary emotions—arousal and anger. He was trying to concentrate on his anger. He could not let himself forget that she suspected him of murder.

But seducing her would be lovely. He would even love to be seduced by her. The mental image *that* thought called to mind caused a familiar stirring in his groin. Embarrassed, he tried to think of other things and willed his blood to cool.

It had been a long time since a woman had caught him so off guard. Never had a female treated him so coolly, so arrogantly. Certainly one had never tried to do him bodily harm. Varya had faced him not as a submissive female, but as an *equal*. An equal in intellect as well as rank. A singular occurrence, that.

Women often seemed content to enjoy his body, but inevitably, their thoughts turned to marriage. He was always honest about his desire never to marry again.

Of course, he kept his reasons for remaining single his own business. Not even the elusive cupid's arrow could induce him to wed again. When conversations began to turn in the direction of the altar, Miles made his farewells. That's what he had done to Bella. That's what he would do to the beguiling Varya With-No-Last-Name.

If she ever let him touch her. She certainly hadn't displayed any interest in his attentions, nor had she done anything to warrant his offering them. Maybe that was what made her so damned attractive in the first place.

Or maybe it was her alabaster skin and clear blue eyes that reminded him of sunshine on Portuguese seas. Maybe he should stop thinking like Lord Byron and get to the musicale before it was too late to do any searching. No doubt Varya was hoping he wouldn't show.

"Well," he said, snapping out of his reverie. "We should be on our way. We'll be late if we don't hurry."

"Oh dear!" the marchioness exclaimed, scurrying toward the door. "Come along, children. Quick now! You know how I detest being tardy."

"Yes, Mama," Blythe replied, her eyes glittering with mirth as she left the room beside her brother. "I know why our mother is in such a hurry—she always is—but what is your hurry, brother dear?"

Miles grinned as they entered the hall. "Why, Blythe. I should think that would be apparent."

His sister stepped into the wrap the butler held out

for her while Miles accepted his greatcoat and hat from one of the footmen.

"Oh? How so?"

Placing his hat on his head, Miles gestured for his sister to step outside into the cool night air before him.

"Because," he replied as the door shut behind them. "I do so hate to keep a lady waiting."

His gaze was like a smoldering weight on her throughout the performance. Keeping her head bowed, Varya concentrated on her playing and avoided looking into his mocking, mesmerizing eyes.

She had been surprised to see him arrive with his family. His sister had smiled warmly at her, and Varya had replied in kind. She knew she had never met the auburn-haired amazon before and could only wonder what Miles had said about her to merit such a greeting.

Many ladies of the ton had tried to befriend her and treated her with uncommon respect. Varya didn't fool herself that any of these overtures would lead to the kind of friendship she had shared with Bella.

These women believed themselves above her, believed that the pleasure of their company was a great favor to a woman who actually *worked* for a living. Her fame and her spotless reputation were the only things in her favor. One wrong step and society would cast her down into the pit. Snobs.

Only Bella had known the truth about her. Bella hadn't cared who she was. The daughter of an upstart Italian businessman had approached the lonely Russian girl without a second thought. A love of music had brought them together, but genuine affection had made them friends.

Pushing thoughts of her friend aside as tears threatened, Varya fixed her gaze on the gleaming keys before her.

Without thinking of the music, she played. Fatigue and nerves made it difficult to concentrate on the emotion the notes usually inspired in her. Instead, her head filled with images from the nightmare that had woken her the night before.

It had been months since she last thought of St. Petersburg and Ivan. No doubt the events of the past few weeks—Bella's murder and her experiences with the Marquess of Wynter—had triggered the horrible memories. She could only hope the dreams would not haunt her for long. Had she not suffered enough already?

Even more disturbing than the familiar dreams of Russia were the strange and unwarranted sensations stirred to life by Miles Christian. Before images of Russia had invaded her slumber, it had been *his* face disrupting her dreams.

Fantasies of soundly humiliating the arrogant marquess had given way to shocking vignettes of his lips crushing hers, of his hands caressing her flesh. How could she have such thoughts of a man she didn't even like?

It had to be Bella's influence. She had heard her friend rhapsodize so often about her handsome and generous lover that it only made sense that Varya would have trouble separating Bella's image from reality.

Even with that thought uppermost in her mind, the knowledge that he was watching her—listening to her—sent a sharp shiver down her spine. Her rigid posture kept her audience from noticing her reaction but it couldn't stop the hairs on the back of her neck from rising or her nipples from tightening almost painfully.

Despite her wandering mind and bewildered body, she made it to the end of the piece without error. It was rare that she ever faltered. Her fingers knew the keyboard so well, she supposed she could play even in her sleep. She could tell from the way the audience vibrated with tension that she had passed her emotions on to them—it was a powerful feeling.

Rising to her feet, she bowed graciously under the applause.

Across the room, the Marquess of Wynter stared at her with eyes that seemed to burn with gold fire. Like a moth, she was drawn to their flame and found it almost impossible to look away.

But she did.

"My dear, you were *marvelous*!"

"Oh, you simply *must* play at my soirée!"

"*Please* say you will come to our dear Sophie's debut next week!"

She made polite conversation with those who converged upon her, asking all the matrons to send her a note reminding her of their invitations. She would be delighted to accept those that her schedule permitted. Even as she gave the appearance of interest in their chatter she watched Miles from the corner of her eye.

His actions mirrored hers. He made conversation, was polite to a fault, but all the while he seemed to be waiting for his moment of escape. It was then that she realized he had not come to the musicale to hear her play. He had come to search for any evidence that might link Lord Pennington to Bella's murder.

The knowledge made her feel strangely bereft.

How had he known about Bella and Pennington? Varya had gleaned the information from reading Bella's journal, but she knew Bella never discussed her past lovers with her current one. Perhaps those gentlemen's clubs were good for something after all.

"I beg your pardon, Miss Varya?"

Turning toward the husky voice, Varya was astonished to find Blythe Christian standing before her, an anxious expression on her striking face.

A long hand extended toward her. "I know we have not been formally introduced. I'm Blythe Christian. I believe you know my brother, Lord Wynter."

Varya accepted the handshake, amazed by the gentle strength of the amazon's grip. "I'm pleased to meet you."

An uncertain smile curved Blythe's lips. "I very much enjoyed your performance." Her gaze flitted to the now silent pianoforte.

"Thank you." Hoping to put the girl at ease, Varya smiled warmly. "I'm always pleased when someone finds pleasure in my music."

"Oh, I did! We were to attend your recital at Lady Penwick's in April, but my brother was called away to the country and we weren't able to go." She licked her lips. "I wonder if you might consider playing at a small soirée my mother and I are planning for the end of the season?"

So that was it. She had been mistaken in thinking Lady Blythe was making an overture of friendship. She simply wanted to hire her. What did she want a friend for anyway? No one could take the place of Bella.

"I would be delighted," Varya replied, schooling her voice. "Just send me a note detailing the time and place."

Blythe's answering smile was more confident this time—one of genuine pleasure. Varya found it next to impossible to harbor any resentment.

"Wonderful! Mama will be so pleased."

"Excellent." Varya was annoyed with this sudden sense of sorrow that washed over her. "Now, if you will excuse me?"

The younger woman looked as though Varya had stepped on her toe. "Oh, yes, of course."

With a slight curtsy, Varya turned to go. A strong hand grabbed her arm, forcing her back around.

Blythe moved closer until mere inches separated them. Her expression was so earnest that Varya could only stare at her.

"Miss Varya, I . . ." She swallowed. "I was very sorry to hear about your friend."

Hot tears blazed at the back of Varya's eyes. No one—not even those who had known Bella—had expressed any sympathy to Varya upon her death. And here was this young gentlewoman who would never—could never—have known Bella, expressing sorrow over her death.

"Thank you," she whispered.

With the slightest hint of a smile, Blythe nodded

and walked away. Varya snatched a glass of wine from a passing footman and concentrated on drinking in small sips until she no longer felt like weeping.

When a group of ladies approached her a few moments later, she was able to pretend nothing had happened. She could even pretend she hadn't noticed Miles watching her from across the floor.

It was then that she realized what Lady Blythe had told her—that Miles had been in the country the night of Lady Penwick's party. That had been the night Bella was killed.

Could it be true? She had no doubt that Lady Blythe believed it, but had she been deceived by her brother, or was he truly innocent?

Some time later, while cornered by Lady Darlington, Varya spied Miles ducking out of the room. She waited a few moments before excusing herself.

"Forgive me, Lady Darlington," she interrupted, placing a silencing hand on the matron's arm, "but I'm afraid I am in need of the ladies' retiring room. Will you excuse me?"

Without waiting for a reply, she turned and hurried from the room. Pressing her back against the cool plaster of the wall, she peered first to her left and then to her right for any sign of Miles.

In the dim light she barely made out his black-clad form at the other end of the hall. The snowy white of his cuff flashed as he slipped into a room three doors down. If all this intrigue was just a ruse to throw her off her suspicion of him, he was doing a good job.

She had to run to catch up with him. Bunching her skirts up in her fists, she hurried after him, a cacophony of rustling silk and clinking jewelry in her wake. Her mother would have a fit of the vapors if she could see her oldest daughter chasing after a man like a hoyden.

Quickly, she opened the door, cast a quick glance around the darkened hall to make sure no one was watching, and dove inside. Her heart somersaulted with excitement and trepidation. What if she was caught?

Gasping for breath, she leaned back against the door, reluctant to step further inside in case she needed to make a quick escape.

Several wall sconces and a lamp on the desk illuminated the room. The walls and furniture were dark and very masculine, covered in shades of forest green and chocolate brown. It looked like every other gentleman's study she had ever seen. Was there some kind of code they had to adhere to?

"Lord Wynter?" she whispered, glancing cautiously around the warmly lit room. He was nowhere to be seen.

"Hell and damnation!"

Varya jumped at the muffled oath, and would have fled the room had the marquess not risen from behind the desk. From his disheveled appearance it was clear that he had been *under* the massive thing.

"You frightened me!" She took her hand away from her breast as her heart began to ease its furious pounding.

"*I* frightened *you*?" The incredulity in his tone would have been amusing if not for the menacing scowl on his handsome face. "Might I remind you, madam, that *you* were the one who barged in here like a pack of wild wolves were snarling at your heels. What the devil are you about?"

His eyebrows were drawn together so tightly that they almost formed a perfect M. Schooling her features to hide her apprehension, Varya replied coolly, "I saw you leave the music room. I assumed you were planning on searching for evidence that might incriminate Lord Pennington. I thought I might offer my assistance."

There, that hadn't been so difficult.

"Get out."

For a moment she was shocked speechless. "I . . . I beg your pardon?"

He looked at her with eyes that were hooded and wary. "The only assistance you can offer me, madam, is by removing yourself from this room. You were quite clear the other night in your wish to separate your investigation from my own. Please leave."

Varya was definitely flustered. "Why you insufferable ape! I have as much right as you do to search this room!"

He shrugged. "Then by all means, search." With that said, he turned his back on her and began peering behind paintings.

She stood her ground, rooted to the carpet by anger and confusion. After telling her to go he was now giving her leave to conduct her own search? Obviously he thought her incapable of finding anything.

"What are you doing?" she demanded as he lifted yet another frame.

"If he's got a safe, it's probably hidden behind one

of the paintings or some other inconspicuous place," he replied coolly, straightening the canvas so that it hung straight.

Varya shrugged and went to the desk.

Miles shot her an impatient glance. "That's too obvious. You'll find nothing there."

But she did. In the lower left-hand drawer, she found a small stack of letters addressed in Bella's handwriting. Grinning triumphantly, she handed them to a glowering Miles.

"The man's a simpleton," he muttered, thumbing through the pile.

Varya chuckled, pleased with herself for having found what he hadn't. "Obviously his wife never uses this room."

He surprised her by dividing the pile between them.

"Would you prefer to have them all to yourself?" he asked, arching a russet brow.

She flushed. He had quite a talent for unnerving her. "No. It will be quicker if we both read—that is, if you plan to share your information with me?" At this point she didn't trust him any more than he trusted her.

His smile was wry. "It will take all my willpower, but I believe I'm up for the task."

They read in silence, scanning each missive for some clue that might convict Pennington. Once in a while, one of them would read a passage out loud. All they discovered was that Pennington had a voracious sexual appetite that seemed to delight Bella. Varya blushed at some of the scenarios her friend had suggested she and the married lord attempt.

Miles tossed the last letter aside in disgust. Varya couldn't blame him for being disappointed, but had he really thought it would be so easy to find the murderer?

She refolded the letters and slipped them back into their previous position in the drawer. She sighed as she stood.

"We've only just begun looking, my lord. I'm sure we'll uncover the truth."

He raked a hand through his hair and met her gaze evenly. "As much as there is no 'we,' madam, I hope you're right. The idea of someone actually getting away with killing Bella makes my gut burn."

Placing her hand on his sleeve, Varya ignored his dismissal. Every instinct she had was telling her that he was no more capable of harming Bella than she was. The realization that she might have actually killed him shamed her.

"You cared for her deeply, didn't you?"

He didn't meet her gaze. Instead, he studied her hand as if he had never seen one before. "Of course I did. I'm not so debauched that I can make love to a woman I don't like."

His tone was biting, but she took no offense. She had a feeling his anger had been brought on not by her impertinence, but by the fact that he had been embarrassed by her observation.

"I would hope not," she replied with mock loftiness. "My opinion of you would fall considerably if you had told me different."

His mouth twisted sardonically. "As if your opinion of me now is a stellar one."

She returned his smile. "It's better than it was the night we met."

They grinned foolishly at each other. Suddenly, Varya became aware that their bodies were slowly drifting closer together. Her heart began to pound in anticipation. Would he kiss her? Did she even want him to kiss her? Good Lord, she did. What the devil was wrong with her?

He was Bella's.

The doorknob rattled, causing both of them to jump back.

Her heart now thumping from fear rather than desire, Varya stared wide-eyed at Miles. He stared back, his face white. What were they going to do? How could they possibly explain their presence in Lord Pennington's private study?

He pointed toward the desk. "Hide!" he whispered.

Varya nodded frantically, hiking up her skirts to run for cover, but at the same time that she moved left, he moved right. They collided at the foot of the sofa, with enough force to knock her well off balance.

Miles grabbed her around the waist. Her hands let go of her skirts and clutched at his shoulders in an effort to steady herself. He took a step forward—

And stepped directly onto the hem on the side of her gown. There was the sound of shredding fabric and gasping breath as Varya toppled to one side. Miles's foot slipped on the silk and he fell with her. He plunged facefirst into her chest as they landed on the hard cushions.

Varya gasped, her skirts billowing around her

thighs. She grabbed him by the ears, trying to extricate him, even as the door flew open.

Within minutes the entire house was buzzing with the *on dit* that the Marquess of Wynter had been found with his face buried in the splendid bosom of the formerly Elusive Varya.

Chapter 5

So this was how it felt to be the mistress of the Marquess of Wynter.

Alone. More alone than she had felt in her entire life.

Varya stood on the balcony that adjoined her bed-chamber. She lifted her face to the night breeze, sighing as its cool fingers drifted through her hair, lifting the heavy mass from her shoulders. She rested her forearms on the wide balustrade and stared out into the darkness. She desperately wanted a glass of vodka.

She wondered if Miles was drinking himself into a stupor, as he had announced earlier.

"By tomorrow morning the whole town will have you known as my mistress," he had muttered gruffly as he escorted her from Pennington's door to her carriage.

"I suppose there are worse things I could be known as," she replied lightly in an attempt to soften his mood. Did he not realize that she felt just as humiliated as he did? After all, it had been *she* with her skirts bunched up around her waist for all to see—not he.

He only grunted and tossed her rather unceremoniously into her coach without so much as a goodnight. For some reason, his behavior left her feeling rather disappointed.

Their audience had been anything *but* disappointed to find them locked in what appeared to be a passionate embrace. None of them had acted surprised, however, and Varya was beginning to realize that Miles's reputation had not been exaggerated.

She also realized that her actions were going to greatly change how people treated her from now on. Some had already begun to regard her with thinly disguised amusement or disgust. A few ladies had even fixed her with looks that could only be described as envious. Who could blame them for wanting a man as handsome and virile as Miles?

She sighed. It would appear that she was not as immune to his charms as she would have liked. She would never admit it out loud, but the heaviness of his body on top of hers had left her with a hot, tingly feeling. His back had been hard and solid beneath her hands, and warm through the light wool of his black cutaway. For one split second, she had been tempted not to pull his head away from her breasts but to press him even deeper into her heated flesh.

And then someone had gasped and she realized they had been caught in a *very* compromising position.

"At least we don't have to explain why we were in the study in the first place," she later remarked as he dragged her outside.

"Trying to find the positive side, are you?" he asked, sparing her a brief glance.

"Yes." She had to run to keep up with him. "Don't you think we should?"

He came to an abrupt stop. "All right. At least they won't expect us to marry." It was said with a decided sarcastic edge, but Varya gave a gusty sigh of relief. Obviously, the marquess wasn't at all accustomed to women *not* wanting to marry him, for he seemed positively startled by her reaction.

After Ivan she had vowed never to marry. There wasn't a man alive whom she trusted enough to hand over complete control of her life. By law a wife was a man's property, and he was free to do what he liked with her money or her person. To put herself so directly under any man's control was to lose her independence, her career, even her own will. In the case of Ivan it might mean losing her life.

A mistress, however, was a different story. A mistress controlled her own money and made her own decisions. If a mistress did not like the way a man touched her, she could leave him. A wife was a prisoner. A mistress was free.

As free as a woman could be nowadays.

Yes, she could live with the stigma of being thought the mistress of Miles Christian. It went against everything she had been brought up to believe, but it would even provide a wonderful cover for them if they chose to continue investigating Bella's murder together.

It would still be her ruin. Having been raised to guard her virtue, she found the thought was somewhat distressing.

"Oh, Bella," she whispered to the darkness. "Why did you leave me?"

For years, her higher social status had given her knowledge and experience that Bella could only imagine. The awe in the older girl's eyes had been the only encouragement Varya needed to spin tale after tale of her opulent life in Russia. It had made the fact that her father had sent her away to school almost bearable.

Only Bella knew how much Varya had wanted her father's approval. Only Bella knew that Varya had never been able to win it.

When Bella ran away from school to become a singer, it had been Varya she had thanked for giving her a dream to chase. Far from feeling proud, Varya had been horrified that her friend had chosen such a path. It wasn't until a few years later, when she herself left the school and forced her entourage to make a sojourn into Paris before returning to Russia, that Varya saw just how free her friend was.

At that time, Bella was a rising star, the darling of Paris. Her lover was a handsome French nobleman who treated her like a rare gem. Bella was in control of her life. She conducted herself like a lady, thanks to Varya's tutelage, and in return, she shared an intimate knowledge of men that had made Varya blush right down to her ankles.

Despite Bella's words, Varya had been completely unprepared for the Marquess of Wynter and his allure.

How Bella had gushed about the man! How many

letters were nothing but "Miles this" and "Miles that." She was certain Bella exaggerated the man's looks and charm. It angered her to see the supremely self-assured Bella make a cake of herself for a man who had no intention of marrying her. And when he broke Bella's heart, Varya's opinion slipped lower still.

Regardless of her personal view of the man, he had meant a lot to Bella and vice versa. He was also deadly attractive. How could she find him so decidedly arrogant yet thrill at his very touch? For that's what the feel of him had been—thrilling. She had actually found herself wondering what it would be like to be his mistress in reality.

She could never betray Bella in such a way. But her friend's memory aside, Varya had not been brought up to be anything to a man other than a wife.

That would never happen now—not that she ever wished it to.

She glanced past the glass doors to the miniature on top of her dressing table. She didn't have to see the faces depicted there to know what their reactions to her situation would be.

Her mother, God bless her, would try to understand but would fail. Ana was not the kind of woman to give in to temptation, and she was certainly no match for the will of Vladimir Vasilyevich Ulyanov. No daughter of his would degrade herself by becoming a man's mistress. Even after almost five years on her own, she didn't know if she could stand up to Papa. Her hands shook as she imagined her father dragging her back to St. Petersburg, back to Ivan, to a life as little more than a prisoner—if she lived that long.

She forced herself to take several deep, calming breaths.

"Everything is going to be fine. No one is going to hurt you," Bella had said when Varya arrived in Paris after that awful night and collapsed sobbing in her arms. Varya forced herself to believe in the words now as she had then.

Bella had coaxed her out of her shell. She'd convinced Varya that isolating herself from society drew more attention than placing herself in the middle of it.

It hadn't been easy, but Varya had stepped into the spotlight. Bella talked her into accompanying her at a soirée in Paris, and for the first time, Varya became known for her own talent rather than position or wealth. When they arrived in London, Varya began building a career of her own.

With Bella's help she'd fabricated a background, shrouding herself in enough mystery to make herself intriguing, but not enough to make anyone suspicious. If she'd had any idea just how provocative her "Elusive" persona would become, she might have been tempted to remain hiding in her boudoir. Instead, she embraced that side of herself and the freedom it brought. Still, when she thought of her father or Ivan, she became the scared little girl again.

Ivan was far away, as was her father. Neither one of them could force her to do anything she did not want. Her father didn't even know if she was still alive, let alone lusting after the man who had broken her best friend's heart.

Lust was something Varya was not accustomed to.

She had listened to Bella's shocking tales of sexual adventures with mild curiosity and burning cheeks, achingly aware that she had reached spinsterhood without ever having known the physical pleasure between a man and a woman.

There was no point even thinking about it. Bella had loved Miles, and Varya could never soil her memory by falling into bed with him. She would not be his mistress.

But she could pretend.

She wondered if Miles would follow through with their farce. Whether he liked the idea or not, pretending to be having an *affaire d'amour* gave them the perfect excuse to be in each other's company, and to be sneaking off together at parties while they searched for clues to the identity of Bella's killer. If only he would continue to pretend, they could solve the mystery together. After all, the one thing they agreed on was that the murderer had to be brought to justice.

Varya sighed and crawled into bed. She'd have to make Miles realize that having her for a mistress was a good thing.

"They're all out to get me," Miles muttered to his unconscious companion. "Every woman I know is part of a great conspiracy to bring me to my knees."

His mother—and every mama on the marriage mart—urged him to remarry, while Blythe constantly reminded him of his notorious reputation. This, coupled with the memory of Varya's lush body beneath his, convinced him that the entire female race was hell-bent on driving him either to the altar or to Bedlam.

No one—not even his mother—seemed to comprehend his aversion to marriage. Was he the only one who remembered Charlotte and the circumstances of her death? She had died bringing Miles's heir into the world. They had all told him it wasn't his fault, but how could it not be?

The loss of his son had been punishment—he was certain of it. He hadn't loved Charlotte, not in the way a man should loved his wife. Oh, he knew many ton marriages in which both parties despised each other and still managed to produce healthy children, but his marriage to Charlotte was different. She had loved him, while he had thought of her only as a friend.

How often had she done something just to please him? All of her gowns were in his favorite colors. All their meals were prepared to suit his palate. They attended the plays that he wanted to see, attended the parties he wanted to attend. Never once did Charlotte even attempt to assert her own will.

She had even gotten pregnant when he decided it was time, although he doubted either of them had much control over that.

Pregnancy had been wonderful to Charlotte. She adored every moment of it, and Miles shared her enthusiasm. He wanted a child as badly as she did, but it was not to be. Charlotte died shortly after the midwife took the stillborn infant from her womb.

Perhaps the rules of society and producing an heir led to the death of his wife and son, but he *knew* he was responsible for it. Of that he was certain.

When they put that tiny coffin in the Christian family crypt, Miles's soul had gone into darkness with it. There had been no light in his life since.

Until a woman with no last name tried to kill him in the name of friendship.

He swished the brandy around in his glass. He couldn't shake the feeling that he was getting into a situation with Varya he would not be able to easily walk away from. Common sense told him to get out while he still could. His cock urged him not to be so hasty. The very fact that he was listening to the latter left a sour taste in his mouth. He took a deep swallow of brandy to rinse it away.

"How can I possibly be attracted to such a woman?"

His companion made no reply.

Miles tried to think about something other than Varya's lush form and intoxicating scent—a hint of cloves and roses.

He glanced around him. White's was fairly crowded, as it usually was after a social event such as Pennington's. He tried to ignore the conversation and laughter buzzing about the club, but it was difficult.

He was the main topic of conversation.

By now, the news that the Marquess of Wynter and the Elusive Varya had been discovered in a clandestine embrace in Lord Pennington's study was spreading like wildfire throughout the ton. Miles had already endured dozens of knowing smirks and nudges from many of his peers.

"Surprised to see you here, Wynter," Lord Darlington had guffawed, shoving a fat elbow into Miles's ribs. "Thought you'd have much more *satisfying* sport than brandy and cards to indulge in tonight." He and his companions laughed uproariously before scuttling off to find a vacant table.

Miles glared after them, becoming increasingly aware that despite the envious and jealous glances cast in his direction, everyone else was wondering what he was doing there as well.

He wanted to stand up and scream that she wasn't his mistress, and that he wasn't the randy goat they all believed him to be. But to do that would require an explanation of why he and Varya had been in Pennington's study alone. Short of telling the truth, which would more than likely ruin their chances of finding Bella's killer if he was a member of the aristocracy, Miles couldn't think of any excuse society would believe over the salacious one they had.

If only the nosy baggage had stayed in the music room where she belonged instead of chasing after him. They wouldn't be in this situation if she had allowed him to take care of everything. But no, she had to be right there beside him.

"Why couldn't she just stay out of my way?" he demanded, jabbing his unconscious companion in the head with his forefinger.

Still no reply.

The fact that she had not chosen a lover from her many admirers before this was what had kept Varya a notch above other women of similar professions. Now that she was believed to have succumbed to Miles's charms, she would be branded a courtesan like so many others.

How would her pride withstand it when almost all

of London believed her to be just another whore? Women who at one time vied for her attention would snub her. Men would no longer try to woo her; they would expect her to give herself to them on demand.

The very thought of anyone trying to force himself on Varya made his blood boil. She might not be his mistress in actuality, but Miles intended to guard her as such. He knew very few would risk his fury.

He took another drink.

"You look as if you just had to shoot your favorite horse."

Without looking up, Miles poured himself another glass. "Care for a brandy, Carny?"

"Don't mind if I do," his friend replied jovially, dropping into the chair opposite him. He ignored their third companion.

"For a man who has secured the most sought-after woman in town as his mistress, you look decidedly glum." Was there an edge of jealousy in his voice?

Miles grimaced. "Jealousy is a childish quality, my friend."

The blond man almost choked on his brandy. "Jealousy? Don't be a fool. What the devil is the matter with you anyway?"

Miles smiled grimly. "My brand-new mistress, as you so thoughtfully pointed out to me."

Carny shook his head, his smile fading into bewilderment. "I'm not understanding you at all. You outswagger us all for Varya's favors, have every tomcat in London green with envy, and I'm to believe that you don't want her?"

Miles finished the brandy in his glass and immediately poured himself another. He was beginning to lose feeling in various parts of his body, but not the parts he had hoped.

He laughed mockingly. "Oh, I *want* her." The brandy gave his voice a slightly raspy edge. "I have serious doubts as to whether she would have me."

His friend stared at him. Miles might have laughed at the expression of disbelief on Carny's face were he not so bent on intoxication.

"But weren't you found in Pennington's study with your hands up her skirts?"

"Of course not!" Miles fairly shouted, appalled. Never mind that when he and Varya fell onto the sofa her skirts had indeed pooled up around her soft, white thighs. He could still feel the satiny smoothness of her breasts against his cheeks. He felt that part of his anatomy which was not yet numb begin to stir.

"That wasn't my intention at all!" Several club members turned interested eyes toward them. He glared coldly at them until they turned away.

"Then why were you there?" Carny demanded in a sharp whisper.

The vehemence in his friend's tone startled Miles. With a narrowed gaze that was beginning to blur a little, he regarded his friend. Why was Carny so interested in his relationship with Varya?

"Because we were trying to discover whether or not Pennington is connected with Bella's murder," he explained, exasperated. "Lud, man! How much have you had to drink?"

Miles could have sworn that his friend was laughing at him. "Did you find anything at Pennington's?" Carny asked.

"No, but later I discovered that many of our acquaintances are several hundred pounds richer this evening, having placed bets earlier as to whether or not 'The Marquess of W would conquer the Elusive V.' " This time his gaze was steady as it met the gray eyes across from him. "Although I believe you suffered a bit of a loss."

Carny winced and turned a dull crimson. He actually looked a little contrite, though he did not attempt to deny it. "I meant no harm."

Miles's jaw clenched. "You do not find making sport of a woman's reputation harmful?"

Carny looked at him as if he had lost his mind. "She's a musician, Miles! One step up from an actress, if that. Regardless of the fact that you are the first gentleman whose attentions she has accepted, everyone in London is well aware of what kind of reputation a woman like Varya has. A very loose one."

Miles's hand shot out and grabbed Carny by the cravat. His reflexes were surprisingly sharp for a man as drunk as he now was. He hauled his friend so close that their faces were almost touching. Just as suddenly, he thrust him back into his chair again.

Carny stared at him, his face ashen. He straightened his waistcoat as curious glances flickered their way. "I have no idea what has gotten into you. No doubt this will all blow over soon. Varya is a mature woman. Surely she knew what would happen. It has no effect on what everyone thinks of you."

Disgusted by the other man's cavalier attitude, Miles shoved back his chair and stood. Towering over Carny, he leaned down and met his puzzled gaze with eyes that looked as if they had been replaced by smoldering coals.

"I already know what everyone thinks of *me*, my friend. Obviously you all believe me to be a greater libertine than I could ever physically hope to be." He straightened and began to back away. "What concerns me now—and God only knows why—is what everyone thinks of *her*."

Chapter 6

❦

Varya had never experienced the cut direct before. She couldn't say that she found the experience a pleasant one.

The invitation to Lady Beckwith-Breyer's ball had arrived several weeks earlier, long before her entanglement with Miles Christian. If she had known how differently people would treat her because of her association with the marquess, she would have stayed at home.

Her abigail, Amy, had gone to great lengths with her appearance—insisting not only on using curling tongs on Varya's normally straight hair, but also on using cosmetics to heighten her already vivid coloring. As a result, her lips and eyes seemed larger, darker against the paleness of her complexion.

Varya had also labored over what to wear, finally deciding on a dark green satin gown with a low square neckline and cap sleeves. Her gloves and slippers had been dyed to match. Her only jewelry was a thick diamond collar and the diamond-studded comb securing the mass of curls on top of her head.

She didn't even try to deny that she hoped to impress Miles with her appearance. Too late she realized her elegant apparel might make her appear to others as if she were trying to rise above her station as a mere musician, especially now that the whole town believed her to be Miles's mistress.

If they only knew.

"Miss Varya . . . How lovely to see you."

Lady Beckwith-Breyer greeted her with great cordiality—and anxiety.

"Thank you, Lady Beckwith-Breyer. It is a pleasure to be here. Tell me, are you well?" The lady was so pale and pasty-looking that Varya thought she would swoon.

"No, no," her hostess replied a little too quickly, her eyes darting around the room. "I am fine, thank you. Please excuse me."

It was then, as the older woman scurried away, that Varya caught several sly glances cast in her direction. The realization that *she* had been the reason for her hostess's distress brought a deep flush to her cheeks. A lady could never be certain of how a fallen woman might be received in society, and no doubt Lady Beckwith-Breyer worried whether Varya's appearance would ruin her party.

Embarrassed, Varya continued through the crowd,

hoping to find a friendly face. She spotted Lady Pennington and Lady Sally Jersey a few feet away, moving through the crowd toward her. After the scene in Lord Pennington's study, Varya had no idea how the lady would receive her.

Lady Pennington raised her impeccably styled blond head, met Varya's gaze coolly, and then looked away as if she hadn't recognized her.

Varya felt the blood rush from her face. Her eyes were locked on Lady Pennington and Lady Jersey as they walked away from her. Lady Jersey didn't even acknowledge her, but Varya could hear her tinkling laughter at Lady Pennington's snub. They were laughing at her!

Mortified, yet outraged by their behavior and the malicious glances other guests were directing toward her, Varya turned to flee.

She whirled around and stumbled directly into the arms of Lord Pennington.

"Oh!" She jumped back as though she had been burned.

He caught her by the upper arms, effectively preventing her from tripping over the hem of her gown.

"Oops!" He favored her with a kind smile before releasing her. "Steady there, my dear."

Varya smiled shakily. "Forgive me, Lord Pennington."

"No harm done. Do not trouble yourself over it. Trying to make your escape, were you?"

She nodded. She tried to meet his gaze, but found it very difficult. She was so embarrassed.

"Well, can't say that I blame you. Must be demmed

uncomfortable for you to be out in society this evening after that spectacle you made of yourself with Wynter in my study last night."

Her eyes widened at the archness in his voice. For some reason his change of manner made it easier for her to raise her gaze to his.

Gone was the kind, older man who had kept her from stumbling. In his place was a very condescending aristocrat. He stared down his hawklike nose at her as if she were the lowliest of serfs. Had he looked at Bella the same way?

"You would have been wise to choose someone other than Wynter for your protector, Varya," he informed her with a condescending air. "He's not exactly known for his discretion."

Her flesh seemed to crawl where his hand rubbed the expanse of bare arm between her sleeve and glove. No one—not even Ivan—had ever caused her to feel quite so dirty. She felt hot rage building deep within her.

"There are plenty of other gentlemen who can keep you in the same style as Wynter, my dear. Gentlemen who will not embarrass you by bringing you out of your customary sphere into society."

Her jaw tightened. "Where I would obviously be an embarrassment."

He smiled. "Exactly." He stepped closer to her, so mere inches stood between them. "Evidently you understand the kind of arrangement I speak of."

She nodded. "I believe so. You refer to the kind of arrangement where the gentleman supplies a lovely little house on the edge of town and pays all the expenses in return for a companion who waits on his every need."

"Yes, that's it exactly." His eyes glittered hotly.

She smiled coyly at him. "By any chance, would you be offering me such an 'arrangement,' my lord?"

Lord Pennington licked his lips, his eyes riveted on her cleavage. Boxing his ears was a great temptation.

"I would be honored to win you away from Wynter, my dear."

Fighting the overwhelming desire to break her fan over his head, Varya fixed him with a narrowed gaze. "And would you tuck me away in a house far from the prying eyes of society? Keep me your little secret?"

"Secret? What secret?"

Varya froze. In her anger she had not been aware of the hush that had fallen over the ballroom. Apparently neither had Lord Pennington, or he no doubt would not have propositioned her within earshot of the Marquess of Wynter.

Tearing her eyes from the earl's ashen face, Varya raised her chin to meet Miles's mocking smile.

It was a mistake. Her breath caught at the sight of him. He had brushed his hair into some semblance of order, save for one unruly burnished lock falling over his forehead. Instead of the formal knee breeches, he wore full-length trousers that emphasized the length and solid muscle of his legs.

"Lord Pennington was just telling me how much he admires your taste, my lord," she replied with mock civility.

"Is that so?" His brow arched as he caught the meaning behind her words.

Their gazes locked and held. Under the glow of half a dozen chandeliers, his eyes seemed unnaturally bright. Staring into their hypnotic depths, Varya found it all too easy to forget about their delightedly scandalized audience.

He bowed over her hand. She couldn't even remember offering it to him. He pressed his mouth against her knuckles. She could feel the warmth of his breath through her glove, and her stomach dropped as if the bottom had fallen out of it.

"You'll excuse us, won't you, Pennington?" Miles asked without looking at the shorter man.

The band struck up a waltz, and he drew her toward the dance floor without a word. He kept his eyes fastened on hers so intently that she found it impossible to look away.

Placing his hand on the small of her back, he pulled her much closer than he ought. She knew she should protest, but she couldn't bring herself to do so. She liked being held by him. She liked feeling his thighs brush hers as he whirled her around the floor as if they were gliding on air. He was an excellent dancer.

"What did Pennington say to you?"

She lifted her shoulders in a slight shrug. "Only that he would be pleased to have me once you were finished."

"Bastard."

The vehemence in his voice startled her. "Not to mention stupid. I am neither desperate nor blind, which I believe a woman would have to be to willingly share Lord Pennington's bed. What Bella saw in him I'll never know."

A smile curved his wide mouth and his eyes glittered with amusement.

"No doubt there are some who wonder what you see in me." He whirled her through a turn so quickly it made her head spin. "I confess to wondering the same thing myself."

Varya's heart pounded against her ribs. "As I am not your mistress, I cannot see that it matters."

"Ah, but you are my mistress—as far as society is concerned."

What difference did that make? It changed nothing between *them*—did it?

"You of all people, my lord, should know that hardly signifies," she replied archly as they twirled around the floor. "Society will believe almost anything."

"Lucky for us, hmmm? Otherwise we would be faced with the rather difficult task of explaining what we were doing in the study in the first place. No doubt it would make finding the murderer quite laborious for us."

"Oh? So now *we're* going to find the murderer, are we? Please don't feel duty-bound to humor me now that a scandal has erupted, my lord. I'm sure I can continue the investigation on my own." Why then didn't she feel as certain as she sounded?

"Ah yes. You did *quite* well. Abducting men at gunpoint is a very efficient way to conduct any kind of investigation, love. I'm surprised you haven't already unveiled the killer." The humor in his voice was thinly guised. Why did he always seem to be laughing at her? And why was she so on edge around him?

"If it weren't for me you'd still be in Pennington's study peering behind his wife's watercolors," she hissed, fighting the urge to kick his shin. "And I am *not* your love."

"Oh, *I* know that, and *you* know that, but everyone else . . ." He shrugged, allowing her to draw the obvious conclusion.

"Well, it didn't take much, did it? Perhaps if you weren't already renowned for your licentious behavior, the assumption wouldn't have been so easily made!"

His face flushed; the good humor disappeared. "Perhaps if it wasn't for your career, the assumption would not have been so 'easily made.' "

"If it wasn't for my career, my lord," she ground out between clenched teeth, "I would never have come to London and Bella's murderer would never be apprehended, because you still wouldn't even know she was dead!"

That silenced him. A tiny muscle ticked in his jaw, and Varya was at once both pleased with herself for getting to him and fearful of his retaliation. Her body tensed for flight.

He steered her through another turn. "You will not create further spectacle by deserting me on the dance floor."

"*I* will not create further spectacle?" She was shocked almost speechless by the absurd accusation.

"You should have known better than to come here tonight. You should have known the gossip would run wild."

Her cheeks flamed with embarrassment. "Believe

me, my lord, had I any inclination as to how I would be received here tonight, I would not have come. Do not concern yourself, however. They still adore *you*."

Before he could reply, the music came to an end and the dancers began to drift away from the center of the room.

Miles regarded her impassively. "Indeed. Well, in the interest of not drawing any more attention to both of us I will leave you now, madam." He bowed stiffly.

Varya didn't even bother to reply or curtsy. Before he straightened, she was already halfway across the floor, the heat of his stare burning into her back.

Miles escaped the crowded confines of the ballroom into the cool night air. As the sounds and stifling heat of the ballroom faded, he inhaled deeply the scent of lilacs and roses. After enduring an hour of scrutiny and speculation, it was good to be outside alone in the dark.

He made his way to one of the darker corners of the terrace. Shrouded by shrubbery, it was no doubt for the sole purpose of providing privacy to desirous lovers.

Fortunately, he found the spot unoccupied and he eased himself down onto the bench with a grateful sigh. He pressed his fingertips to his forehead, rubbing away the ache that pressed against his skull. He was too old for the high drama he had been taking part in all evening.

How could he have behaved so badly toward Varya? One minute he had been teasing her, and the next they had been practically tearing each other's throats out. Never before had he been so deliberately cruel to a woman. But never before had a woman so provoked him.

What difference did it make whether she was or wasn't his mistress? This public scrutiny was ridiculous. He was a single man. Varya was an unattached woman, not a chit right out of the schoolroom. Many of the people pointing fingers and making snide remarks were engaging in clandestine affairs with the spouses of friends, even having children by them. He lived in a society of hypocrites, and there was very little that could be done about it, other than wait for their interest to move on to something else.

Miles gazed up at the sky. It was a clear night, and the stars twinkled and glittered like diamonds. He watched as one of the stars streaked across the heavens. In the dark, he could pretend he was miles away from Varya rather than just outside the room where she was dancing with Lord Dennyson. Right at this very moment, he could almost pretend they had never met.

Almost.

Who was she? How had she ended up living with Bella in France? Her house and manners indicated that she was quite wealthy. She did not perform often enough to make a fortune from it, so where did the money come from?

More importantly, why did she get under his skin the way she did?

Perhaps because she was one of the few women he had ever met who hadn't thrown herself—or her nearest relative—at him? He raked a hand through his hair in frustration. He didn't have any answers. Very un-usual for him.

He sat there for quite some time, allowing the soft breeze to wipe away the sticky perspiration the heated ballroom and layers of evening wear had induced. It felt good finally to be comfortable and alone.

He didn't give much thought to the voices that were approaching him until a female voice rang out with a very familiar accent.

"Just what is so important that we have to discuss it out here, Lord Carnover?"

Miles's jaw dropped. Varya? Carny? What the devil?

"I want to know what kind of game you're trying to play with Miles."

"I beg your pardon?"

Miles smiled at the ire in her tone. Apparently he wasn't the only man capable of drawing her claws.

"Filling his head with this nonsense about discover-ing the identity of Isabella's murderer. It's all a scheme to get your hooks into him, isn't it?"

Careful, Carny, he thought, well aware of the fading bruise on his temple. *She'll knock you senseless.*

"My relationship with Miles is none of your con-cern! Think of me what you will, my lord. I do not care."

Miles chuckled softly.

"I'll tell you what I think of you, madam. I think you turned down every other man who made an offer to you because you're a lying opportunist using Bella's murder as an excuse to snare one of the wealthiest ti-tles in all of Britain!"

Miles started. He had never heard Carny speak that way to a woman before. Anger began to worm up from within his belly. His hand went to the shrub, about to push it aside so he might confront his friend. To his surprise he heard Varya chuckle, and he paused.

"Snare him? Oh, my lord, I'd like to believe you might find me smarter than that. What man of Miles's rank would ever lower himself to marry a mere musician?" She laughed.

"I remember the generous offer you made me several weeks ago, Lord Carnover, and I remember that marriage was not on the list of what *you* wanted from me. Tell me, are you speaking out of concern for your friend, or are you simply trying to find an excuse for my apparent preference for Miles over you?"

Now *this* was an interesting turn of events. Carny had said nothing about Varya refusing an offer from him.

The silence that followed her question betrayed Carny's guilt.

"Lord Carnover, I did not choose Miles as my protector." Varya's voice was calmer now, soothing even. "If he told you that the rumor was started because we were investigating Bella's death, then he told you the truth. If we had not been caught together in Lord Pennington's study I would be carrying on as I always have."

Miles had to press his ear against the foliage to hear Carny's softly spoken disbelief.

"You mean to tell me that Miles hasn't wooed you?"

"Yes. You needn't take it as an affront to yourself or

as a danger to your friend. My relationship with Miles is purely platonic, I assure you."

Miles made a face. Even though he had told Carny that there was nothing between them, it irked him that Varya found him so easy to resist.

"It seems I have made quite an ass of myself," Carny remarked.

Yes, you have, Miles agreed.

"It is something I have learned to expect from your sex, my lord." There was laughter but no censure in Varya's voice.

"You're too kind," Carny replied with a dry chuckle. "May I escort you back inside?"

"No, thank you," she replied lightly. "I don't think my reputation could survive an association with both you *and* the Marquess of Wynter. I'll return in a few moments."

"As you wish."

Miles waited until Carny's retreating footfalls died away before stepping from his hiding spot.

"You handled that quite graciously."

He had the pleasure of watching her jump and whirl around, indignation flashing in her sapphire eyes.

"Sinking to eavesdropping, my lord? How petty."

Still angry, was she? Miles smiled. "Not so petty as you if the charges Carny laid were true."

She frowned. "You know very well that they are not."

"Do I?" He paused to smell a white rose that blossomed on the trellis. "You sought me out—and in a very attention-grabbing manner, I might add." He raised a questioning brow. "Perhaps it is not Bella's murderer you wished to catch, but her former lover?"

He just barely managed to grab her wrist before she could strike him, but wasn't quite quick enough to escape her foot. It connected with his shin with bone-jarring force.

"I've been wanting to do *that* all evening!" She glared at him, her eyes dark with indignant rage.

"That's quite a temper you have, madam," he ground out, resisting the urge to rub the spot where she had connected. He held fast to her wrist.

" 'Tis only you who brings it out of me, my lord."

She tried to free herself from his grip, going so far as to pry at his fingers with her free hand.

"You insufferable man! Let go of me!"

He smiled at her exertions, but had no intention of letting her go just yet. The throbbing in his shin was worth the knowledge that, if nothing else, she was truthful in her desire to catch Bella's killer.

"Bastard!" She clawed viciously at his fingers.

Tightening his hold on her arm, Miles yanked. She fell against him with a surprised yelp, and her free hand slammed into his chest. He grunted at the impact, but maintained his footing.

She sneered at him, her body rigid where it touched his. For a moment he half expected her to spit in his face, so foul was her expression.

The warm fullness of her breasts pressed against his torso. He wondered if she could feel his heart pounding against his ribs through the layers of clothing that separated them.

Miles smiled. He was tired of all this arguing. He

was tired of pretending she didn't affect him. "There's so much fire in you, Varya. I think you are one of the most intriguing females I have ever met."

She continued to watch him warily, but some of the stiffness left her body. She seemed to be at a loss for words, something that surprised him.

"If you hadn't been forced into this farce of ours by circumstance," he began, his voice sounding strange and husky to his own ears, "would you have chosen me over all the others as you told Carny you had?" As he spoke them, the words astonished him. What was he doing?

He relaxed his hold on her arm, and as she withdrew it, peeled off her glove to bare the flesh underneath. The bruises he had given the night of their struggle were dark against her pale skin.

"I'm sorry for this," he murmured, balling the silk in his fist. "Does it hurt?"

"A little."

He brought her hand to his lips, planting feathery kisses along the sensitive flesh on the inside of her wrist, up to her palm. She gasped softly. He nipped gently at the tip of each finger, savoring the salty-sweetness of her skin.

He released her, and his hand came up to caress her cheek. He gazed down at her, searching for any indication that she wanted him as desperately as he wanted her. Her eyes were closed, her lips slightly parted. Her chest rose and fell in shallow breaths. So she wasn't immune to him after all.

"Would you have chosen me, Varya?" he asked again, plucking a rose from the trellis. He brushed his lips against her forehead, her temple, and the soft skin of her cheek, trailing the petals of the rose along her throat, down to the expanse of creamy flesh revealed by the neckline of her gown. "Would you?"

Without waiting for her reply, his lips claimed hers. Her mouth opened and he could taste champagne on her breath.

She didn't try to fight him. Her free hand gripped the lapel of his coat as if to pull him closer. Her tongue met his as it slipped past her lips. His heart leaped traitorously within his chest, and Miles knew that he would soon be lost.

Reluctantly, he let her go. Taking a step back, he studied her flushed face as he fought the urges that threatened to consume him. Her lips were moist and red; her nostrils flared with every panting breath. She seemed to have difficulty pulling herself together. *Good*. Lord knew he wouldn't be able to reenter the ballroom until a certain part of his anatomy righted itself.

She opened her eyes, but instead of desire in their dark blue depths, he saw a raw vulnerability that frightened him. She looked like a woman going to meet her executioner rather than one succumbing to passion. He reached for her.

"No!" she cried, jerking back from his grasp. "No, I wouldn't have chosen you!"

"You lie," he chided gently, his fingers brushing her cheek.

Varya pulled away from him as if his touch burned. Her eyes were wide and wild against the pallor of her face.

"You mustn't ask me such questions," she whispered hoarsely. "Please do not ask me again."

With that, she turned and fled down the steps into the garden and into the darkness without a backward glance.

Miles stared after her, stunned by her behavior. Why had she so fervently denied her desire for him? He had felt it, as hot and consuming as his own.

He stared down at the glove in his hand. It wasn't much, but that flimsy scrap of silk would be a suitable excuse for calling on her the next day.

Then perhaps he would learn why she had lied.

Chapter 7

Lord Finch-Barrows: *Fat and sweaty*.
Lord Malbray: *Hairy palms*.
Lord Pennington: *Lecher*.

Varya sighed and lifted her quill from the paper. So far, none of Bella's paramours had presented himself in a very flattering light.

She looked down at the last name on her list. She had written it with a great deal more flourish than the others.

Miles Christian: *Dangerous*.

With a disgusted snort, she crossed off his name, dipping and redipping her quill until there was nothing but a large black blob where the words had been.

Her attempts to put him out of her mind had been futile. She had managed a brief respite during the few hours sleep she had gotten after returning home from the ball. Even then, he had been her last thought before falling asleep, and her first thought upon waking.

How could she ever face him again after making such a fool of herself the night before?

She had hidden in the garden maze until she could stand to stay there no longer. By the time she had found her way to the exit, most of the guests had already departed. Miles was one of them. She made her excuses to Lady Beckwith-Breyer—who had been all too happy to see her finally leave—and called for her carriage.

Lady Pennington and Lady Jersey were waiting for Lady Jersey's carriage, since Lord Pennington had departed earlier for one of his clubs.

Varya stood in stony silence for as long as she could bear, listening to Lady Pennington's stage-whispered slurs against her character. Lady Jersey tittered and giggled, and tapped her companion's arm with her fan when she uttered an especially biting comment.

When her carriage finally pulled up in front of the walk, Varya turned to Lady Pennington and fixed her with a sweet smile that was anything but sincere.

"Lady Pennington," she began, meeting the woman's haughty gaze. "Would you do me the courtesy of thanking your husband for the flowers he sent me after my performance at the King's Theater the other night?" She watched in satisfaction as the blond woman's face darkened.

"But please tell him that in light of my current

arrangement with the Marquess of Wynter, I must regretfully decline the generous offer he presented to me earlier this evening." She bowed her head slightly in parting and forced herself to descend the steps to the street in a slow and regal fashion. She would have preferred to hike up her skirts and run, but her pride refused to allow it.

Sighing, she tried to return her attention to the list, but the invitation she had received that morning caught her eye. It was from Lord and Lady Rochester, one of the haute ton's more liberal-minded couples. Their gatherings were renowned for their sexual exploits. Guests would often bring their spouses and meet new lovers during the course of the visit. It was not unusual behavior at any such gathering. Varya had been invited to their house party scheduled to begin that Thursday. Since it was still the season, the party would last only until Sunday so guests would not be away from the delights of London for long.

She didn't want to go, especially not alone, but Lord Rochester had been another one of Bella's conquests. Varya was beginning to comprehend that no matter how kind and sweet a friend Bella might have been, she had absolutely no scruples when it came to the opposite sex.

Still, she owed it to her friend to continue her search for her killer, even if it meant attending Lord and Lady Rochester's hedonistic party. She would feel so much safer if Miles were to accompany her, but she wasn't sure she had the courage to go with him if he asked.

No man had ever affected her senses as he did. With

Ivan she had feared for her safety. With Miles she feared for her heart. In some respects, that made him the more dangerous of the two.

A knock at the door interrupted her thoughts.

"Enter!"

Piotr stepped into the room, his stocky frame seeming almost small in the large doorframe.

"Forgive me, Excellency, but that man is here to see you."

Varya's smile was tolerant if somewhat shaky. "I assume by 'that man' you mean the Marquess of Wynter?"

Her servant nodded.

"Show him in, Piotr, and please refrain from calling me 'Excellency' in his presence."

"Yes, Excellency." He bowed and backed out of the room.

Miles. Varya laid a hand against her midriff as if it might quell the uneasiness there. She hadn't expected to see him so soon. What would she say? More importantly, what could he possibly have to say to her?

She stood, brushing at her skirts to smooth out any wrinkles in the soft lavender muslin.

He entered, looking dashing in a wine-colored coat and buff trousers; his hat and gloves in his hand. He sketched a small, stiff bow.

Varya swallowed, unsure of what to say other than "Good day, Miles."

"Good day." He held out a square of fabric to her. As she took it she realized it was the glove he had removed the night before. Her fingers brushed his as they closed around the silk. Heat suffused parts of her body she had never known to feel warm before.

"Thank you," she whispered, her voice hoarse. "Will you sit?"

"I will, thank you."

That he seemed as uncomfortable as she felt did little to soothe her nerves. She left her position by the desk and followed him to the sitting area, seating herself on the chaise. He took the chair across from her.

They sat in tense silence. Varya stared at a point just beyond his shoulder, while Miles twiddled his thumbs and glanced about like a caged animal.

He cleared his throat, and finally folded his hands. "How are you?"

"I am very well, thank you," she replied softly. "And you?"

His smile was strained. "Fine, fine. I received an invitation to a house party at Lord Rochester's country seat this morning."

"So did I."

"Ah." He nodded, tense as he sat on the edge of the seat, as if any second he might bolt for the door. Did he regret his actions the night before? Or had the kiss left him as shaken as it had left her?

"I think I might go," she began, as if the idea had just occurred to her. "Lord Rochester was one of Bella's lovers." *Just like Miles*, she reminded herself.

"Yes. I know."

"Oh yes. Of course." A movement by the door caught her attention. She almost sighed in relief at the interruption. "Ah, Piotr. Vodka. Good."

The manservant entered the room and set the tray on the low table between them. He shot Miles another one of his intimidating glares, only slightly less hostile this time.

Miles smiled weakly and took the glass she offered him. He drank deeply, hoping the potent liquor would boost his courage. Out of the corner of his eye he saw Varya's eyes widen at his behavior. He lowered the glass, but it was already empty.

"Would you care for another?" Her voice betrayed her bewilderment.

He shook his head.

"I think I may attend the Rochesters' party as well," he said in a careful tone.

"Oh?"

"Yes."

"It probably would be a good idea for both of us to be there in case one of us finds evidence linking Lord Rochester to Bella's death," she agreed somewhat lamely.

"Exactly."

The ticking of the grandfather clock in the corner seemed abnormally loud in Miles's ears. The flesh underneath his stiff collar and cravat was moist with sweat and beginning to itch.

"We could go together." Hesitantly, he raised his gaze to meet hers. What the devil was the matter with him? He hadn't been nervous with a woman for years.

The color had deserted her face, to be replaced by two bright crimson circles high on her cheeks.

"I don't think that would be wise."

"More fuel for the gossips, I suppose. Perhaps we should arrive separately."

"I think that would be for the best."

He stared at her, suspicion tickling the edges of his mind. "Is it the gossips you wish to avoid, or my company?"

She jumped to her feet, as if to dodge the question.

"I have a list of Bella's suitors. Perhaps you'd like to take a look?" She hurried over to the desk.

He rose and moved to join her by the desk. With a gentle tug, he took the fluttering parchment from her hands and read what she had written.

"Nice penmanship."

"Thank you."

He began to chuckle. Some of her comments were hilarious, scathing even. Unfortunately for the gentlemen she referred to, they were all accurate.

"Lord Dennyson drools. How cruel of you to mention it, Varya!" He laughed heartily.

She tried to snatch the paper out of his grasp, but he held it out of her reach until she ceased her futile attempts.

He smiled, pointing to a huge inkblot. "Was that me?"

She blushed. "Yes."

"Ah. What damage did your stinging wit do to my manhood?" He held the paper up to the sunlight streaming through the long, narrow windows.

"I said you were too arrogant for your own good," she replied waspishly.

"No you didn't."

She made another grab for the list.

He held it above his head, which might as well have been a mile away for all of Varya's futile stretches as she tried to snatch it away.

"No," he insisted, squinting. "I think I see a D." He eyed her skeptically. "Surely you didn't call me dastardly"? He gasped mockingly.

"No!" She succeeded in rescuing the paper from his fingers and clutched it tightly against her.

"I know." He turned a smug smile toward her. "You said that I was *dangerous*." He waggled his eyebrows suggestively.

Instead of the indignation he was expecting, she went completely still and white. For a moment he feared she might faint.

Realization coiled heavily in his stomach. That was exactly what she had written.

"I must seem very silly to you, don't I?" She sank down onto the chaise, subdued. The paper slipped to the carpet.

Alarmed by her distress and hurt by her accusation, he seated himself beside her. He hesitated for a few brief seconds before reaching out and taking her hands in his. She tried to pull away, but he held fast.

"Varya."

He sighed when she didn't respond and continued speaking to the top of her head, "You must understand that I would never set out to purposely shame you—"

"Shame me!" She bolted to her feet, yanking her hands free of his loosened grasp. As she turned to face him, he watched her expression change. Gone was the wounded pride she had shown moments before, replaced with a mask of fury.

"How could I feel anything but shame when I'm attracted to you?"

This certainly wasn't what he had anticipated. He stood. "What the devil do you mean by that?"

"I am talking, my lord, about the fact that Bella loved you. How can you expect me to betray her this way? I am thoroughly disgusted with myself." She threw her hands into the air. "I don't even particularly like you!"

Miles didn't know whether to laugh or feel hurt. "I believe insulting my character gives you leave to call me by my first name, Varya. Let us not stand on ceremony."

She scowled at his teasing, but remained silent.

"All right," he conceded. "If you want to be like that—I don't consider you a particular friend either." She raised a brow. "And I trust you about as much as I would trust Napoleon—perhaps a *little* more."

Her jaw dropped at that confession, and he moved closer. Standing only inches away, he lifted her chin with his finger.

"But that doesn't stop me from wanting to kiss you. Bella's friend or not."

Varya stared at him, her eyes like giant sapphires against her alabaster skin. Desire glowed in their depths as her lips parted in unconscious invitation. It was insanity, but it was obvious that she wanted him as much as he wanted her . . .

"I think you should leave."

Her words hit him like a wet glove. Gone was the passion he had seen in her eyes, replaced by cool determination and . . . was it . . . regret?

"Are you certain?" he asked gently. Surely she didn't mean it.

"Yes," she whispered, turning her head away from his touch. "Please. Go."

Miles took a step back, suddenly wanting very much to be out of her presence. No woman had ever rejected him before and Varya's refusal left him with the very bitter taste of wanting something he could not have.

"Your loyalty to Bella is admirable." Stiffly, he walked toward the small table where Piotr had left his hat and gloves.

"I vowed never to be any man's property, Miles," came her husky reply. "Even were it not for Bella I could never consent to being your mistress. You value your control far too much for my liking."

He stopped and turned. She faced him with all the bearing and dignity of a princess, despite the slight tremor he had heard in her voice.

"I was asking you to be my friend, Varya. Perhaps even my lover—not my mistress. There is a difference." He set his hat upon his head. "If you happen to change your mind, you know where to find me." And then, with all the dignity befitting his station, he bowed in her direction and strode from the room.

"Are you certain you want to do this?"

No. He wasn't certain at all. He held the key, heavy and cold, in his hand. It hovered before the lock as though being repelled by the house itself.

"Yes," Miles replied grimly. He shoved the key into the lock and twisted. He dreaded what he might find in Bella's house, dreaded the memories and ghosts that waited for him across the threshold.

The door swung open with an alarming squeak that sent his heart pounding. Only silence—no ghostly apparition—greeted them.

Carny entered first. Miles stood on the step and stared into the dusty dimness. It seemed so wrong that this house be quiet and empty.

A deep breath, and he stepped inside. A chill raced down his spine as the heat of the day met the cool interior of the house.

"What do you hope to find?" Carny asked, trailing a finger along the dusty top of a little oak table.

Miles shrugged. "I have no idea. Answers? Redemption, perhaps."

Carny shot him a puzzled glance, but Miles ignored it. Instead, his gaze swept the room, lingering every once in a while on a familiar ornament or trinket. Bella had been dead for almost two months and Varya had not yet packed up all her things. He could only imagine how difficult it was for her to enter this place. It filled him with sorrow just to be there. After all, he had bought the house.

After their affair had ended Bella insisted on paying him rent. He accepted only because she loved the little house more than some people loved their children. Whether she had indeed paid him money he had no idea. His solicitor would have collected it for him. Miles had made a point never to see Bella again. And he hadn't. He hadn't even known she had returned from her tour of the continent. He wondered if she had even gone.

"The Runners have already been through here, Miles. All the evidence has either been found or ruined. What makes you think you can find something new?"

"Because I knew her," Miles replied, not even bothering to look at his friend. "And because I owe it to her to look."

Leaving the tomblike hall, Miles slowly climbed the stairs. He did not pause on the next floor, but continued on to Bella's bedchamber. If there was anything to be found, he'd find it there.

He stepped inside, and almost gasped aloud as reality hit him—this was the room she had died in. He had already known it, but it was still shocking to see it. Someone had come into this room as a guest—a lover—and had killed her! Foolish, trusting Bella! The mental image brought the taste of bile to his mouth.

Like the pieces in the entrance hall, the furniture in Bella's room had not been draped with holland covers. Dust clung like mold to the dainty dressing table and armoire. The bed hangings were dull and lifeless, shrouding the rumpled sheets like a widow's veil. The bed had not been touched since Bella's murder.

"You shouldn't look at this." Carny spoke from behind him.

Miles turned, the spell broken. "Carny, I've seen friends blown apart on the battlefield. An empty room cannot compare." No, for imagining what took place in this silent room was no doubt worse than any reality. He imagined Bella being terrified, tortured, when in fact she probably died fairly quickly.

"There wasn't much of a struggle," he remarked, voicing his thoughts out loud.

Carny shook his head. "She knew him."

"Varya says Bella was dressed to receive a lover. Obviously she wouldn't expect him to kill her." He moved toward the bed. "The bed is relatively neat as well. He did it quickly."

"He had to." Carny stepped up beside him. "If Bella had screamed all of London would have heard her."

An image of Bella's face frozen in a silent scream flashed in Miles's mind. He shook it away. He couldn't help her if he allowed emotion to get in the way.

A ray of sunshine filtered through the gauzy drapes to splay across the bed. A strand of gold glimmered on the pink sheets.

Frowning, Miles picked it up.

"What have you got?"

He held it up to the light. "A hair—dark blond."

"Could belong to one of the Runners," Carny suggested, but he didn't sound convinced.

"It could." Miles wasn't convinced either. "Or it could belong to our murderer."

"Still, it doesn't give us much. Half the men Bella slept with have blond or light hair."

Miles smiled grimly. "It would exclude those of us who don't, however."

Carny eyed him keenly. "You think Varya will believe your innocence now?"

"I'd like to think she and I are beyond that, my friend." But yes, he hoped this might reinforce her belief.

"Do you want to look around some more?"

Miles shook his head. He'd didn't want to spend another moment in that house.

"No. We'll come back later. I've seen enough." God, just seeing the room had shaken him. What had Varya suffered finding her best friend dead in that airy chamber? She had spoken of it only once, her grief barely concealed. Had she anyone to share her grief with?

They left the house in silence.

"Can I drop you somewhere?" Carny asked as he opened the door of his carriage.

"I think I'll walk, thank you. I have some . . . business to take care of."

His friend nodded, his gaze averted as he climbed into the coach.

"I will be at White's tonight if you care to stop by for a drink."

Miles smiled. Sometimes he needed a reminder of just what a good friend Carny was.

"Perhaps I'll see you later."

It was Carny's turn to smile. "Or perhaps fate will be kind and you'll be otherwise engaged."

Miles doubted it. "Perhaps." Shutting the door with a resounding thud, he waved goodbye to his friend and sent the coachman on his way.

He took a few steps before turning back to the house. Its clean red brick stared back at him—empty and bleak. An unexpected surge of anger washed over him.

I'll find who did this to you, Bella. I'll find him and make him pay.

It wouldn't bring Bella back, but it would give her

some justice. And perhaps it might give Varya and Miles himself some peace of mind.

He turned away.

He hadn't walked for long before his thoughts turned to Varya. What kind of man was he to want her so badly? She was Bella's friend. He ought to respect that as she did. He knew Varya desired him, but it was her friendship with Bella that held her back. As much as he admired her for it, he couldn't help but wish she were a little less noble.

Like himself.

Yes, it was low of him to pursue her, and a guilty conscience hounded him, but he could not let her go.

For the life of him he could not understand why she intrigued him so. Perhaps it was the feeling that she kept as many secrets as he did. Something in her eyes told him that she too had seen the face of death and managed to escape. Perhaps she might be the one to understand him.

"What if I'm wrong?" he asked out loud, smiling in embarrassment as a passing lady and her maid eyed him dubiously.

Even Bella, who claimed to have fallen in love with him, whose memory Varya held so dear, had first been attracted by the size of his purse rather than by his character. If he was wrong about Varya, the folly could prove fatal. A wise man would stay as far away from her as possible. A wise man would say goodbye before he found himself in over his head.

But the idea of one day saying goodbye to Varya left him with an odd hollow feeling in the pit of his stomach. She had turned his world upside down and had taken away the boredom that had caused him to take up working for the government. Since he had met her he hadn't given a second thought to playing spy for the government. He left that to Carny without regret.

Would his life go back to being as spiritless as it had been when she walked out of it? He just couldn't return to a life of Parliament, parties, and playing spy games with Carny.

There could be no future for him and Varya—not much of one, anyway. All he could give her was his protection, possibly his heart, although he wasn't certain that was much of a prize. He could never make her his wife, never give her children. Quite frankly, he doubted that it was in him even to make a woman happy.

And that's what Varya was. A woman. She wasn't some young chit tossed into his path by a greedy mama. She wasn't a bored *lady* out for a clandestine affair. She was everything that was unexpected and exciting, and she made him feel as though there was some life left in his bones.

She scared the hell out of him.

The musical dissonance of breaking glass woke Varya. Her head pounding from the rude awakening, she bolted upright in bed, the blankets falling around her hips. Straining her ears to ascertain where the sound had come from, she heard more crashing.

And voices.

"Katya?" she said softly.

Silence.

With her heart hammering and her stomach twitching with fear, she crawled out of bed and slipped on the thin silk robe that had been draped over a nearby chair. Barefoot, she padded over to the door. She opened it cautiously and peered out into the dark hall.

The sounds were coming from downstairs. She could barely make out the faint outline of Piotr's bulky form as he carefully made his way down to the lower floor. He took the main staircase so that anyone trying to harm her would have to go through him.

Silently, she followed, trusting that he would be able to protect them both.

They reached the landing below and moved like two shadows along the wall. The sounds were growing louder now as they approached the study.

Piotr glanced over his shoulder at her, motioning for her to keep back. Nodding, Varya was not surprised that her faithful servant had been aware of her presence, even though she had no idea how she had given herself away.

Piotr threw open the door of the study. It crashed against the wall, startling the two black-clad intruders. Varya could hear their curses.

A shot rang out, then another. Someone yelled in pain. She heard the sounds of a struggle, raised voices, then nothing.

Cautiously, she moved toward the door. She gasped in fright when Piotr suddenly appeared in front of her with a lamp. He gestured for her to enter the room.

The vandals were gone. They had climbed out the window and slid down the rope suspended from the stone flower box below the window. The rope glowed almost white in the moonlight.

"They had a gun," Piotr told her, setting the lamp on the desk. "They shot at me, but missed. I shot back and hit one in the arm. He will hurt for a few days, I think." He lit another lamp. Varya hauled the abandoned rope completely into the room before turning to survey the damage.

She sucked in a sharp breath. The room was in a complete shambles. Books were strewn everywhere. The drawers had been removed from the desk and the contents flung all over the floor. Paintings had been torn from the walls, trinkets swept off the shelves. Even the cushions off the furniture had been tossed to the four corners of the room.

"What were they looking for?" Piotr scowled. Nothing appeared to be missing, but there was no doubt that the burglars had indeed been looking for something.

"I have no idea," Varya replied automatically, but then it clicked. There was only one thing in her possession that someone could possibly want to see, and *someone* was afraid he was mentioned in it.

Bella's journal.

Chapter 8

So this was where he slept at night.

Accepting the hand the liveried footman offered her, Varya alighted from her carriage. Once she was on the ground, her gaze flickered appreciatively over the creamy façade of the Palladian mansion. The portico had been fashioned to resemble an ancient Grecian temple, practically obscuring from view the high windows set into the smooth stone walls.

By English society standards, the house was the epitome of wealth and elegance. By Russian standards, it was a plain summer cottage. Varya could not fault it, however. She'd much prefer it over the cold mausoleum in which she had grown up.

Lifting her skirts, she hurried up the steps to the

door. "I'm here to see Lord Wynter," she told the pleasant-looking butler who answered her knock.

Lifting her chin defiantly, she dared him to refuse her entrance. After all, it was highly unseemly for an unchaperoned woman to call upon a gentleman in his home. But it was Katya's morning to go to market and Varya had been too anxious to see Miles to wait for her servant's return.

The butler merely smiled and stepped aside for her to enter. Was Miles in the habit of receiving lone women in his home at all hours? Or was this servant the only nonjudgmental personage in all of England?

"Come this way, miss. I will inquire as to whether the marquess is at home this morning."

Surely Miles would not refuse to see her? The thought raced through her anxious mind as she followed the gray-haired man through the Grecian-styled great hall and up the wide marble staircase. Being seen with her in public was one thing, but having her in the same house as his mother and sister might be too much even for him.

How she had fallen. If the ton only knew her true identity, those doors that were now shut to her would open, and all of London would fumble for her favor. But there was no sense in thinking of it. It would never be. She was the Elusive Varya and she was a mistress.

She was deposited in a large withdrawing room and left there while her escort continued to his master's bedchamber. For a moment, Varya was tempted to throw all her breeding to the wind and follow him, just so she could catch a glimpse of Miles in such intimate circumstances. But she had not forgotten herself so completely just yet.

She seated herself in a comfortable winged-back chair upholstered in amber velvet. Weary from the long sleepless night that had followed the burglary attempt at her townhouse, she relaxed her rigid posture and leaned back against the soft cushions. She closed her eyes, grateful for the peace and feeling of security that seemed to surround her in this house.

Miles was here. Something inside her was convinced that he would know what to do, that he would make her feel safe again.

"Oh! Good morning."

Varya jerked upright at the breathless voice, her eyes flying open in dismay.

Blythe crossed the room toward her, an amazon in amethyst silk. A cautious smile curved her lips.

"Forgive me. I . . . I did not mean to disturb your meditation."

Varya smoothed her hair, her cheeks warm with embarrassment. Gone was the woman who greeted her so warmly just a few nights ago. As Miles's sister, Blythe should not have any knowledge of his mistress, let alone an acquaintance with her, but Blythe was too polite to cut her directly.

"Please excuse me. I'm afraid I didn't sleep well last night." Realizing how that must sound, Varya's cheeks flamed even hotter. She lowered her gaze to the carpet and prayed that the woman would leave.

Blythe eased her statuesque frame into the chair opposite her. Her feline eyes, so like her brother's, were bright with what Varya thought might actually be sympathy. It only added to her discomfort.

"I assume that you are here to see Miles?"

Folding her hands tight in her lap, Varya nodded. "Yes. Normally I would not presume such impropriety, but I have something of great importance to discuss with him."

"Oh." Now it was Blythe's turn to wonder. "I thought perhaps you had come to discuss the musicale I mentioned to you at Lady Pennington's."

An icy chill cut through the heat infusing Varya's face. "I assume you will want to withdraw your proposition." It was not a question—she knew the answer.

"No," came the startling reply. "I would like to continue as planned."

Varya raised a brow at the rebellious smile that curved the younger woman's full lips. Maybe Miles's sister wasn't the excruciatingly correct lady Varya had first believed.

"Will you take tea with me?" Blythe inquired, relaxing in her chair. "I'm absolutely uppish if I don't drink at least four cups a day."

Varya had never considered tea a cure for irritability. Too much of it had just the opposite effect on her.

"I would enjoy a cup, thank you."

As if by magic, a maid appeared carrying a tray with a silver tea service on it. Evidently the servants were well aware of their young mistress's habits.

"I realize we are both in a difficult situation, but I would like for us to be friends. Do you think that possible, Varya?" Blythe asked once the maid had left the room.

This was definitely not what Varya had expected. It was scandalous even to consider it, but she had no friends in London and was surprised to realize that she desperately wanted one.

"I think that very possible, yes." Emotion made her voice hoarse to her own ears.

The redhead looked up from pouring their tea. Her smile was genuine, dazzling. "Then I am no longer impertinent for calling you by your Christian name. I'm afraid Miles has not seen fit to tell me your last."

"He does not know it."

Blythe's arched brow and silence made Varya swallow uncomfortably. She knew how strange it must sound that she had not seen fit to tell her lover her family name. She couldn't very well refuse to tell Blythe now that she had made such a point of bringing it up.

"It is Ulyanova."

Blythe's nose wrinkled. "I believe I'll just call you Varya, if you don't mind?"

Varya smiled. "No, I don't mind."

"Good. Cream and sugar?

"Please."

Varya took the delicate china from her and raised the cup to her lips.

"Might I ask you a question of a rather . . . delicate nature, Varya?"

"Of course."

"What's it like to be a man's mistress? Oh dear."

Varya wiped her mouth with the back of her hand and stared in horror at the tea sprayed all over the table and the hem of Blythe's gown.

"I suppose I should have waited until you had swallowed."

"I can't believe I was so clumsy. Please, forgive me." She began dabbing the mess with her serviette.

"It isn't your fault. Sometimes I don't know when to keep my mouth shut—one of the pitfalls of being the only daughter, and spoiled rotten."

Varya glanced up and saw the rueful smile on the other woman's lips.

"I don't mind your frankness. I'd rather you voice your thoughts to my face than behind my back."

"Has it been so very awful for you?"

The genuine sympathy in her voice touched Varya. She couldn't remember the last time someone had expressed such an honest concern for her well-being.

"Not so very bad," she replied truthfully. "Perhaps it is society's poison tongue that drives away your brother's other lovers." How easy it was for her to pretend she and Miles had actually been intimate.

Blythe's expression was sullen. "I wouldn't know. As a *lady* I'm not supposed to know such things."

Swallowing past the lump in her throat, Varya lowered her gaze. "You must believe me completely without morals."

"Oh no!" Blythe assured, reaching across to give her hand a gentle squeeze. "I don't think that at all, although I'm quite certain that my brother's reputation will not suffer as yours. It's so unfair."

"No doubt society will forget all about me when Miles finds someone else." Why did it hurt to say it aloud?

Blythe frowned. "Given different circumstances,

wouldn't you like to have a long relationship with him? Perhaps marry him?"

"Lord, no!" Seeing the bewildered look on the other woman's face, Varya felt compelled to go on. "It's not that I don't . . . *care* for your brother, I just don't have any desire to marry."

"Have you ever been married?"

"No."

Blythe frowned. "Why not?"

"A wife becomes her husband's property," Varya reminded her bitterly, "as does everything she owns."

"But you can have an agreement drawn up to protect your money and investments."

Varya smiled indulgently, wondering if she had ever been so naïve in the ways of the world.

"No piece of paper can ever prevent your husband from doing exactly what he likes with you, Blythe."

"Maybe not," Miles spoke from the doorway, "but the bride's older brother might be able to talk some sense into him."

Varya's heart leaped at the sound of his voice, despite his disapproving tone.

He strode into the room. His hair was damp and brushed back from his face. He was impeccably dressed in a chocolate brown coat and biscuit-colored breeches. She inhaled the faint scent of sandalwood, spices, and something faintly sweet. He always smelled so wonderful.

"Good morning, my lord," she said politely.

He bowed. "Ladies."

Blythe stood. Varya had to crane her neck to look at her face.

"Miss Ulyanova has come to visit you, Miles, and so I shall leave you to your privacy."

Miles appeared puzzled by this announcement. "Thank you, Blythe."

She smiled sweetly, said her goodbyes to Varya, and crossed to the door in a few steps.

Once the door had closed behind her, Miles lowered himself into the chair his sister had occupied just moments before.

"Ulyanova, is it?"

"Yes."

"Interesting." He poured himself a cup of tea.

Varya noticed just how large his hands were. He had trouble holding the pot by its delicate handle, so he curled his fingers around its base to pour.

"It's quite common, actually." *Liar*.

He arched a brow, but said nothing.

Varya sipped her tea, waiting for him to break this thin barrier of tension that had sprung up between them the moment he entered the room.

He did not keep her waiting long.

"Varya, I understand your experience with men is probably vast compared to that of my sister, but I would have her decision to marry be her own, and not influenced by someone whose view of men has been colored by unfortunate incidents."

Varya smiled coolly. "As you wish, Miles. I have no desire to harm Blythe in any way."

"I didn't mean to imply that you did," he said softly. "Now, can I assume that you are here because you gave some thought to my offer—"

"It is grievous, don't you think," she interrupted, having no desire to discuss his "offer" so soon, "that a woman such as Blythe, who must marry, rarely sees a gentleman acting in any way other than his best behavior before the wedding? Oftentimes a woman never knows what kind of man she has married until it is too late."

"That is unfortunate, yes. But you must remember that Blythe has the benefit of a very influential family, who would never allow anyone to treat her in a fashion she did not deserve. Now, why don't you tell me—"

"Then she is a lucky young lady, indeed," she agreed, setting her empty cup on the tray. It bothered her deeply when he mentioned the presumed difference in their social standing.

"It has been my experience that no matter how good the family name, one is still quite capable of selling his daughter off to the highest bidder, regardless of his moral character."

"Did someone try to sell you to the highest bidder?" he inquired, his tone careful.

"Lord no," she countered, realizing she had said too much. "You have already pointed out that you and I are not of the same sphere, and we both know that such arrangements are usually made only among the aristocracy."

He regarded her for a moment, long enough to make her uncomfortable.

"Obviously I have offended you. Please forgive me. Perhaps you should tell me your reason for such an early visit." He gazed at her patiently.

"Of course." She suddenly felt very sheepish, and didn't like it one bit. "Piotr and I caught two house-breakers in my study last night—"

"What?" Gone was his relaxed manner.

It was as though she had been caught in the middle of a cannon blast. Gingerly, Varya laid her hands over her ears and waited for the ringing to stop.

"I don't believe I need to repeat myself."

He reached across the scant distance between them and gripped her shoulders painfully. "Were you hurt? What did they take?"

She winced, and he loosened his hold.

"I am unharmed, and they didn't take anything."

Miles released her and stood. He moved toward a window, sipping his tea as if it helped him to contemplate the situation.

"I believe they were searching for Bella's journal."

He turned to face her with a scowl. "Why?"

"Because it's the only thing I've ever had in my possession worth stealing—particularly if the thief was connected to Bella's murder."

"They could have been after your jewels," he suggested. "Money, perhaps personal papers?"

Varya thought it was somewhat unlikely. Even though she had plenty of valuable items in her possession, no one in England knew anything about them.

"How many women do you know who keep their jewels in the study?"

Shaking his head he frowned. "I hate to admit it, but I think you're right."

"It had to happen eventually," she retorted caustically.

Miles glowered at her. "Retract your claws, harpy. I meant that your theory disturbed me because it means you are in danger, not because I was surprised by your astuteness."

"Oh." How many more times would she make an idiot of herself that day?

"Who among Bella's acquaintances know the two of you were friends?"

"Everyone. We were often seen together—we performed together quite a bit."

"So it wouldn't have been difficult for the murderer to discern your relationship?"

Varya's brow furrowed. Where was he going with this? "No. We never tried to hide our friendship. Why would we?"

Folding his long arms, Miles ignored her question. "Did you ever meet any of Bella's lovers?"

"No, Bella was very discreet. Other than you she rarely spoke of any by name unless the affair was long over. What I do know I gleaned from her journal, and even then she refers to some of the men by their initials only."

"Did you tell anyone about the journal?"

She shook her head. "You?"

"Just Carny."

"Can he be trusted?"

He shot her a glance that spoke volumes as to what he thought of that question. "With my life."

"Perhaps the killer already knew. If he was Bella's lover, he might have seen her writing in it."

"If that was the case, why wouldn't he have taken it then?" He scratched his chin.

"Perhaps she was blackmailing him or had threatened to reveal some secret if he didn't leave her alone? Or perhaps he hadn't known about it until recently."

Miles nodded as if her theories made sense. Varya smiled smugly, happy that for the first time that morning she didn't feel as though she had said the wrong thing.

"If that's the case and he knows you have it, you could be in grave danger."

Her smile faded. "I know."

"I think I should perhaps take a look at this journal."

Varya was loath to part with the one piece of evidence she had against Bella's lovers, but she had to admit that Miles might be able to find clues where she had failed.

"Because you think you might find something I missed or because you have such little faith in my capacity to reason?" There was no need of her being so prickly with him, but the man had an annoying way of making her feel as though she were under a magnifying glass.

A sardonic smile curved his lips. "Because I might recognize some of the initials. Many of these men travel in my circles. Her killer has to be somewhere in those pages if your suspicions about the break-in are correct. If that offends your dignity, I apologize, but I believe finding Bella's murderer is more important than my pride or yours. Don't you think?"

He had her there—and very neatly, too. Her back rigid, Varya nodded. "Of course. You are welcome to read it."

"Thank you." He took a breath. "I also think you

should hire some extra men to act as guards. I know a few ex-military men who could use the work and can be trusted to do a thorough job."

Varya nodded. She would never find Bella's killer if she were dead as well. "Would you arrange an interview with them for me, please?"

"I'll take care of it this afternoon," he promised.

"Thank you." She stood. "Now that we have that settled, I really must be going."

He looked startled. "So soon?"

Her smile was dim. "I think it's best, do you not? It is not good ton to entertain your mistress in your house, is it? My visit has already put you at risk for some very impertinent remarks." *And if I don't leave now I'm going to throw all my principles to the wind and agree to be your mistress for real.*

"Yes, of course. You are correct."

Her smile grew a little, but still felt rather pathetic. "It had to happen sometime."

He chuckled, but he didn't appear to be any happier than she felt.

"When will I see you again?"

She gazed at his suddenly sober face. For a split second, she had the absurd desire to reach up and trace the outline of his jaw, just to touch him.

"Tomorrow, no doubt. I'll meet you at the Rochesters' estate." Before she could do anything she might regret, like throwing herself at his feet, she brushed past him and hastened to the door.

"Varya . . ."

Against her better judgment, she turned. The hopeful expression on his face was almost painful to look at. He was a dangerous man as far as her heart was concerned. He had already proven his ability to affect her emotions with a single word or phrase. One touch and she melted like butter near an open flame.

"May I . . . that is, would you—"

She cut him off. "Yes." Was she losing her mind? "I have never been to Vauxhall Gardens. Perhaps you would like to accompany me this evening?"

He grinned. "I would, yes."

She could feel her smile trembling on her lips. "I will be ready at eight."

"I will collect you at five minutes past."

She nodded. "I look forward to it. Good day, Miles."

"Good day, Varya."

Then, before she could possibly do or say anything else, she whirled around and practically ran to the front hall. The butler opened the door for her and she flew down the steps to her carriage.

Blythe joined Miles at the window. Together, they watched Varya's carriage as it moved down Wynter Lane.

"I like her," Blythe informed him. "I know I shouldn't, but I do."

Miles smiled thoughtfully. "So do I."

Chapter 9

"**H**ow do I look?"

Laughing with a mixture of nervousness and delight, Varya pirouetted around the drawing room. The skirts of her indigo gown twirled around her ankles and the simple diamond pendant around her neck glittered in the lamplight.

Katya clapped her hands together in front of her bosom and sighed. "*Prekrasnaia.*"

A smile spread across Varya's face at the housekeeper's praise. "Do you really think I look beautiful, Katya?"

"She does not lie," Piotr told her in a voice as gruff as the expression on his homely face. "Why is it you want to look beautiful for this Englishman?"

141

Katya shot him a dark look. "You be quiet! What business is it of yours?"

"It's all right, Katya," Varya intervened, trying not to chuckle. "Piotr just doesn't want me to get hurt." She directed a meaningful gaze at her faithful protector. "He will just have to learn to trust my judgment."

The stony-faced Russian nodded curtly but said nothing. He held Katya's unwavering gaze for a few seconds before grumbling under his breath and looking away. Katya flashed Varya a triumphant smile. It was all Varya could do not to laugh. Piotr and Katya seemed as attached to arguing as they were to each other.

The sound of the knocker striking the front door echoed throughout the house. Varya's heart leaped at the sound. Her wide gaze flitted from Piotr's stern countenance to Katya's smiling one. "It's him."

With one hand pressed against her chest in an attempt to calm the erratic pounding there, she gripped the back of a chair with the other in case her suddenly wobbly knees decided to give out on her. Why did this man have such an irritating effect on her? And worse yet, why did she like it? She should be wary of his attention, not pleased by it.

Katya elbowed the scowling Piotr. "Don't just stand there, you idiot. Let him in!"

Muttering in Russian under his breath, Piotr reluctantly shuffled off toward the front hall.

Varya glanced to see Katya smiling warmly at her.

"I have waited ever since you were a little girl for the right man to come and capture your heart." She held out her arms. "Now he has come, and you are so beautiful."

Dumbfounded, Varya allowed the larger, older woman to pull her into a fierce embrace. Being hugged by Katya was like being hugged by a small bear. It was several seconds before Varya could catch her thoughts or her breath.

"Katya," she admonished, pushing free of the woman's ironlike arms. "Miles is not 'the right man.' "

Her housekeeper released her, a knowing smile on her thin lips. Katya had worked for her family long before Varya had been born. There had been a stiff English governess to teach lessons and manners, and the merciless nuns at the school where she had met Bella, but whenever Varya had needed a friend, Katya had been there for her. The Russian woman had given her more affection than her mother and father combined. When she fled from Ivan she had been able to leave her family behind in St. Petersburg, but not Katya.

A large hand patted her cheek. "Ah, my *golubchik*, always denying with your head what your heart already knows."

Varya watched as the older woman lumbered away. She felt as if she had missed something. Katya only referred to her as her "little bluebird of happiness" when Varya's life had been on the brink of a major upheaval. She had never been wrong before.

"She is wrong now," she muttered at the chair. Now she held on to its back for fear that Katya had broken one of her ribs.

"Talking to furniture? I'm not certain, but I believe that might be one of the first signs of madness."

Slowly she brought her head up, smiling sheepishly.

"Good evening, Miles," she chirped between clenched teeth. "Why didn't Piotr announce you?"

He grinned—at her distress, no doubt. "He told me if I was going to make a habit of being here I could announce myself."

Varya pressed the back of one hand to her forehead. "I suspect my servants must be overindulging in vodka in their spare time. It's the only explanation for their behavior tonight."

Miles chuckled. "Never mind them." He crossed the carpet in three strides and gently pulled her hand away from her face.

She gazed at him in fascination as he cupped her hand with his long fingers, and raised it to his mouth. Sensation jolted her entire body as his lips brushed the sensitive inside of her wrist. It felt as if the blood was dancing in her veins.

His gaze locked with hers. His eyes seemed to blaze from within with an ethereal light, flames of gold against pale green ice. She couldn't look away.

"You are beautiful," he whispered, releasing her hand.

Her throat constricted painfully. "Thank you," she replied hoarsely. "Between you and the servants, that seems to be the general consensus."

He tilted his head to one side, as if studying her every feature. In all her years in public life, never had she felt such blatant scrutiny. "Then it must be true."

She chuckled, warmth suffusing her cheeks. "I suppose it must."

"We should leave before I decide to kiss you." His lips curved in invitation.

"Yes, I suppose we should." But her feet showed no sign of movement.

Laughing, he offered her his arm. "Shall we?"

Her fingers curled lightly around his forearm, all too aware of the hard muscle beneath her hand.

"Why not?"

It was a perfect evening.

Vauxhall was crowded, but not overly so. Most of the patrons were simply glad to see summer had finally arrived after the unusually long winter England had suffered through that year. It was early June, and a lady needed nothing more than a light Spencer or shawl to be comfortable out of doors.

The pleasure gardens was one of the few places in England where class distinction mattered little. Lord and laborer trod the same paths marveling at the fireworks exploding in the sky. There were many of Miles's acquaintance who shunned Vauxhall for that very reason—why mix with riffraff? Miles simply didn't care who else enjoyed the gardens, just as long as they didn't interfere with his evening.

He was proud to be seen with Varya on his arm. She was stunning in a velvet gown, a dark gray cloak, and a matching chapeau modeled after a gentleman's top hat. Were it not for the skirts swaying rhythmically around her ankles, she would almost appear to be a young buck out on the town.

It had been too long since he had ventured out in public with any woman, let alone one believed to be his mistress. He had forgotten how intoxicating a sudden breath of perfume on the breeze could be, knowing that the heady scent belonged to the beauty beside him.

"Are you enjoying yourself?" he asked as they dined in one of the supper booths.

She glanced up from her plate and fixed him with a smile that warmed him from head to toe.

"This ham is sliced almost as thin as paper," she replied merrily, "but other than that, I'm having a marvelous time. Thank you so much for bringing me, Miles."

"Thank you for suggesting it."

She finished off the last of her ham and daintily wiped her mouth. "Would you care to take a stroll?"

"I would, yes," he replied, not minding for one minute that she had committed a faux pas by asking him first.

They left the booth and moved toward the south walk. The last dying rays of the sun painted the horizon in shades of orange, yellow, pink, and violet. Torches were already lit along the paths, casting a warm, dim glow across the entire garden. Miles felt extremely comfortable and content—a feeling deepened by the secure pressure of Varya's hand on his arm.

"Where does that path lead?" she asked, pointing to the right and lifting her chin to gaze at him questioningly.

Miles smiled. The walkway she had pointed to was even more dimly lit than the others and shrouded by trees. "That's the Lovers' Walk."

"Oh!"

He chuckled at her shamed expression. "Come, I as-

sure you that you will be completely safe with me."
His quickening pulse belied the seriousness of his
words.

Varya smiled gratefully and wrapped her arm more
tightly around his. "I confess I would like to see it."

"Then you shall," he replied, steering them toward
the darkened walkway. "I cannot believe you've never
been here before."

She shrugged. "I have been busy with concerts and
haven't made many friends. It would have seemed
odd to come here with Piotr or Katya, and Bella never
had any interest in it."

"No," he agreed, shaking his head sympathetically.
"Bella liked to stay indoors." In bed. It was lowering to
realize that he had stayed with Bella as long as he had
only for the sex. The more he learned about her, the
more it appeared that they hadn't had anything else in
common.

Other than Varya. Had Bella realized how fortunate
she was to have such a loyal and devoted friend? Probably. Miles did not want to interfere with such a bond,
but there was a little voice inside him urging him to
take a chance and make Varya his own.

"What about you? Do you come here often?"

He shook his head. "Not for years. My wife, Charlotte, used to enjoy watching all the different people
milling about." A rueful smile tugged at his lips. "She
had a childlike fascination with the fireworks. Her eyes
would be as round as saucers for the entire display."

Varya tilted her head, her gaze far too knowing for
his comfort.

"Bella mentioned you had lost your wife. Do you miss her?"

"Sometimes." He looked out into the darkness, blindly watching the crowd ebb and flow around them. "She was a good woman. Our families had known each other for years, and I doubt that anyone, even Carny, could boast knowing me better than Charlotte did. She was my best friend."

Varya's fingers tightened on his arm. Did it bother her hearing him discuss his late wife? The dead were so much easier to be jealous of—there was no possible way to compete with a memory.

"Bella was my best friend."

The loneliness in her voice surprised him. She spoke as though Bella had been her only friend.

"You must miss her very much."

Varya nodded, and Miles's heart twisted at the pain on her face. "I do. Did you love Charlotte?"

"No," he replied honestly—brutally so. "I loved her as a friend, not as a woman. We married and produced a child out of duty and she died not knowing true love. She knew—even dying she knew that I would mourn our son more than I would her." His chest tightened with the admission.

Varya stopped walking and turned to him. Miles was compelled to meet her gaze. There was no blame in her eyes, just simple sorrow.

"I'm so sorry."

He shrugged stiffly. "It was a long time ago."

"No. I'm sorry that you felt the need to punish yourself all these years for something that was beyond your control."

Her words stunned him. Is that what she thought?

"Varya"—he gripped her shoulders—"it was my fault. I killed Charlotte."

Flesh stiffened beneath his hands. He had genuinely repulsed her now.

"How did you do that, Miles?"

With her head tilted like that she looked just like an inquisitive child. What would it take to prove to her how desolate he was?

"The baby—*my son*—was too large for her to birth."

She stared at him in confusion. "That's ridiculous."

"Look at me!" He stepped back and held out his arms.

"You are very fine," she replied.

Growling in frustration, Miles grabbed one of her gloved hands and placed it palm to palm against his own. The difference was staggering.

"I married her because I was supposed to. I got her with child because it was expected. And then I killed her because my child was too large for her little body to birth."

Her fingers curling around his, Varya brought his hand to her lips, brushing it with a gentle kiss.

"Charlotte and your son did not die because of you, Miles."

He tried to jerk his hand away, but she held it with more strength than he would have believed her to possess.

"Charlotte died because of blood loss or infection, or whatever killed your son took her as well. Healthy women do not die just because their child is big. Do you understand me?"

He wanted to. Oh, how he wanted to!

"But the doctor—"

"Was a man, and your sex knows nothing about women and their bodies, no matter how much you like to boast the opposite." She released his hand. "This self-pity doesn't suit. Stop it."

Dumbfounded, Miles could only stare as she linked her arm through his again and continued down the path.

Could it be that she was right? Part of him wanted to absolve himself of the guilt he'd carried all these years, another was loath to relinquish it so easily.

Resolved not to give the matter another thought until he was alone, Miles tried stuffing it to the back of his mind. He would not allow this morose behavior to destroy his evening with Varya any more than it already had.

"Shall we stay for the fireworks?" she asked, her head brushing his shoulder.

"If you wish." However, he wasn't ready to share her with the crowd again just yet. "But let us enjoy the rest of the walk first."

They had just turned the corner and were about to enter the Lovers' Walk when a feminine voice called out, "Miles!"

They stopped and turned toward the sound. Under the lamps, Miles watched patiently as a gentleman and lady made their way toward them. His pleasure in the evening evaporated suddenly as a sliver of light fell across the woman's all-too-familiar features. He stiffened. For a moment, he nearly believed she was a ghost. After his conversation with Varya, it was almost too much.

"What is it?" Varya asked, her voice low. He could see her gaze darting curiously between him and the approaching couple.

He wouldn't lie to her—not when she would find out for herself the next day when they arrived at the house party.

"Charlotte's sister and her husband," he replied, unable to meet her gaze.

"Oh."

Miles felt her trying to move away from him, as if she hoped to disappear somehow.

"Don't you dare desert me in front of them," he growled. "Not if you want to search their home tomorrow."

Varya's wide-eyed surprise at her realization that Charlotte's sister was Lady Rochester faded as her shock gave way to what Miles could only assume was pique. He should have told her of the connection earlier, but inviting her to his sister-in-law's home for sex hardly seemed the proper thing.

Gathering herself, Varya lifted her chin and regarded his former family with a regal air. Miles would have laughed were he not dreading the meeting.

"Miles, how good to see you." Lady Caroline Rochester stepped toward him with a wide smile on her lovely face—a face that looked even more like her late sister's now than it had five years ago. Her hand reached out for his.

He complied, surprised by the gesture. "Hello,

Caro. Robert," he replied, mustering all the enthusiasm he could, but failing miserably.

Fortunately, both Lord and Lady Rochester were too preoccupied surveying Varya to notice his discomfort. He had hoped to prevent Varya from falling prey to their blatant and sometimes vicious curiosity. Unfortunately, now he had little choice but to make the introductions.

"Delighted to meet you, Miss Ulyanova," Caroline gushed when the deed was done. "Rochester and I had the pleasure of seeing your performance at the King's Theater several weeks ago. Never have I ever heard anything as lovely as your music."

Miles's eyebrows flew up in shock. Was this truly Charlotte's sister standing before him? For the years since his wife's death, a bitter and sullen woman had occupied Caroline's body. He was surprised and delighted to think perhaps that woman had finally been replaced by the warmhearted girl he remembered.

Varya relaxed at her kind words and accepted the praise with grace. Miles was strangely proud of how she conducted herself in company. She treated everyone with the same warmth and ease. A title never impressed her, and he wondered once again if she was a member of the upper class. Her profession wasn't that of a lady in the social sense, but she had certainly been taught to act like one. Her past was a mystery begging to be solved.

"We're off to Rochester House tomorrow," Robert mentioned. "Will we see you there, Miles?"

Miles thought he detected a sneer in his former brother-in-law's voice, but his expression was the very essence of affability.

"Yes. Varya and I have decided to attend."

Miles looked down at the woman at his side. Varya's eyes were calm, her expression serene. He decided then and there that he didn't care what social sphere she had been born into. She was worth a dozen highborn ladies in his mind.

"I'm looking forward to it," Varya said politely, breaking the tense silence.

"As are we," Robert replied, and this time Miles was certain of the snide undertone in his cultured accent. "Perhaps you'll deign to *entertain* us, Miss Ulyanova?"

A polite nod. "I would be quite pleased to, Lord Rochester."

Miles glared at the other man. Varya may not have interpreted Robert's double entendre, but he certainly had. He hoped the savageness of his expression would tell his former brother-in-law clearly that he had no intention of sharing Varya with Robert or anyone else. How Caroline bore Robert's licentious behavior, he would never know.

Robert returned his animosity with an innocent smile. "Come, my dear, we must let these two resume their stroll." He gave his wife's arm a not so gentle tug.

Caroline surprised them all by grabbing Varya's hand as her husband pulled her away. "I am so pleased that you will be joining Miles, Miss Ulyanova. I've long since wanted to make your acquaintance."

A sweet smile curved Varya's lips. Miles's heart twisted at the naked sincerity of it. By defying her husband and society's dictates by being so openly kind to a woman deemed beneath her, Caroline had just made herself a new and devoted friend.

"I look forward to seeing you as well, Lady Rochester."

"Caroline," she corrected, and then they were gone. Caroline practically tripped over her gown trying to catch up with her husband as he yanked her behind him.

"He was very charming," Varya remarked dryly as they resumed their stroll.

"He's a bastard," Miles growled.

She chuckled. "Well, since they also went in the direction of the Lovers' Walk, why don't we choose an alternate end for our evening?"

"Such as?" he asked, turning to face her.

"Why don't we go back to my house?"

He stared at her in disbelief. Had it been so simple? Was she finally going to be his?

"Are you certain?"

She was silent, but the smile she gave him was so full of promise that Miles felt himself growing aroused by the images it called to mind.

Luck was finally on his side.

"That's one thousand pounds you owe me, Your Grace." Varya smiled triumphantly as she fell back in her chair.

"That's my *lord*." Miles hiccupped.

She frowned, waving aside his words. "It is not. I played it."

He squinted blearily at her. "What the devil are you talking about?"

"You tried to claim my card as your own." She wagged a finger at him. At least she thought it was only one; it appeared to be two.

"I didn't say 'card,' I said 'lord'!"

She winced at the volume of his voice. "What's *He* got to do with it? Really, Miles, you are being a ridit . . . ridict—sore loser."

Miles tossed his cards on the table and rubbed his face with both hands. "My head hurts," he groaned.

Varya raised her brows, wondering if all Englishmen were such poor drinking companions. She splashed another liberal amount of clear liquor into his empty glass.

"Have some more vodka, you'll forget all about your head." She filled her own glass as well, spilling a few drops on the table's felt-covered top. "Oops."

She glanced up to find him watching her strangely. "What?"

"I've never gotten foxed with a woman before."

She grinned, happy to be the first. "I've never gotten drunk with a marquess before either. Let's go sit somewhere more comfortable."

With the bottle in one hand, and her glass in the other, Varya stood and moved toward the thickly cushioned sofa. Her knees felt shaky beneath her, and she realized that she was indeed well on her way to being "disguised," as the English so politely put it.

The bottle landed on the small side table with a resounding *thud* as she sank deep into a corner of the plush brocade-upholstered sofa. Her fingers absently stroked the ice blue fabric.

"Am I your first marquess?" he asked, falling down on the cushion beside her.

Hadn't she just told him as much?

"Yes," she replied slowly, hoping it would sink in this time.

Suddenly, he was looming over her. A mixture of surprise and excitement coursed through her relaxed body. He was so close she could feel the warmth of his breath against her cheek.

He took her glass, placing it beside the vodka on the table. The vodka sloshed against the rim, spilling a little onto the polished wood.

He propped himself up on his elbow, and she felt his fingers tug at the pins that held her hair up. "I want to be your last marquess, Varya."

She had no problem with that. It was very unlikely she'd ever drink vodka with someone of his social status again.

"I want to be the last," he murmured against her temple, his breath sending a delightful shiver down her spine. "The last and the only man."

Realization washed over. Her loyalty to Bella raised its head long enough to be driven back to the far recesses of her mind. She didn't want to be loyal to Bella just then.

"Will I be your only woman?" she whispered, both fearing and anticipating his answer. Surely it was the vodka causing her to act this way. She didn't want to be his only woman, did she? That kind of commitment bespoke a vow she'd sworn never to make.

His fingers combed through her hair, draping it over the arm of the sofa, fanning it around her like a halo. It was such a delicious sensation; she sighed in delight.

"You can be whatever you want," he answered. "I don't think I'd ever find another to compare to you."

His mouth came down on hers before she could say anything. Soft and warm, his lips coaxed hers into parting and closing almost rhythmically. His tongue slipped past her teeth, hot and moist against her own. She moaned softly, wrapping her arms around his neck.

Even if she had wanted him to stop, it would have been next to impossible to push him away. Her muscles were languorously heavy.

He tugged at her skirts, pushing them above her knees. The warmth of his hand against her bare thigh was possibly the most sensual thing she had ever felt. She felt a tingling sensation in the pit of her stomach, and she knew that it was because of him, not the vodka.

Her fingers tangled in his hair, tenderly stroking the silky russet strands. Her hips rose beneath him, pressing against the hardness of one muscular thigh.

As if sensing her body's growing arousal, his fingers slid up her leg to her hip, bunching her gown around her waist. The vodka had completely robbed her of any inhibitions. Her legs parted, her body begging for his intimate caress.

"Oh God," he groaned against her mouth.

"Yes," she panted.

"No!"

Varya bolted upright as he heaved himself off her. Bewildered and tipsy, she could only watch as he staggered across the room. He grabbed blindly at the back of a chair, almost pulling it over in his effort to gain support.

"What is it?" Good Lord, was he suffering some kind of fit?

He shook his head, his back to her.

"Damn it, Miles! Look at me!"

He did. His face was white and drawn. His expression could only be described as a mixture of discomfort and regret. Had kissing her been so awful?

He started to reach for her, but then pulled back and pressed his hand to his stomach as something akin to fear contorted his features.

"Miles, what is the matter? I'll have Piotr send for a physician."

Truly frightened, she leaped to her feet and ran across the room toward the bellpull to summon Piotr.

"No!" Miles gasped from behind her. "I don't need a doctor."

She whirled around. "Miles, you look horrible and I'm worried. Please tell me what is wrong?"

She got her answer not even two seconds later when Miles made a low sound that seemed to rise up from deep within him, fell to his knees, and cast up the contents of his stomach all over her Aubusson carpet.

Chapter 10

He longed for death.

Surely even hell would be preferable to the pain he was now in. His eyelids felt as though they were lined with shards of glass. His skull throbbed with every motion of the carriage.

Miles made the trip to the Rochesters' country estate with the windows covered. The carriage jostled from side to side and seemed to hit every rut in the road. He lay prone in the corner, praying either for the headache powder he had used to take effect or for the angel of death to smite him.

"Just what did you do last night that brought about this wretchedness?" Carny asked from the seat opposite him.

159

Miles grunted and pressed his hands to his aching head.

"Let me guess," his friend continued mockingly. "It has something to do with the Elusive Varya."

Miles was heartily sick of that damned nickname. Opening his eyes as far as the pain would allow, he summoned what he hoped was a glare.

"I knew I would regret inviting you along."

Carny chuckled. "I seem to remember showing up on your doorstep this morning and inviting myself. You were too concerned with keeping your head out of the chamber pot to stop me."

"As you say." The powder began to take effect, alleviating Miles's agony enough for him to open his eyes without feeling as though his brain might squeeze out through the sockets.

Carny frowned and propped one boot against the carriage wall. "What happened last night? I haven't seen you this foul-tempered in ages."

Miles was touched by his friend's concern, but he wasn't about to confess that he had vomited all over Varya's music room and then run out of her house.

He'd never been so humiliated in all his life. And that Varya had witnessed it was not to be borne. How could she ever see him as a lover now? No doubt she would take one look at him and burst out laughing.

"I don't want to talk about it, Carny. Stop pestering me."

"She's really gotten to you, hasn't she?" he persisted.

Miles said nothing.

Carny chuckled and shook his head. "She must be very talented in bed. Is that it?"

Miles shot him a warning glance.

Carny's face paled. "My God, you're not falling for her, are you?"

Miles frowned. His annoyance at Carny overrode the ache in his head. What a ridiculous notion. So why did his heart lurch at the words?

"Of course not." Then as an afterthought, "I like her exceedingly well."

The blond man snorted.

Sighing, Miles rubbed his forehead. "What is so wrong with that? Is it not possible for me actually to like a woman?"

Carny raised an insolent brow. "And just what do you like so *exceedingly* about her?"

Miles was taken aback by the question. Pushing himself into an upright position against the squabs, he considered his reply. "Well, she's intelligent and witty. She's beautiful and talented and easy to talk to . . . Oh, what now?"

Carny was smiling despite the scowl directed at him. "You *are* in love with her."

Miles opened his mouth to protest, but his friend stopped him by gripping his arm.

"I think that's just wonderful, my friend. I just want you to know there are no hard feelings. My intentions toward her were not quite so noble as yours, but that's all water under the bridge, eh? I wish you both happy."

"Damn it, I'm not in love with her!" Miles shouted,

his head reverberating in agony. Was he was going to have to do his friend bodily harm before he got that point across?

This time Carny laughed out loud. Dabbing at his eyes with the tip of his finger, he sniffed and replied, "Oh yes, you are."

"Was there anything in particular I could help you find, my lady?"

Varya jumped. *Caught. Damn.*

Slowly, she closed the desk drawer. Lifting her chin imperiously, she willed her heated cheeks to cool and met the curious gaze of the servant who had stumbled upon her just as she was about to sneak a peek into Lord Rochester's desk.

It wasn't right to attempt a search without Miles there, but the temptation was overwhelming. And since she couldn't be certain that Miles was even going to show up, she had convinced herself that she wasn't truly deceiving him. In her excitement, she hadn't given any thought to being caught.

"Yes," she answered quickly with a shaky smile. "I was hoping that I might be able to find some writing paper. I would like to send a letter to my . . . dress-maker."

A flicker of disbelief crossed his face before the butler, or whatever he was, schooled his features once again into bland indifference. Varya thought he would have been used to the eccentricity of the various London visitors.

But she wasn't aristocracy, was she?

"I'll see that a supply of paper and ink is sent up to

your room, my lady. May I ask which chamber you are staying in?"

"I believe Lady Rochester called it the white room." Who in the devil was she going to write to? She supposed she would have to write to someone or else her request for paper would look suspicious.

"I'll see to it right away." He turned to walk away and paused. "Lady Rochester and her guests are in the west sitting room, my lady, if you should care to join them."

Varya took the hint. He wasn't about to leave her alone in his master's private domain.

"I would like that, thank you." Plastering a stiff smile on her lips she stood and exited the room ahead of him. Where was Miles when she needed him? No doubt he would have sent the patronizing little rodent on his way and they could have continued their search.

No doubt His Lordship was still in London nursing a wicked headache and feeling quite ashamed of himself. She had tried to tell him that being sick from drink was nothing to be embarrassed about, but he had run from her house as though an army of Cossacks were on his heels.

If he chose to stay behind in London with his tail between his legs while she braved this . . . debauchery, she would never forgive him. Already she had been propositioned by two dandified lords who had a hard time accepting refusal. Luckily she had been rescued by Lady Rochester.

Part of her had been glad that Miles had chosen to be ill when he had. What if she had actually allowed him to make love to her? She was heartily ashamed of her behavior—not because it was wanton, but because she hadn't cared that Bella had loved him. She hadn't cared at all about her loyalty to Bella—she had wanted Miles inside her, and nothing else had mattered.

She *still* wanted him.

With that very thought echoing in her head, she turned the corner and stepped out into the front hall. If she wasn't mistaken, the west sitting room was down the opposite corridor.

"Varya!"

Miles and Carny stood inside the doorway, obviously just arrived. Oddly, Carny appeared to be happier to see her than Miles did. In fact, Miles looked as if he had just bitten into something quite bitter. His pride, no doubt.

She sketched a polite curtsy. "My lords, I am pleased to see that you have *both* arrived safely."

"Lord Wynter was a tad under the weather when I called on him this morning," Carny informed her with a knowing smile, tipping his hat. "I'm afraid it was exceedingly easy for me to invite myself along."

Her gaze shifted to Miles. His face reddened at Carny's reference to his hangover.

"Are you feeling better now, my lord?" she inquired. His face was pale, his eyes heavy, but other than that he appeared to be in reasonable health.

"Obviously," he replied brusquely, not quite meeting her gaze. "Am I not here as promised?"

She raised both brows. He was certainly in fine form. Why was he angry with her? Did he regret kissing her now that he was sober? It hurt more than she cared to admit that he might feel some remorse for his actions.

"You could have sent a note excusing yourself if the idea of traveling pained you." Yes, a note would have been fine. Then she could have made her own excuses and departed. It would have saved her the humiliation of his present indifference.

"I gave my word, madam, and when I give my word I keep it. Perhaps you are unfamiliar with such behavior, but I strive to be a gentleman."

"Miles!" Carny gasped, staring at his friend in horror.

The words stung like a slap. Did he imply that she had no breeding? That she was incapable of giving and keeping a promise? Was this the same man who just last night told her he wanted to be the only man in her life?

"Indeed," she replied icily, watching the dull flush creeping up Miles's cheeks deepen. "And you are *nothing*, Lord Wynter, if not a gentleman. Now, if you'll excuse me, I'm expected in the drawing room."

Without even a backward glance at the man who preoccupied so many of her thoughts, Varya made the most dignified exit she could.

By six o'clock, all the guests had arrived and were installed in their private chambers, preparing themselves for dinner at eight. No doubt preparations for the secret assignations to follow had been made much earlier.

Alone in his room on the second floor, Miles paced and cursed himself for being such an idiot.

He had behaved abominably toward Varya upon his arrival. He could find no excuse for it other than that he was still embarrassed over ruining her carpet, and that he had given in to the burning desire to prove Carny wrong in his assumptions.

He was *not* in love with Varya, but that was no excuse for his rudeness. He would have to apologize as soon as he saw her, which—he checked his watch— would be in approximately twenty minutes, when the company congregated in the drawing room before dinner.

He didn't know why Carny's insinuations had made him so uncomfortable, but he had a few suspicions. Love made a man weak and open to attack. He supposed that was a good enough reason for not wanting to experience the emotion.

His reasons were not quite so noble, however.

He tried to justify them. He reminded himself that he knew nothing about her. At the very least, she had something to hide. A voice somewhere inside scolded him for being so distrustful, but it could not be helped.

She obviously had money, but he didn't want to hazard even a guess as to how she had acquired it. Ladies of the upper class did not swill vodka like most people drank tea. He knew from firsthand experience how vile the stuff was. Ladies did not run about Covent Garden at night abducting men at gunpoint. Nor did they engage in murder investigations.

No, if Varya were a true lady, her parents would

have had her safely married off by now. There was a chance that she could be a widow, but that still didn't explain her lifestyle.

Miles considered himself very open-minded, but not even he would consider falling in love with and marrying a woman he could not fully trust.

Trust and love were important facets of a successful marriage. His parents had enjoyed such a bond and had shared a happy life together. After what had happened with Charlotte, he wanted more than society's idea of a "good match."

It had been his experience that those kinds of marriages, no matter how agreeable in the beginning, always ended in despair. And he would not allow himself to fall in love with a woman he could not marry. He had already married a woman he had not loved. Better to be alone than cause the unhappiness of so many people.

He believed it.

Truly.

Regardless, his fears did not excuse his boorish behavior. Varya had given him no reason whatsoever to suspect that she entertained notions of marrying him. He doubted she would even consider such a thing, given the opinions on marriage he had overheard her confide to Blythe.

They could probably be lovers. He knew several ways to prevent pregnancy, and with each of them having a separate life, there was no fear of their growing too attached. Marriage forced such intimacy upon people, forced them into close quarters and gave them a false sense of security. Even with Charlotte he had believed they would live to an agreeable old age together—maybe have another child or two.

The death of his son and wife had been senseless. He would not risk such pain again. He could not bear it.

But there went his head, making up things for him to be worried about when the only thing that should concern him was apologizing for being such an ass. Imagine how Varya would laugh if she knew he actually fretted over falling in love with her! Why, she herself would call it a ridiculous notion.

He wondered how she would react if she ever discovered he had hired an investigator to look into her past.

A brief knock sounded against the door. "Time to face the lions, old man," Carny announced, sticking his head into the room.

"Then let's do it," Miles replied, giving him a gentle shove out the door. "The quicker this evening is over with, the better."

Could anyone see her heart pounding in her throat?

Well into her second glass of champagne, Varya was very careful to appear nonchalant as Miles and Carny entered the room. It was very difficult, given the rush of heat that hit her as soon as her gaze fell on Miles. Lord, everyone there believed her to have intimate knowledge of the man's body, and she couldn't help blushing like a schoolgirl!

Even though she was playing the part of a mistress, it made her very uncomfortable to be in company with so many men and women who obviously weren't married. Even worse was the fact that she knew several of the gentlemen's wives, who no doubt didn't know or didn't care where their husbands were.

But the real slap in the face was her reaction to Miles. She was supposed to be *angry* with him, for heaven's sake, not holding her breath waiting for him to notice her!

She was still confused by his rude treatment of her earlier, but she refused to allow it to ruin her evening. If she had to spend the evening watching endless scenes of licentiousness unfold, she would make the best of it. She certainly wasn't going to become part of it. She would stay as far away from Miles as possible, and if he wanted to speak to her, well then he—

"Good evening, Varya."

She almost spat champagne back into her glass, startled by his silent approach. Thank God her back was to him. Her eyes watered as she choked on the bubbly wine.

"Good evening, Miles," she replied coolly, once she had composed herself. She turned to face him. "Where's Carny?"

Miles glanced over his shoulder and pointed to a small group of guests across the room. "I believe he's chatting with that lovely young widow even as we speak."

"How very mercenary." She sipped her champagne and tried to look everywhere but at him.

"Varya," he began softly, "I would like to apologize for my behavior early. It was uncalled for."

She met his gaze evenly. "It wouldn't have been had I given you cause for it, Miles."

He had the good grace to blush slightly at her censure.

"I had no reason other than bad manners." He took her hand. "Please say you'll forgive me."

She nodded, struggling to maintain her poise even though she wanted to throw herself into his arms. "As you wish. But if it happens again, I won't be so forgiving."

"Of course."

Something in his smile made her frown. It was almost as if he had predicted her responses. The arrogance! He hadn't had any doubt that she would forgive him. Well, she meant it. He got only one chance. As attracted as she was to him, she wasn't one of his little bits of muslin whose actions he could anticipate and manipulate.

Dinner was announced, and the hostess paired off all the guests according to seating arrangements. Varya was very near the end of the procession, a fact that made her chuckle softly to herself.

"May I ask what is so funny, madam?" her escort inquired jovially.

She shook her head. "Nothing, sir. Do you think we shall make it to the dining room before the food grows cold?"

Even though she entered the dining room much later than Miles had, she still found herself sitting beside him. He was so attentive and so charming that Varya finally relaxed and put his earlier rudeness out of her mind. She actually enjoyed herself. She tried a bit of almost everything the servants offered, and kept her wineglass filled.

"Will you be attending Prinny's soirée at Carlton House next week, Wynter?" Lord Dennyson asked.

Miles nodded, swallowing a bite of pheasant before answering. "I plan to." He glanced at Varya. "Would you like to go?" he asked her in a low voice.

She nodded, pleased that he had invited her. She had yet to see the inside of Carlton House. There had been talk of her playing there, but no invitation had ever come.

"I would like that very much," she replied softly.

"I thought as much." He smiled warmly. "Especially since Czar Alexander will be there."

Her fork clattered loudly against her plate.

"Are you all right?" Miles's gaze held obvious concern—and something more. For a split second, she thought she saw suspicion in his gaze. That would not do.

"No, no. I'm fine." She fixed the other guests with what she hoped was a sheepish smile and not a grimace. "I'm afraid I was overcome by the prospect of being in the company of a fellow Russian, let alone the ruler of my homeland."

"Yes," Lady Dennyson agreed. "I suppose when one is unaccustomed to such exalted circles, the notion of being admitted would be a tad staggering." She smiled condescendingly. "Fortunately, you will not be alone. Lord Dennyson and I will be there, along with a few others." She gazed very pointedly at Miles.

Varya could have cut the woman's tongue out, and from the expression on Miles's face, he would be glad to help her. She might as well have called Varya common.

"Indeed, Lady Dennyson," Varya replied with a forced smile. "I daresay I will not be alone in my awe of the czar if you are there as well."

Lady Dennyson did not seem to know whether she had just been insulted or flattered. Apparently she chose to believe the latter, because she smiled before returning her attention to her plate.

"I wonder if Princess Caroline will be there," Carny remarked, drawing their attention away from Varya. She smiled her thanks. He winked.

"After that scene at Covent Garden Monday evening, I should hope not!" Lord Dennyson chortled.

Society had been vastly amused when Caroline showed up at the theater where her husband was entertaining Czar Alexander and his other guests. She'd presented herself to the czar and was well received, a feat the regent's mistress had not achieved.

"It's a wonder Prinny's even hosting the bash." Robert chewed a bite of pheasant. "It's no secret he blames the czar's sister for his daughter's latest rebellious streak. Talk has it that the chit wants to have a say in who she marries."

"I don't see that she did anything wrong," Caroline spoke in defense of the regent's only daughter.

Robert caught her hand in what looked like a loving gesture, but Varya could see Caroline's flesh turn white under the force of his grip. Her mouth tightened in pain.

"My dear, perhaps it would be best if you did not speak of things of which you have no knowledge?" His tone was syrupy-sweet.

A tight coil of anger suddenly wound its way up

from Varya's belly. Robert reminded her of Ivan—ruthless and controlling. No doubt Caroline hated these parties of his—everything in her demeanor said so—but Robert clearly ruled his house—and his wife—with gleeful brutality.

"If there is one thing a woman *does* have a good knowledge of, my lord," she joined in with forced lightness, "it is the prospect of a loveless marriage. Perhaps your wife, like us all, simply relates to feeling like a horse on the auction block?"

Several other women at the table laughed and voiced their agreement. Varya seemed to be the only one who noticed the glare Robert directed at her. She fought a frisson of fear and haughtily raised a brow in a silent dare. She would not allow him to intimidate her as he did his wife.

"I, for one, would never dream of underestimating a woman," Carny announced, once again refocusing the group's attention on himself.

Varya could not get away from the table fast enough. Her appetite had slowly dissipated beginning with Miles's casual reference to Alexander and culminating with Robert's oppressive treatment of his wife.

She made her excuses as soon as dessert was over.

"Pray, do excuse me," she said as she stood. "I believe I have overindulged in Lord Rochester's fine wine and am now suffering for it. I think I might go rest a bit."

Lady Dennyson voiced her disappointment, of course. She had so *hoped* that Varya might entertain them at the pianoforte.

Varya wanted to tell her just what she could do with the pianoforte.

"Are you ill?" Miles caught her just as she was about to leave the room.

She nodded, suddenly very tired. "It is just the headache, but I believe I should lie down."

His eyes bored into hers, as if trying to discover whether she was telling the truth. Luckily for her, she was feeling ill. Very ill.

"I'll check on you later," he promised.

She nodded. "Please do," she murmured, not really caring if he did or not as long as he woke her when it was time to search Lord Rochester's study. "I want to be alert when we conduct our search."

"Don't worry about that now. Just get some rest."

She smiled weakly. "Thank you."

Varya turned and left the room. She was halfway up the huge flight of stairs leading to the second floor when she felt the hair stand up on the back of her neck. Pausing, she glanced over her shoulder.

Standing in the middle of the foyer, watching her, was Miles. The expression on his face made her shiver. It was more than suspicion or curiosity. It was a look of sheer determination, and Varya knew that if she wanted to keep her secrets she would have to guard them very carefully from now on.

Chapter 11

❝**F**ind anything?❞

"Nothing."

It was just after three o'clock in the morning. The household was quiet; all the servants were in their beds, and all the guests were in someone else's.

Miles sat back on his haunches behind the desk and sighed. He had gone through every drawer and still had found nothing. Perhaps he should have woken Varya; she seemed to have a talent for understanding the deviously minded.

Which was exactly why he had decided not to wake her. She had *too much* talent for spying and searching. Her strange behavior at dinner had resurrected his suspicions toward her, reminding him that even though he had feelings for her, she was still hiding something.

"What about you?" he asked, peering around the desk as he shut the drawer.

Carny carefully adjusted the painting he had just hung back on its hook. "Rochester doesn't have any wall safes."

"Damn. I was hoping we wouldn't have to search the family rooms." Miles stood and stretched his cramped legs. This investigation had him feeling horribly inadequate.

"It might be a good idea anyway. You never know where he might have hidden any letters or personal items Bella gave him." Carny began randomly rifling through the few books on the shelves.

"According to Bella's journal, they exchanged letters."

Carny turned toward him, his expression pensive and shadowed in the lamplight. "Did Varya ever mention what happened to Bella's personal effects?"

Miles shook his head. "No. The only thing she's mentioned is the journal."

His friend sighed. "I wish you had woken her. I'd like to know if she has any other possessions of Bella's. If we could read some of the letters these men sent her, it would be more helpful than looking for what she sent them."

Miles almost slapped his forehead with the palm of his hand. Why hadn't he thought of that? Because he spent most of his time trying to solve the mystery of Varya's past rather than Bella's murder. He should be ashamed of himself.

"I thought it best not to involve her. Her behavior tonight was definitely suspicious."

Carny turned to face him, an open book in his hands, his expression incredulous. "*Her* behavior? I am loath to tell you this, my friend, but her behavior has been more consistent than your own."

"How so?" Miles leaned his hip against the edge of the desk and folded his arms across his chest. This was hardly the time or place to get involved in a debate with Carny, but he was perversely interested in what his friend had to say.

"Well—" He placed the book back into its slot on the shelf. "You've twice threatened me with bodily harm since you met her."

"You deserved it."

"Did I? You've never threatened me in all the years I have known you."

"I fail to see how—"

"*And*"—Carny smiled knowingly—"you haven't been spending as much time at the clubs as you used to—"

"It's become bloody tedious, that's all." Miles pretended great interest in the tips of his fingers.

Carny laughed. "I'm sure it seems so, when you've better ways to spend your time."

Miles's head snapped up. "Don't you start that again." He pointed a warning finger at his friend.

The blond man feigned indignation. "I wouldn't dream of such a thing." The grin on his face betrayed that he was lying through his teeth.

Miles sighed. "Didn't *you* find it odd that she seemed so distressed at the possibility of seeing the czar?"

"Not at all." Carny began shifting knickknacks on

the shelves, presumably in hopes of finding a hidden compartment. "I live in daily despair of ever laying eyes on *our* sovereign, and I'm a peer of the realm." He cocked a brow. "If Czar Alexander is half as odious as Prinny, I'm not at all surprised the dear woman doesn't want to meet him."

"She's a 'dear woman' now, is she?" Miles snorted. "I seem to recall someone calling her a 'lying opportunist.' " He smiled smugly.

Carny shrugged. "I was mistaken. Do you suppose she might have left Russia for political reasons?"

"It's possible. Treason would be ample enough reason to fear coming face to face with the very monarch you tried to depose. But she doesn't act like someone with a political agenda."

Carny shrugged. "Whatever it is, any woman who can bring you to your knees deserves my highest regard."

"Carny . . ."

He held up his hand. "I know, I know. You are not in love with her. If I say one more word you will forget we are friends. Blah. Blah. *Blah*." He rolled his eyes.

Miles couldn't help but chuckle and shake his head.

"Find anything of interest?"

They both jumped. Miles sat hard on top of the polished surface of the desk, while Carny juggled a fragile porcelain shepherdess. He caught it before it could hit the floor, and sighed in relief.

Varya stood just inside the doorway, clad in her nightgown and wrapper. Her hair spilled around her shoulders like a dusky cloud. If he were of a poetic bent—which he wasn't—Miles would have likened her to the queen of the Amazons, so fierce was her expression. Since her anger was directed at him, he put aside any thoughts of poesy.

Carny smiled, leaving Miles to do the explaining.

"No. As a matter of fact, we haven't."

"You should have woken me." She moved almost menacingly across the carpet. "Perhaps I can be of assistance."

"You were sleeping so soundly and I—" He fell silent as she shot a furious glare at him. The look spoke volumes as to what she thought of his explanation.

He shrugged mentally. Fine. If she didn't want to hear him out, that suited him just fine.

"I believe I'll leave the two of you alone to sort this out," Carny announced, waggling his finger as if they were two unruly children. He moved toward the door, and then stopped.

"Varya, do you have any of Bella's personal belongings?"

Her brow wrinkled. "I have some in storage at my house. Why?"

"I believe we might be able to find some clues among her correspondence. Would you mind if I came by some afternoon and had a look?"

"I suppose not."

He smiled. "Excellent. Well, good night." He slipped silently out of the room.

Varya turned her attention back to Miles. He straightened his spine under her distrustful stare. *He* had nothing to feel guilty for. *He* wasn't the one acting more suspicious than a fox in a henhouse.

"You couldn't wake me, but you could rouse Carny?"

"I didn't want to endanger you—"

"He knows everything?"

"Yes. I told you I had confided in him. Carny's done this kind of work before. He's very good. I trust him completely."

Her dark eyes narrowed. "But you don't trust me."

"Now, Varya—"

"I suppose I can't blame you." She placed a finger thoughtfully against her cheek.

"You can't?" This certainly wasn't what he had expected.

She smiled. It made the hair on the back of his neck stand up on end.

"Oh no. How can you be faulted for distrusting a woman who does not talk about her past?"

"Well, you have to admit—"

"Everyone knows women generally aren't allowed the same freedom as men. We can't travel as extensively alone; we can't behave as recklessly. Women are expected to behave in a more decorous manner than men. Therefore, a woman who appears to have had a fulfilling life, but does not talk about it in detail, must have something to hide."

"Well—"

"And," she continued, stepping up so that their bodies were almost touching, "everyone knows that it is men who are generally secretive and untrustworthy."

"Exactly." He frowned. That wasn't right at all, was it?

Sighing, she shook her head. "If you wish to distrust me based on the grounds that you do not know all the details of my past, then do so." She jabbed him in the chest with a finger. "Just keep in mind that I know very little about you, nor have I asked to."

He licked his lips. "What would you like to know?"

She waved her hand dismissively. "Nothing. Unless there is something you wish to tell me, I have no desire to hear about your past. Is there something you wish to know about mine?"

Despite the sincerity in her words, Miles couldn't fight the feeling that she would lie if he asked a question she didn't want to answer.

He shook his head. "No. You are right. I apologize for my behavior." She had been correct when she told him he should be on the stage.

She gazed at him wearily, but nodded in vindication. She moved around the desk and knelt behind it.

"What are you looking for?" He turned to watch her examine the intricately carved oak.

"Have you checked for secret compartments?" She was already running her hands along the inside of the desk.

He snorted. "Read many gothic novels, Varya?" He frowned as she pressed one of the scrolls near the center of the desk, and heard a decided *click*. She shot him a triumphant look as a small compartment popped open.

"I prefer to think that you have too little imagination, Miles, as opposed to my having too much." She reached into the small hole.

His jaw clenched tightly. "Secrecy and deviousness do not come as easily to me as they do to some, apparently." When she did not respond to his taunt, he asked, "How did you know to check for a secret compartment?"

"My father had one in his desk," she replied, obviously deciding that they had traded enough barbs for one evening. "It was where he kept all the papers he didn't want us to see." She withdrew a stack of papers from the hole. "For me, the temptation proved too great. One day I peeked through the keyhole and saw him press the mechanism. As soon as I had the chance, I read his papers."

"What did you find?" He took the stack from her hands.

"A list of candidates for my hand in marriage." She smiled wobbly at his indrawn breath. "I never looked in that compartment again."

"Serves you right." He kept his tone light as he brought the candle closer. Later, he would discover the truth behind the pain in her eyes, but not now.

For now, he wanted to revel in her discovery. How long would it have taken him to find that nook? He thought he had gone over that study with a fine-tooth comb. As much as he wanted to conduct this investigation without her, he couldn't deny it would go much more quickly with her help.

Varya rose to her feet, furtively wiping her eyes. He pretended not to notice to spare her pride even though it was torture not to take her into his arms.

He divided the papers between them. They sat in comfortable silence as they read.

"Bella liked to write letters," Miles commented, rubbing the back of his neck.

"And Robert liked to keep them," Varya replied,

tossing one aside with a disgusted snort. "Why, I don't know."

"Not much wonder he kept them hidden from Caroline. Besides it being bad form to parade a mistress in front of one's wife, a gentleman wouldn't want his wife to find out he liked to wear ladies' lingerie."

They laughed together and Miles dropped the letters he had finished reading. "There is absolutely nothing here that could implicate Robert as Bella's killer."

Varya sighed. "Not a thing, though I don't know how I shall ever look at Lord Rochester with a straight face again."

"You'll have to if you don't want to cause any suspicion."

"I know. I suppose it will help whenever his arrogance becomes overwhelming. I shall simply picture him in a silk peignoir." She shook her head and began gathering up the papers. "I had no idea Bella was so . . . inventive."

Miles chuckled. "The two of you seem a very unlikely pair. How did you become friends?"

"Bella took me under her wing when I first arrived at school," she confided, sliding the stack back into the compartment. "I'd never been away from home before. I was so frightened, easily intimidated. Bella defended me against the other girls until I learned how to stand up for myself."

"And you remained in touch after you returned to Russia?"

Varya nodded, her lips tightening and Miles was even more certain that whatever had driven Varya to London had happened in Russia.

"When I joined Bella in Paris, she introduced me to many of the theater managers she knew and helped me find work." Her expression grew thoughtful. "She was a good friend."

"As are you, to be hunting down her killer."

She shrugged. "You're helping me."

"I suppose I am," he replied, unable to take his eyes off her. "I have a feeling I might have been the reason she asked you to come to London."

Varya met his gaze evenly. There was no censure in her expression. "Yes. She was . . . distressed."

"And I was the only lover she ever discussed with you?"

"Yes." A slight smile. "I remember being mortified that she discussed such things with me. Now I wish she had at least mentioned some of the others. It might have been helpful."

Miles took her hand in his. Her fingers were long and slim and cool against his.

"You know I never meant to hurt her." It was a statement more than a question, but Varya nodded.

"I know that now. I'm sorry I tried to kill you."

They laughed at that, breaking the solemnness of the moment. Miles couldn't take his eyes off her smiling face.

She looked lovely in candlelight. Her thick black hair framed a face as pale as cream. His gaze drifted down the long, graceful column of her throat to the V of her wrapper. The soft, silky material draped seductively over her shoulders, skimming across her full breasts to fasten between them. His mouth suddenly felt very dry.

"You're staring at my breasts."

He gasped loudly, almost choking.

"How rude of you to mention it," he replied hoarsely, pressing his fist against his chest.

She leaned forward, smiling seductively as she pushed her torso forward. "Perhaps someday I'll let you touch them."

His jaw dropped.

She straightened and stepped away. "But if you ever act without me again, you'll never get the chance."

By the time he found his voice, she was gone.

She was walking down a long, dark corridor. Searching. She was searching for something. She didn't know what, but she knew she would find it soon.

Sinister shadows reached out for her, raising the hair on the back of her neck with their feathery caresses. She shivered despite the heat and quickened her step.

The house was completely silent except for the distant hum of voices. She remembered there was a party going on downstairs in the grand ballroom. She could dimly make out the first strains of Mozart as the orchestra began to play. The music filled her with a sense of dread. Odd, she always used to enjoy Mozart.

There was a door slightly ajar at the end of the hall. Lamplight peeked out around it. Slowly, she moved toward it, her heart hammering painfully against her ribs. She didn't want to go inside the room, but she couldn't stop. A force greater than her own will was propelling her legs.

The door swung open, allowing her full access to the room.

It was Ivan's bedchamber. The crimson draperies and heavy oak furniture seemed debauched and sinister in the lamplight.

Ivan knelt over the still figure of a girl on the bed, his profile to her. He was nude, his large body knotted with thick muscle. His buttocks flexed as he pumped himself into her. His grunts mingled with her fearful gasps. His hands were wrapped around the girl's throat; his face was flushed with exertion and sexual pleasure. He was strangling her.

Varya's horrified gaze went to the girl, who turned terror-filled eyes toward her.

She ran toward the bed as the girl began to thrash underneath Ivan. Her flailing arms bounced off his arms and chest with as little consequence as a child's.

"Get off her," she screamed, tearing at his hair. He loosened his grip on the pale throat. She felt her nails rend his flesh, drawing blood, and she fought all the harder. She had to save the girl. He turned on her, snarling and she froze.

"You're mine now, Varya," Ivan growled.

It wasn't Ivan.

Varya jerked upright in bed, a cry tearing free from her throat.

It was Miles.

The grin on his face was so broad it made his cheeks ache, but it felt good, euphoric even. Varya wanted him, and despite his nagging distrust of her, he wanted her too. If it hadn't been for his decision to search the study on his own, he might be in her bed at that moment.

He glanced toward the door that connected their chambers and wondered if she was still awake.

Determinedly, he strode toward the door. He raised his fist to knock, and heard a sob from the other side.

"Varya?" A jolt of fear ran through him as he opened the door.

The drapes were tied back, allowing the room to be illuminated with silvery light. The pale furnishings and fabrics glowed eerily under the moon's aura. Out of habit, his gaze scanned the room looking for any threat.

In the middle of the chamber was a large four-poster bed, and in the middle of that, amid tangled, stark white sheets, sat Varya.

For a moment, all Miles could do was stare. She looked like an enchantress with her tousled hair and flimsy negligée that left very little to the imagination.

His gaze went to her face, and he saw her eyes widen briefly at seeing him, as if he were a childhood monster come to life.

"Varya?" He moved toward her. Her fear seemed to give way to relief as he came closer. "What is it? I heard you cry out."

"I had a bad dream," she replied as he sat down on the bed beside her.

"Would you like to talk about it?"

"No." She leaned back against the pillows. "I would not."

He wished she would open up to him but he could not force her trust. And to be honest, it wasn't trust he wanted from her right at that moment.

"Then don't talk. Would you let me kiss you, Varya? Would you?"

Her gaze locked with his. He sat silently as she searched his face, letting her find what she was looking for. Finally, she nodded.

Miles groaned at her acquiescence. This glorious, unorthodox woman surprised him at every turn. Despite the warnings from his brain that he shouldn't allow himself to get so close to her, he drew nearer.

Varya closed her eyes as his head lowered to hers. His fingers splayed along her back, pressing her closer. Almost as soft and light as the touch of a feather, her lips parted as his mouth brushed hers.

She was his.

Chapter 12

Heat.
  All Varya could feel was a burgeoning warmth. It radiated from his skin, and made her head spin.

She wound her arms around his neck, pulling him closer as her tongue met his. The silk of his dressing gown was cool against her flesh, but she could feel the heat of his hard, muscled flesh beneath it.

Never would she have thought the feeling of two tongues sliding against each other could be so . . . exciting. Pressing her body against him, she could feel his growing arousal against her thigh. A heady sense of power raced through her at the knowledge that she could have such an effect on him.

The memories of Ivan were no match for the touch

of Miles's hands and lips. The images that had haunted her since that night in St. Petersburg began to waver and fade under his gentle assault on her senses.

A feeling of peace settled over her. She felt safe and strong in his arms. Suddenly, she knew that not only did she trust this man with her life, she trusted him with her very being.

It was terrifying and exhilarating at the same time.

Strong hands slid down her back and along the curve of her hips to stroke her thighs. The thin silk of her gown bunched under his fingers, creeping stealthily upward so that she was left bare from the waist down.

Varya's heartbeat quickened and she shifted her hips, unconsciously trying to urge him to touch her more intimately. A pulse drummed heavily within her, driving her more than any craving had before. Instead of slipping between her legs as she wished, his strong fingers kneaded and caressed her buttocks. She whimpered in frustration.

Soft, warm lips moved across her jaw and down her throat, planting feathery kisses along the exposed skin just above the lace of her gown's low neckline. His breath raised goose bumps where it teased her flesh. Her nipples tightened in anticipation, aching for the heated caress of his mouth.

Varya tried not to think about how he sent her senses reeling. She didn't want to analyze her body's fevered reaction to him. Her fear would ruin the moment, and she didn't want these wonderful sensations ever to stop. Tomorrow she might regret her actions, but for now she would think of nothing but how wonderful it felt to have Miles's body against hers.

"So beautiful," he murmured against her breast. "So incredibly beautiful."

His hand slid up to cup her breast. Slowly, his thumb traced torturous circles around her puckered nipple. A sharp gasp of delight escaped her lips. Miles yanked the neckline of her negligée, pulling it down to expose her flesh. The savagery of the action betrayed his passion. A low growling sound rumbled from his throat as he took her nipple into his mouth.

A shock of incredible pleasure shook her, arching her back and making her gasp in pleasure. Bella had told her a man's touch could be exquisite, but she had never prepared her for *this*.

"Oh, Miles!"

His hand was on her thighs again, nudging between them as his tongue laved her breast. It was torture—torture that felt incredibly wonderful.

Her fingers tangled in his hair, holding him to her. Her body hummed with the tension that seemed to start between her legs. She parted her thighs so that he could touch her, gasping as his fingers slid into that part of her that burned for his touch. The muscles in her thighs tensed and relaxed almost rhythmically.

His fingers moved inside her, spreading warm dampness to her outer flesh, making her writhe impatiently as the throbbing in her loins built to a sweet agony.

Miles lifted his head long enough to move to her

other breast, his tongue flicking at the puckered peak greedily.

Varya moaned, nearly delirious with pleasure. She bit her lip to keep herself from making vows she knew would be better left unsaid.

His thumb rubbed gently against her most sensitive spot; the tiny bud throbbed acutely with every stroke. Deftly, he manipulated her flesh so that the pleasure was almost too intense to bear. He seemed to know how to sustain the delicious torment until Varya thought she might go mad.

Then he sent her over the edge.

Ripples of incredible release shuddered through her body. Incapable of thought or speech, she felt her mouth go slack. She heard a high, keening cry, dimly aware that it was coming from her own throat.

When she finally came to her senses, it was to find him watching her intently. His face was flushed; his eyes bright with unspent passion. His expression was tenderly hungry, affecting her even more than his touch had.

"Thank you," she said breathlessly, not caring that her body was still exposed to his gaze.

He chuckled somewhat hoarsely. "It was my pleasure."

"No, it wasn't." Boldly, she reached out and caressed the bulge tenting his dressing gown.

His body jerked at the touch. Empowered, she moved to slide her hand inside the robe . . .

"Let me give *you* pleasure." She knew his member was the key to a his sexual fulfillment, and she wanted to give Miles the same experience he had given her. The need to share this moment was overwhelming.

He smiled ruefully, seizing her by the wrist and moving her hand away from him. He shook his head. "No."

It was as though a bucket of cold water had been tossed on her, and she drew back from him.

"No?"

"Not here." He reached for her, pulling her close once again. "My pleasure lies in being able to make love to you in your bed. I want to take my time. I want to make you scream with pleasure. I don't want it to happen in someone else's house, someone else's bed."

She stared at him, wondering if she had heard him correctly. Had he actually demonstrated a streak of discretion? Somehow, she found the admission heart-warming—just as she found her own behavior disgusting. She had no willpower when it came to him, and her loyalty to Bella meant nothing when he held her in his arms.

Gently, he lowered her onto the sheets. Where the warmth of his body had been was now chilled.

"Get some sleep," he told her, rising to his feet. "We'll talk in the morning." He didn't even try to hide the fact that he was still very much aroused.

She said nothing. He strode to the door that separated their rooms.

"Sleep well, Varya."

She turned her back to him. "I can't wish you the same, Miles."

"I know." The door clicked shut behind him.

What had just happened? Why did the incredible passion he had given her now feel cold and empty? And why did it hurt so much that he had treated her more like a lady than his mistress?

Wrapped in her guilt and confusion, Varya fell into a deep and dreamless sleep.

Miles couldn't sleep. His mouth still tasted of her, his fingers smelled of her. He still wanted her, and his mind was whirling with questions, and a profusion of images that ranged from erotic to disturbing. He thought of Varya, her body open to him, and sighed in frustration.

He was getting too close to her. What had started as a mild distraction had blossomed into something heady and sweet, and decidedly dangerous. He could have taken her. Could have spent himself on her delicious body until these confusing thoughts swimming in his brain couldn't even summon the energy to form.

He couldn't bring himself to use Varya so cheaply. He didn't want the maids to find the evidence of their passion on her sheets and giggle about it in the laundry. He wanted their first time together to be special, meaningful.

He had never wanted that with anyone before. He was fascinated by her, enslaved by her. Completely and utterly besotted with her.

And still he did not know her.

What frightened him the most was that not only did he want to know everything about her, right down to her favorite color, he wanted to feel that he might be able to share all of *his* secrets with her.

Damn, this poetic nonsense had to stop. He didn't particularly like this new melancholy, romantic side.

Rolling over onto his back, he gave up on pursuing sleep. His mind was far too busy, his body still too heated for rest. Had Varya found sleep yet? No doubt she had tumbled into a languorous slumber despite her anger at him. Sexual pleasure often had that effect.

He felt guilty for leaving her after making her feel so vulnerable, but he couldn't stay with her and not make love to her. The temptation of her body was almost too great to resist, as his actions earlier had proven.

Was he so quick to forget his mistrust of her? How could he even entertain having a relationship with her when he was certain she was still hiding something? He'd have his answer soon enough. If the investigator he had hired didn't find out her secrets, Miles would himself the night of the regent's party.

Even though he feared the outcome, Miles would personally see to it that Varya was introduced to Czar Alexander.

When Varya woke the next morning she was astonished that she had actually managed to fall asleep with Miles only a room away—his wonderfully talented fingers had drained every ounce of energy from her body.

Stretching languidly, she tried to keep her mind from dwelling on the passionate response his touch had brought out in her. Such thoughts would only make her hungry for more, and he had already made it clear that he would not make love to her until they returned to London.

Only two more days. She could survive.

An uncommonly bright smile graced her lips as she slipped out of bed. A part of her felt guilty for throwing herself so wantonly at the man Bella had loved, but she pushed it aside.

Gone was the doubt and fear of the night before. In the light of day, it was easy to understand Miles's reluctance to make love to her for the first time in a strange house. She had no idea what the experience would be like, but if it was anything like the pleasure he had already given her, she certainly didn't want to risk the rest of the house knowing about it.

Besides, it wouldn't do for the maids to find virgin's blood on her sheets.

She washed quickly, scrubbing away the heaviness of sleep from her face, and the scent of Miles's flesh from her own. She rang for her maid and set about selecting a morning gown.

Not quite a half hour later, she entered the sunny breakfast room, feeling more lighthearted than she had in years.

That she was alone in the room surprised her. It was by no means early morning, but surely everyone hadn't eaten already? She stopped and listened. The house was quiet except for the distant sounds of the servants going about their daily business.

Shrugging, she helped herself to the buffet of buttered eggs, ham, sausage, cheese, and bread. The food was still warm, so obviously she couldn't be all that late.

She seated herself at the table, ravenously attacking

the food on her plate. A cup of tea followed—the crowning glory to a full stomach. But now that her hunger had been sated, it was time to discover where everyone else could possibly be.

She wandered out the front door. She inhaled a deep breath of the fresh, sweet air. The odor of flowers, grass, and horses pleasantly assailed her nostrils. The air here was much preferable to that of London. Perhaps she should consider purchasing a house in the country.

There was no one on the lawn. She shrugged and started around to the west side of the estate. The thick grass tickled her ankles through her stockings as she skirted around the corner. Still nothing.

This was very odd. Perhaps they were all on the back lawn playing horseshoes or some other inane English game. She lifted her skirts a few inches so she might move a little more quickly and hastened toward the back lawn.

It was a cockfight.

That was the only word she could think of to describe the scene that met her as the grassy area that framed the courtyard came into view.

Almost everyone on the guest list surrounded two gentlemen who were pummeling each other. Well, actually one was doing all the pummeling and the other was simply receiving.

Much to her astonishment, the ladies seemed to be taking more enjoyment from the pugilists' battle than the gentlemen who also looked on. So many squeals and titters, and not one swoon in sight.

Varya moved closer. As she did, she noticed several curious—even envious—glances shot her way. Peculiar. A slight tremor of dread crawled up her spine.

"Oh, Madam Varya," Lady Dennyson greeted her breathlessly, her florid face quivering with excitement. "How romantic! Just like a knight rushing in to defend your honor!"

"I beg your pardon?" Varya stared at the woman as if she were mad. What did *she* have to do with this exhibition of masculine stupidity?

"Lord Wynter, of course!" the older woman gushed. "Lord Pennington made a *very* rude comment about you in front of him. Lord Wynter, gentleman that he is, gave Lord Pennington a chance to retract his statement, but Lord Pennington continued his slander—by the way, my dear, I want you to know that *I* don't believe one single word of it—and wouldn't you know Lord Wynter couldn't stand by and allow him to say such things!"

Varya's head swam.

"He demanded Lord Pennington give him satisfaction," Lady Dennyson continued, "and when Lord Pennington refused to duel over 'a mere bit of muslin,' Lord Wynter struck him! I do declare, I have never seen a man knocked so far by a single blow as Lord Wynter knocked Lord Pennington!"

She patted Varya's hand and winked knowingly. "You're a very lucky young lady, my dear."

Horrified, Varya turned her attention to the fight. Miles had Lord Pennington by the shirtfront. The tips of the battered earl's boots barely brushed the grass. She winced as Miles's fist met his opponent's nose with a resounding *thwack!* Pennington's head snapped back.

Miles seemed unaffected by the blood his opponent was losing. In fact, he was speaking—grunting—at the nearly unconscious man. Varya hated to admit she almost felt sympathy for Pennington, despite his previous insult toward her character.

"You"—*smack!*—"will"—*whooomp!*—"apologize!"—*thud!*

Lord Pennington crumpled to the ground in a whimpering heap. His mistress rushed to his aid, pausing only for a second under the baleful glare of the Marquess of Wynter.

Varya could only stare, her eyes wide. She wouldn't have thought Miles capable of such violence, not for her. Not for anyone. For one brief second, she remembered the image from her dream, of Miles with his hands wrapped around the girl's throat, crushing the breath from her body . . .

No, it was just a dream. A dream that reflected nothing but her own confused mind.

"Varya, are you quite all right? You're very pale."

She turned to find Caroline watching her closely, her dark gaze filled with concern.

"Wh-what happened?" She gestured toward Pennington. She didn't quite believe the fantastic tale Lady Dennyson had told her.

Caroline flushed. "He was saying some horrible things about you. I think he was trying to embarrass Miles. Instead, Miles hit him."

"Because of me?" This was all too ludicrous—not to mention horrid and surreal.

Caroline nodded, a frown marring her brow. "I've never seen Miles act this way before. He must care for you very much."

A bubble of near-hysterical laughter broke free of Varya's throat. Either she was going mad, or the rest of the world was.

She looked up to catch Lady Dennyson grinning broadly at her. Her plump jowls jiggled as she nodded and winked.

It appeared to be the rest of the world after all.

A large, strong hand caught her arm in a death grip. She gasped as the flow of blood through the limb was effectively cut off.

"We need to talk," Miles growled, dragging her around to the garden door of the house, and inside where no one could hear them.

Varya stumbled silently behind him, for no other reason than the hope that if she remained quiet he would soon release her arm, which had already gone numb.

Once inside the privacy of the small back parlor, he did release his hold on her. Varya winced at the prickly sensation as feeling began to return to the appendage.

"What the devil has gotten into you?" she demanded, borrowing one of his favorite expletives.

The finger he pointed at her trembled slightly. Varya was willing to wager it wasn't fear that made it do so.

"I just made a bloody ass of myself, and it's all your fault."

"*My* fault? Come now, Miles. Weren't you capable

of making an ass of yourself long before you ever met me?" *Oh yes, Varya, bait him.*

He flushed angrily. "You know perfectly well what I mean. I just fought a man because of you!"

He was insane, ridiculous, maddening—and strangely desirable in his anger, misplaced as it was.

"I did not ask you to beat Lord Pennington senseless, Miles." She folded her arms across her chest.

"Why did you not tell me he offered you a carte blanche that night at the ball?"

She shrugged. So that was it. No doubt Pennington's version of the story strayed mightily from the truth. "It didn't seem important."

"Didn't seem important!" he thundered. "It might have prepared me for his attack on your character!" His eyes narrowed. "You refused him, didn't you?"

Varya felt ice settle in her soul. "If I had a pistol I would shoot you."

"Don't you threaten me." The finger he had jabbed at her just moments before turned on himself. "I'm not to blame for this . . . fiasco!"

"You've spent much time blaming me, Miles, and very little explaining how you reached that cunning conclusion. I suggest you start before I begin searching for something to gut you with."

Something ignited in his eyes. "If you hadn't insisted on being part of this investigation there would be no need for us to continue with this farce—"

"Oh, shut up!"

He stared at her in astonishment.

Varya shook with every step she took toward him,

her body tight with rage. Her finger struck him squarely in the chest.

"You may have been able to use that excuse *before* last night, Miles, but not now. A few hours ago you became intimately acquainted with my body. Were you coerced into such behavior?"

"No, but—"

"Were you proposing marriage?"

"Lord, no!" His face was white.

She smirked. "Then guess what, Miles? I *am* your mistress—your whore, or however Lord Pennington put it."

"You are not a whore!" His hair stood up where his hands had plowed through it.

She smiled at his vehemence. "You and I both know that. I don't really care what the rest of the ton believes. Do you?"

"Yes!"

Varya choked on her laughter, all of the fight gone out of her. "I appreciate you defending my honor, Miles, but you can't go around beating everyone who insults me. You'll spend all your time engaging in fisticuffs."

"Laugh at me if you will, but every insult to you is an insult to me. If you won't think of your own reputation then I'll have to, if for no other reason than to keep us both from public ridicule!"

Her eyes narrowed at his tone. "It was *your* reputation that made our charade so easily believed, *my lord*. And please forgive my impertinence, but beating Lord Pennington for voicing his opinion of me is hardly conducive to avoiding the public eye."

Miles snorted. "If you had been a respectable woman, it never would have happened—" He froze, as if realizing what he had just said.

Varya recoiled as if slapped. All along, she had told him that she didn't care what people's opinions of her were but she did care. She cared about his opinion. Now that she had it, it felt as if she had been his boxing opponent instead of Lord Pennington.

"Varya, I—"

She held up a trembling hand. "Don't say another word, I beg you. You've made your point"—she swallowed hard—"quite clear." Before she could make a complete fool of herself, she turned on her heel and forced herself to walk calmly down the corridor, holding the tears at bay until she reached the sanctuary of her chamber.

Miles watched her retreating form with a mixture of remorse and disgust. Remorse for what he had said, and disgust for everything else he had ever done to hurt her. Every time she started to get close he pushed her away. What was wrong with him?

"Well done, Miles," came a familiar jeer from behind him.

"Go to hell, Robert," he muttered without turning around.

"I always thought you had a way with women. Certainly, you never lacked for attention in Spain or Portugal, or even after your return." He stepped closer, gesturing as though a thought had just occurred to him.

"In fact, I returned home only two months after you

did, and you had set up that exotic singer by then. What was her name?"

"Bella," Miles whispered. "And Varya's nothing like her."

A soft, cruel laugh came in response. "I guess not. Well, buck up, old boy. I daresay you told Pennington the truth."

Even though he knew better, Miles turned to his former brother-in-law, awaiting his next remark.

"She's not your whore—anymore." Robert laughed loudly at his own wit and strolled off in the same direction Varya had gone, leaving Miles standing alone. A state he now found distinctly uncomfortable.

He waited two hours before attempting to see her. He spent the first hour riding about the estate, trying to figure out just what he was going to say that could ever undo his earlier words. The second hour he spent bathing and choosing the proper attire in which to make his apologies.

Finally presentable, he knocked on the door that connected their rooms, wishing he had some kind of gift in case words weren't enough.

There was no answer.

He tried the knob. The door swung open to reveal a maid striping the sheets off the bed. She jumped when she saw Miles.

"Beggin' your pardon, my lord."

"I'm terribly sorry," he apologized, feeling a little embarrassed at having been caught barging into Varya's room. "Can you tell me where I might find the lady who has been using this room?"

The girl flushed. "She's gone, my lord."

Certainly he couldn't have heard her correctly. "Excuse me?"

The maid swallowed, obviously unwilling to be the one to deliver bad news to one of her master's house-guests.

"She packed up and left for London over an hour ago."

Chapter 13

A respectable woman indeed!

Varya yanked her hat from her head with a snort and tossed it unceremoniously on the plush cushions beside her.

If Miles Christian, lowly Marquess of Wynter, only knew what manner of woman he was dealing with! If they were in Russia, she could buy and sell his smug hide like some people purchased stockings. The man was an ass. What did he know of respectability? Without his title he'd be nothing more than a very rude, arrogant, handsome, extremely attractive . . .

"Pompous fathead!" she seethed under her breath.

"Are you quite all right, my lady?" her maid asked tentatively.

Varya met her wide-eyed gaze with a deliberate

turn of her head. "Do you have a husband, Amy?"

The girl seemed startled by her curt question. "Why no, my lady."

"A lover, perhaps?"

Amy blushed prettily. "Aye. Jack's his name, my lady. We're to be married someday."

Varya nodded absently. "You're not afraid of being under his control?"

Her maid frowned. "His control? Jack's never tried to control me, ma'am."

"You lie," she retorted in disbelief.

Amy looked indignant. "I can assure you I do not lie, my lady! My Jack is a good man—treats me like his equal, he does."

Varya was instantly contrite. The girl so obviously believed in her lover's affections. "I'm sorry, Amy. I did not mean to offend you."

"It's nothing, ma'am."

Perhaps things are different for the lower classes, Varya thought. Certainly there weren't fortunes and titles at stake with those marriages not of the gentry and aristocracy. How odd that women of rank had less freedom in their lives than their maids.

She shuddered as she imagined what life under Ivan's domination would have been like. He wouldn't rant and rave about her reputation. He'd simply force her to be the model wife.

After Miles's gentle, passionate embrace the cruelty of Ivan's nature seemed even more frightening. Under his hands she would have suffered painful beatings and sexual perversity. No doubt he would have eventually broken her mind as well as her body and spirit.

She had done the right thing by running away. There was no cowardice in escaping men such as Ivan and her father.

Her father had not been physically cruel, but he had ruled his family with a will of iron. Silence was sometimes a greater punishment than a slap. Being excluded from family functions, banishment from social entertainment—something Varya adored—had been a favorite punishment. He had been cold and distant, but he had never struck them. He didn't have to. His word had been final and no one ever dared dispute him.

Except for Varya. The first and only time she had ever opposed her father had been when she left, breaking the betrothal contract with Ivan. She wondered if her father had vented his wrath on his wife, Ana, or on Stephon and Natalya, Varya's younger brother and sister. It had been almost five years. Had he forgiven her yet?

Five years. It was a long time to go without contact with one's family. She wondered if they thought of her as often as she thought of them. Did they think her dead or alive? And Ivan—had he married someone else, or was he waiting for her to return so that he could crush her throat with his bare hands as he had the maid's . . . ?

"My lady, are you ill?" Amy leaned forward on her seat, her plain face wrinkled with worry.

That was the second time that day that someone had inquired after her health. She really must learn to school her features to better hide her inner emotions.

She thought she had mastered the art, but the entrance of Miles Christian into her life had drastically lowered her defenses.

"I am well, thank you, Amy. When do you and your young man plan to be married?"

Again the younger woman colored. "As soon as we have enough money saved, my lady. My Jack don't want me to have to work after we're wed."

Varya's eyes narrowed. "Why?"

Amy's blush deepened. "On account of all the gentlemen, ma'am. Jack don't—doesn't—like when I accompany you to house parties and such because of the gentlemen who get fresh."

Nodding, Varya felt strangely agitated by the maid's words. Men may *proposition* a pianist, but they tended to take what they wanted from servants like Amy.

"Amy," she said suddenly, "I'm going to let you go."

The girl's face crumpled. "Oh please, ma'am, don't! I don't encourage any of 'em, I swear!" She buried her head in her hands.

Cursing her folly, Varya leaned toward the sobbing girl. It took all her strength to pry Amy's hands away from her face. Good Lord, but the girl was strong!

"Amy, I'm not letting you go because I'm angry. I'm letting you go so you can marry your Jack."

The sobbing abruptly ceased. Watery, red-rimmed eyes stared at Varya in astonishment.

"But without the salary I make working for you, my lady, we can't afford it." Her eyes welled up as her voice caught on the last two words, and Varya feared she would start bawling again.

"You don't need your salary. I want to give you and

Jack money to start your life together." Why? So that someone might have a chance at the happiness Varya knew she would never find. She simply couldn't trust her freedom to someone else.

"Oh, my lady! You are too kind!"

"I just want to see you happy," she replied a trifle gruffly, once again leaning back against the squabs. "Now, how does one thousand pounds sound?"

Amy fainted.

By the time Miles had ordered his valet to pack up his belongings, instructed his coachman to follow with the carriage, and gotten a suitable mount from a smirking Robert, his *mistress* had at least a two-hour head start on him.

Miles offered to buy the velvety gray stallion from his former brother-in-law. Not just to catch up to Varya, but to keep the other man quiet. Miles knew Robert often needed extra blunt to pay off gaming debts, and even Rochester wasn't stupid enough to risk losing such a sale just to vex the Marquess of Wynter.

He had to be mad, Miles thought angrily as he and the stallion flew over the rough road to London. The promise of the sweet, hot nest between Varya's thighs had to be the only reason he would even consider chasing the bothersome baggage all the way to London.

"You are in love with her."

The memory of Carny's words almost knocked Miles out of the saddle and he drew back sharply on the reins. The stallion reared in annoyance, pawing wildly at the air with its front legs.

Heart hammering, Miles fought to soothe the irate

beast. The stallion ceased its efforts to throw him and pranced nervously. Miles spoke to him in a low voice, saying nothing in particular, just allowing his gentle words to calm the horse's agitation.

What the devil had happened? He had heard Carny's voice as clear as day. Had it really been only in his head?

Mad. He *was* going mad.

Falling in love with Varya? It was ludicrous! She went against everything he was brought up to look for in a wife; she was beneath him socially—a harridan, and secretive. She—he stiffened. Had he just thought of her in terms of marriage?

Falling in love with her would be bad enough, but marrying her was out of the question! Poor Charlotte would be the first and only Marchioness of Wynter during his lifetime. He had married her out of duty, and look what had happened.

Even if he loved Varya with all his heart—a feat he was not capable of—she would never be his wife. He would not go through that kind of guilt again.

Why was he even entertaining the idea? Carny was an idiot. He had no idea what he was talking about. Miles's feelings for Varya equated to curiosity and lust, pure and simple. He wanted her body and the answers to her many puzzles. Once he had those he would lose interest, as he always did. Then his life could go back to how it had been before the night she kidnapped him.

He spurred the stallion on. He had no idea what he was going to say to Varya once he caught up with her. He supposed he would have to apologize. After that, he was going to put all his energy into getting into her bed.

The sooner he bedded her, the sooner she would be out of his system. He hated the crude bent of his thoughts, but there could be no denying how badly he wanted her. The sooner he had her, the sooner his life could return to how it had been.

"Dull."

This time Carny's ghostly presence inside his head didn't spook him as badly.

"Go to hell, my friend," Miles muttered between clenched teeth, and dug his heels into the stallion's flanks.

"Don't worry about unpacking just yet, Amy."

"Ma'am?" The young maid looked up from the trunk she had opened.

Varya smiled wearily. "I wish to rest for a while. You may put the clothes away later." She stood by the bed, resting her heavy head against a carved oak poster. "Why don't you inquire among some of your friends, ask if any of them want a position as a lady's maid. I shall need a new one once you are wed."

A delighted flush darted across the maid's cheeks—much preferable to the pallor of her earlier faint.

"Certainly, my lady. I know of several girls who would make excellent maids for you."

Varya's smile grew. "I only need one. Ask them to come around some day next week."

"Of course. Shall I help you undress now, ma'am?"

Varya nodded. "I'm afraid I'm too tired to do it myself, Amy." She felt as weak as a kitten. The past twenty-four hours had robbed her of all her energy. She didn't want to think of Miles, Ivan, or her father. She didn't want to dream of Bella's broken body or the marriage she had narrowly escaped. She just wanted the blissful cocoon of sleep.

Amy deftly unfastened the dozens of tiny hooks down the back of her gown as Varya held on to the bedpost for support.

Once she was left wearing nothing but her shift, Varya sagged onto the bed and allowed her abigail to unwind the thick coil at the back of her head. The rhythm of the brush pulling through her hair made her eyelids droop and her breathing shallow. She felt herself beginning to lean to one side as her tired body refused to hold itself upright any longer.

Amy helped her into bed, removing her stockings and garters before tucking the soft blankets up around her chin.

"Thank you, Amy," she mumbled sleepily.

"You're welcome, my lady. Sleep well."

Once she heard the chamber door click shut behind the maid, Varya rolled over onto her stomach. The sheets were soft and cool against her exposed flesh. They smelled of outdoors and the rose-scented soap all her linens and clothing were laundered with.

She closed her eyes, easing the ache in her head. Bunching her pillows, she snuggled deep into their downy softness, waiting for sleep to overcome her.

She dreamed.

She dreamed that Miles was there with her, his large, muscular body stretched out next to her. His golden skin was velvet against her own. The hair on his chest was thick and springy beneath her palms, and darker than the russet mane that framed his face.

He was watching her with those catlike eyes of his, the heat of his gaze causing her heart to flutter madly in her chest.

His long fingers combed through her hair, stroked her face, and caressed her so intimately her body throbbed. His hands seemed to be everywhere at once.

"This'll be an easy job," he told her in a voice that wasn't his.

"Wh-what?" A fog of passion hung low over her mind, dulling her senses. "What are you talking about?"

"Don't worry, sweet. I'll make it painless."

"I d-don't understand." Something wasn't right. Frantically, she struggled to wake.

Then she felt it.

Miles was gone, replaced by stifling blackness. Something heavy was pressed against her face. Roses, she smelled roses.

Panic-stricken, she came awake to the realization that one of her pillows covered her face. She tried to push it off her, but it wouldn't move. Fear washed over her. She groped wildly, and found the strong, hairy forearms of the man who straddled her.

She fought, lifting her knees and slamming them into his sides. He grunted, and she felt him fall to the side. He loosened his hold long enough for her to draw breath, but the pillow was quickly pushed back into place, suffocating her. Her nails clawed at his arms; she heard him hiss in pain.

Blackness swamped the edges of her mind. Every

breath she drew resulted in nothing more than a mouthful of fabric. There was no air. He was going to kill her.

Like Bella. Oh God, she was going to end up dead like Bella and no one would ever know who killed her. No one but her servants would care. Katya and Piotr would notify her parents and tell them she had been murdered. Would her parents weep for her? Would Miles?

Miles.

If she had stayed with Miles at Rochester's none of this would be happening. She would be humiliated but at least she'd have been safe. She would have forgiven him. Now he would never know. She would never know what it felt like . . .

Darkness engulfed her.

Then suddenly, the weight was gone. She knocked the pillow off her face and threw it so it couldn't be used against her again. Greedily sucking air into her lungs, she hauled herself into a sitting position. Her eyes widened in surprise as the door to her chamber shook, splintered, and finally flew open.

Miles.

"Where is he?" he demanded, bursting into the room like a pouncing feline.

"I think he must have escaped over the balcony," she wheezed, gesturing toward the gaping French doors.

Miles's scowl deepened. "The balcony?" His gaze followed hers. "Have all your lovers been so cowardly that they run at the sound of someone approaching?"

The venom in his tone was nothing compared to the

stunned astonishment that washed over Varya. She stared at him, wondering if he was out of his wits.

"My lovers?" She slumped against the headboard. "You think that man was my *lover*?"

"What else am I supposed to think when I come to your bedchamber and find the door locked and hear a man's voice from inside?"

He was jealous. Varya would have laughed in his face if she weren't overcome by the urge to smash it.

"Perhaps that he was trying to kill me? Honestly, Miles, sometimes you can be such an idiot." She pulled a pillow up to her chest and hugged it against the sudden chill that had fallen over her.

For a moment he appeared to be almost pleased by the revelation, and then his face paled considerably. He rushed out onto the balcony, only to return seconds later with a length of rope.

"Well, now we know how he got in, but I'm afraid thanks to my stupidity he got away."

Varya didn't reply; she didn't know what to say. Wearily, she pulled the counterpane up over her shivering limbs.

"Are you hurt?" Miles asked, practically tripping over his feet in his effort to get to her. The fear and concern etched on his face shocked her. He cared. He truly cared what happened to her. The knowledge filled her with joy—until it felt as though she might burst with emotion.

"You saved me," she whispered.

He looked startled. "I suppose so, yes. Did he hurt you?"

She laughed shakily. "No, but he tried, Miles. He

was going to kill me." Her eyes filled with hot tears as
the shock finally set in. She hadn't wept in front of anyone in years, and was uncommonly proud of the fact,
but she was undone by his unexpected tenderness.

Miles brushed away the first hot, salty drop that
trickled down her cheek with the pad of his thumb,
but as the rivulets became more than he could manage,
he switched to his handkerchief.

The soft linen smelled like him—spicy yet strangely
sweet. Varya found herself sniffing just so she could
breathe in that comforting fragrance.

"I don't suppose you got a look at his face?"

She shook her head. "He came in while I was
asleep. Why did you come?" She raised her gaze to his
face, holding her breath as she waited for his answer.

He flushed. "When I found out you had left, I bor-
rowed a mount from Rochester and gave chase." His
gaze was earnest as it met hers. "I am truly sorry for
what I said to you this morning—and for the stupid
assumption I made upon barging in here."

She knew how difficult it must be for him to say
those words to her, and that made his apology even
sweeter. "You should be."

He chuckled as he drew her into his arms. "I deserved that, I know."

Sighing, Varya snuggled against him. She despised
weakness, but right now she felt too safe to care if she
needed him or not.

His hands stroked her hair as his cheek brushed the
top of her head. "I don't know what I would have
done if I had arrived to find you dead."

The raw emotion in his voice made Varya's throat clench.

"Don't think about it. I'm safe now."

"I know, and I am so glad for it." His lips pressed against her forehead as he began to rock her gently, like a father rocks a frightened child.

"I'll find whoever attacked you, Varya, and I'll take care of him, but I don't want to risk your safety again for that damned book of Bella's."

She frowned, smart enough to realize that her safety certainly came before the investigation, but not wanting to give up so easily.

Horror struck as something occurred to her. Gripping the sleeves of his coat, she tilted her head back to stare at him. "He got past the guards, Miles. How did he get past your guards?"

He paled. "I don't know."

"What if he comes back?" Terror had her firmly in its grip. "Even if I give you the book, how will he know I no longer have it? How can I ever feel safe in my own home while he's out there?"

He calmed her with gentle shushing noises and tender caresses. Still, his silence unnerved her.

"What are we going to do?" Tears of frustration and fear burned the backs of her eyes.

Miles thought for a moment before answering. Wiping her tears away, he met her gaze evenly.

"I'm going to move in here with you."

Chapter 14

Varya choked. "No."

Miles carried on as though he hadn't heard her, "If I move in here with you, we will both be able to rest easier."

She snorted at the irony of the statement. Not bloody likely.

But he carried on, ignoring her. "Obviously, the men posted outside are not enough. With someone actually in the house, it will be much harder for anyone to get to you. I'll put new locks on the windows and doors and speak to all the staff about keeping a watch for suspicious-looking characters . . ."

"People will talk." Could she bear having him under her roof? It was a dream come true and a nightmare at the same time. So close she could touch him.

He chuckled softly. "Varya, no one will think any-thing of me staying here at night. You're my mistress, remember?"

As if she could have forgotten.

"What will your family say?" Blythe was the closest thing she had to a friend in London, and Varya didn't want to risk their fledgling relationship. And she cer-tainly didn't want to embarrass her friend or Miles's mother.

"I'll explain the situation to them. Once they un-derstand your safety is at stake, I'll have their full support."

He would not be dissuaded. The idea of him sleep-ing under her roof, watching her every move, was dis-concerting. What if he spoke to Katya? Her faithful servant already saw Miles as a handsome prince, come to rescue Varya from her tower prison. If Katya told Miles who she really was, he would treat her differ-ently, and probably notify her parents out of his mis-guided sense of honor. She would not give up her freedom after enjoying its sweetness for so many years.

"Where will you sleep?" she blurted out, and then blushed furiously. Why, of all things, had she asked him *that*?

"Where would you like me to sleep?"

His voice was soft, almost a caress. She closed her eyes and shivered.

"There's another bedchamber connected to this one," she murmured. She opened her eyes and quickly looked away from his hot gaze. "But I don't think your staying here is necessary. I'll have Piotr move in there." Mother Mary, but she *wanted* him to stay with her.

"I'll have some things brought over from Wynter Lane," he replied, ignoring her again. His fingers trailed along the curve of her bare shoulder, causing her to shiver once again.

"Shall I sleep in that adjoining room, Varya?"

He wanted her to invite him to her bed; she could hear it in the husky timbre of his voice. She knew he would not touch her unless she touched him first. Could she do it? Could she forsake her loyalty to Bella now that he was offering her what she wanted so badly? Wouldn't Bella want her to grab what happiness she could?

"No," she replied, lifting her gaze to his as she came to a decision. "You'll sleep with me." God help her. She might be a fool, but she wasn't stupid enough to let him slip through her fingers.

He inhaled sharply, making her smile. She took his hand in hers and placed it on her breast. His thumb brushed against her taut nipple, sending a shiver straight to the place between her thighs.

When he stood, Varya lifted her head so fast it hurt her neck. She winced. "What are you doing?"

Grinning, Miles gestured at the chamber door. It was wide open.

"I think it's best to close it, don't you? Unless, of course, you'd prefer to leave it open?"

She felt her cheeks suffuse with heat. "No, close it."

He did, securing it with a chair as he had broken the latch when he kicked the door in. As he walked, he removed his jacket and tossed it on the sofa.

Wetting her lips, Varya watched with wide-eyed interest from her seat in the middle of the bed as his nimble fingers deftly unknotted his cravat. The discarded muslin fell to a soft puddle on the carpet.

His waistcoat landed on her dressing table when he threw it, knocking over the miniature of her parents. *All the better*, Varya thought. She didn't want to feel the weight of their painted gazes as she became his mistress for real.

"Shall I continue?" he asked in a teasing voice, pulling the tails of his shirt free of his trousers.

"Please," she replied in kind. This lighthearted approach did much to calm her.

He paused a few feet away from her, grabbed the bottom of his shirt, and raised his arms. He leaned forward, pulling the fine linen garment over his head.

His hair was mussed, curling slightly around the strong column of his throat as he straightened. She could see the knotted muscle beneath his golden skin flex as he pulled his arms free of his shirt sleeves.

He tossed the shirt aside.

Lord, he was beautiful. His shoulders were wide and muscular, curving into thick, well-defined biceps. His chest was broad and covered with soft auburn hair—just as in her dream. The curls trailed down along his rippled abdomen, tapering when they reached his narrow waist.

A jagged scar marred the perfection of his torso. The narrow strip of pink, satiny flesh began high up on his ribs and ran almost to his navel.

"The war," he replied when he noticed her stare.

Rising up on her knees before him on the bed she held his gaze. "Does it hurt?"

"Varya, I don't think this conversation is conducive to sexual arousal." His expression was one of distaste.

Varya caught one of his large hands in both of hers. "Does it hurt?" she persisted.

He stared down at their joined hands. "Sometimes." His voice was soft, distant.

She turned his hand over in hers, bringing the palm to her lips. She kissed the soft inner flesh, working her way out to his fingers. The salt of his skin was on her mouth; she flicked her tongue over the tips, nipping softly with her teeth.

A soft gasp slipped past his lips, and Varya felt the fingers of his free hand slide through her hair. Emboldened by his touch, she released his hand, and turned her attention to the scar so close to her face. Softly, her lips brushed the satiny flesh. The hair on his torso tickled her cheek; she pressed her face against his warmth.

Slowly she felt herself being lowered onto the bed; her shift rode up around her thighs. She became aware of the heat between her legs, the puckering of her nipples, and the pounding of her heart.

It seemed as if she had waited all her life for this man; giving him her body was just a small part of what was happening between them.

She refused to think about the rest.

Cool air touched her breasts as he peeled back the front of her shift—a shocking contrast as his warm hands settled over the taut flesh. Varya moaned as he gently rolled one hard nipple between his thumb and forefinger.

"So damned beautiful," he muttered, lowering his head to capture the other nipple between his lips. Mercilessly, his tongue flicked the aching bud.

Her hips jerked against him as a jolt of erotic pleasure coursed from her breasts to the very center of her sexuality. A delicious ache was building inside her.

His hands were tugging on the straps of her shift, hauling them down over her arms in a clumsy attempt to remove the flimsy garment. She shifted her body to accommodate him. When the gauze finally pooled around her feet, she kicked it away.

Then he was gone.

Bewildered and drugged with desire, Varya leaned up on her elbows. "What are you doing?" He wasn't leaving her, was he?

Hopping on one foot, Miles struggled to remove one of his boots. "I think it's only fair that we both remove all our clothing, don't you?" He grunted as the boot finally came free, almost losing his balance in the process. "Although we might both be well into our dotage before I get these godless boots off."

Varya chuckled as first one boot then the other sailed across her chamber. Her laughter faded as his hands went to the falls of his trousers. The usually smooth front bulged with his hard arousal. She watched in fascination as he peeled the snug-fitting fabric down his legs.

Good Lord, it was really going to happen. She was finally going to experience the pleasure of a man's body.

Standing naked before her was the most beautiful man she had ever seen. From the top of his head to his powerful torso and the long, muscular columns of his legs, he was as perfect as Michelangelo's *David*—with one *large* difference.

He moved toward her like a great cat, muscles rippling, every step measured and sensual. Her stomach fluttering in anticipation, Varya fell back against the coverlet as he crawled onto the bed, sliding between her thighs as though he belonged there.

The hard length of him probed her moist flesh as he leaned over her, brushing his lips against her face and throat with feathery kisses. It was almost too much for her to bear.

As he supported himself on one forearm, his free hand toyed with her nipples, manipulating the aching peaks until she moaned aloud with pleasure. She wanted him inside her, wanted to feel her body wrapped around his, wanted him to take her in all those different positions Bella had told her about until they were both too exhausted to move.

Never had losing her control felt so *right*.

He slid down her body, his mouth blazing a fiery trail along her flesh. He paused only for a moment at her breasts, sucking ardently on her nipples until she writhed in exquisite agony. The ache deep within her was acute now, begging to be relieved.

"I want you, Miles. Now." Her voice was low and husky, and sounded strange to her own ears.

He lifted his head, releasing her nipple. The pink skin glistened with wetness from his mouth. His eyes seemed to be pools of molten gold, reflecting her own wanton image.

"Not yet," he told her softly, "but soon." He moved down her rib cage, kissing and licking her hot flesh. His tongue probed lightly at her navel before moving to the generous flare of her hips and down one thigh.

Varya felt his weight slide from the bed. His hands gripped her hips, pulling her derriere to the edge of the mattress.

"What are you doing?" She gasped as his lips brushed the sensitive skin of her inner thigh. Despite her shock, she felt a flood of warmth inside as her flesh throbbed in anticipation.

The light stubble on his cheeks rubbed erotically against her softness. His breath was cool against her.

"Worshipping, I think," came his reverent reply as his lips trailed up her thigh to that part of her that burned for his touch. She jumped as his lips touched her in the most intimate of kisses.

"Oh my," she whispered. Bella had never told her about *this*.

"You're so wet," he muttered hoarsely, trailing a finger along her warm cleft. "God, I want you."

His fingers opened her for his tongue. A spasm racked the muscles in her thighs as his mouth claimed her. His tongue was soft, hot, and wet, and the feel of it against her flesh was almost too incredible to bear. Raising herself up on a wobbly arm, Varya reached down with the other to tangle her fingers in his soft hair, pressing him closer.

His gaze met hers over the expanse of her soft belly. Heat flooded her body. She should be embarrassed, but it was so arousing to watch as his mouth caressed her. His tongue brushed her most sensitive spot and she moaned out loud.

"More!" she cried as his tongue rubbed the throbbing bud with excruciating deliberation.

The sensation was too much. His tongue moved relentlessly; his fingers held her open. She fell back against the bed; her hands pulled fervently at his hair as her hips bucked beneath him. "Oh yes, yes . . ."

Her breath was coming in short, feral pants. The sweet pressure between her legs was building—soon, soon.

"*Yes!*" Her body exploded with pleasure. Spasms of delectable warmth raced through her torso and limbs, leaving her muscles feeling heavy and liquid.

Miles rose above her, reveling in the fact that he had pleased her. Her countenance was tranquil, but he wasn't finished with her.

He stood, hooking his arms underneath her knees and holding them wide. He watched as the head of his shaft parted the flesh that had perfumed his hands and face. His head fell back. She was so tight, so wet.

Too late he felt the thin barrier fall beneath his siege, felt a twinge of discomfort as his own sensitive flesh plowed into her. He heard her startled gasp in unison with his own. Wide blue eyes stared up at him.

"Virgin," he croaked.

She nodded, shifting beneath him in a way he could only term uncomfortable.

"Why didn't you tell me? I thought . . ." *Oh yes, Miles. Tell her what you thought.* "I thought you had done this before."

She shook her head, wincing as he withdrew from her. Gently, he lowered her legs, staring in fascinated horror at the smears of blood on his rapidly deflating shaft.

Gingerly, she slipped off the bed and inched away from him. Miles had no idea what to do. The only other virgin he had ever been with was Charlotte, and she had been his wife—he had expected it. But Varya wasn't his wife, and he hadn't wanted to hurt her.

"Are you all right?"

She slipped her arms into the sleeves of a satin dressing gown, tightly cinching the belt before turning to him. He knew he should dress, but he couldn't seem to bring himself to move.

"I'm fine. A little sore, but I suppose that is to be expected. I'm afraid no one ever told me that it could be so—uncomfortable. Is it always like—this?" There was no need to define "this."

He flinched. "It's worse for some women than others the first time." He moved toward her. "Varya, if I had known—"

Her gaze met his and the coolness in her eyes stopped him. "You assumed that I had been with other men."

He began pulling on his trousers. "Yes."

"Because of what I do?"

He hated the suspicion in her voice, and he was too ashamed of himself to answer. He had thought she had been with other men. Her profession and her passion had persuaded him. How could he have known?

"You thought I was a whore, despite my telling you that I did not have a protector." Her tone was bitter.

"You said you didn't *need* one," he reminded her before he could stop himself. "You said nothing about never having had one." He shoved his feet back into his boots.

"So, you just assumed—"

"Yes." He pulled his shirt over his head. "Just as you assumed I was Bella's killer." He moved toward her. She didn't pull away when he slipped his arms around her.

"I'm sorry for what I thought," he murmured against her hair. "I'm sorry I hurt you. We've both made horrible misjudgments about each other. Will you at least grant me the opportunity to make it right?"

He felt her nod against his chest and released her. "I'll take that as a yes." He reached for his waistcoat.

"I suppose I truly am your mistress now."

How resigned she sounded. Had she believed that being a mistress would be better than the life she already had? Why hadn't she married? She had been untouched, and her beauty and fortune made her a very desirable wife for someone of her class. Why?

"No," he corrected, combing the tangles from her hair with his fingers. "You are not my mistress."

Her gaze met his. To his astonishment, her eyes were dry.

"Then what am I?" she whispered.

His head lowered. "If you'll have me, I'd like to call you my wife," he said softly, just before his lips met hers.

"Did you let him inside you?"

Varya came up out of the bath sputtering, soap bubbles flying from her lips and nose. She swiped a hand across her face, clearing away the suds.

"Katya!"

The Russian woman shook her head ruefully. "You did."

Varya's cheeks burned with embarrassment. Her shame could not have been greater if her own mother had discovered her with a lover.

"It's none of your concern," she replied haughtily, instantly regretting her tone. She scrubbed viciously at her face to hide her crimson cheeks.

"No, of course it is none of my concern," Katya said stiffly, her voice low and thick with her heavy accent. "I have only watched you go from being raised to be the wife of a prince to being a nobleman's *nariakha*!"

Varya flinched at the Russian word for "whore." Calling herself Miles's mistress would be easy to get used to, but hearing herself described in those base terms was degrading—especially coming from Katya. She refused to tell the older woman that Miles had actually proposed afterward. Then she would have to explain why she had refused.

"You forget your station," she mumbled, not willing to admit how much the words had hurt.

The woman who had been like a mother to her braced a meaty hand on either side of her ample hips, and stared down at her with a countenance that refused to be bullied.

"No, *golubchik*. I have not forgotten who I am. It is *you* who has forgotten. So busy you have been—pretending to be something you are not. So busy that you do not remember who you are, but *I* remember." One fist came up to her impressive, bombazine-clad bosom. "You are Varvara Vladimirovna Ulyanova, daughter of Vladimir Vasilyevich, and you are a Russian pr—"

"I know who I am!" Varya cried, leaping to her feet in the tub. Water sloshed over the sides, soaking the marble floor of the bathing chamber. "I do not need you to remind me." Her voice was shaking, her body trembling.

Jerkily, she climbed out of the tub, handfuls of suds running down her wet flesh. Katya held a towel; she snatched it out of her hands without thanks.

"So you do remember," the older woman continued, seemingly unperturbed. "Is there a chance that you now carry your knight's child?"

"He is not my knight," Varya answered brusquely. She remembered the moment Miles had taken her virginity, his disappointment, and his shrinking male member. Even though she had not been expecting the sudden pain, she knew that a man had to deposit his seed inside a woman to impregnate her. She also knew, thanks to Bella, that this was a somewhat messy procedure. There had been no mess after Miles withdrew from her, only a little blood. Her own blood, which had called to mind that horrible night in Ivan's room.

"No. There is no chance of a child." At least she hoped there wasn't, but if there was, she'd deal with that when the time came.

"Good." Katya nodded. "I will show you how to use a sponge soaked in vinegar to prevent conception. I did not think I would have to teach you until after your wedding."

But there would be no wedding—ever. After escaping both her father and Ivan, Varya had no intention of putting herself under any man's control, not even if that man already claimed her heart. She was Miles's as long as he wanted her, but she would never be his wife. She simply didn't think she could trust a man that strong-willed with her soul.

But she wanted to. Telling him no had been so much harder than she ever could have dreamed. The hurt and disappointment on his face had cut her so deeply she almost changed her mind.

"I'll never be a bride, Katya," Varya said harshly, detesting the older women for her disappointed tone, and hating herself for being the cause of it. "So you'd better teach me everything you know."

Chapter 15

"Drink?"

Miles lifted his head. "Hmm?" He hadn't heard anyone else enter the room.

Blythe stood by the liquor cabinet, a decanter of claret in her hand and an amused glint in her eyes.

"I asked if you would like a drink."

"Please." Absently, he brushed a speck of lint from the arm of his jacket and tugged at his shirt sleeves so that the snowy white cuffs peeked out from beneath the stark black of his evening attire. Any diversion was preferable to thinking about the night ahead.

Two days had passed since Varya's refusal of him. Two days he had spent playing the scene over and over in his mind, wondering how he could have done it differently—wondering what he had done wrong.

Of course he had handled it badly.

"You only want to marry me because you've taken my maidenhead."

"Not only because of that."

Where were his smooth words then? *Stupid. Stupid. Stupid.*

Why didn't he tell her how he felt? He should have told her that he wanted to marry her because he couldn't imagine spending the rest of his life without her. He should have told her he was willing to face all his demons for the chance to wake up beside her every morning for the next fifty years.

Of course, two days ago, in the shock of having taken her virginity, none of this even occurred to him. It was only since her curt dismissal and the agony of spending forty-eight hours watching her house, guarding her without being able to touch her or comfort her, that he realized just how deep his feelings for Varya were. He didn't know what he could possibly say to her to fix things, but he could make certain no one tried to harm her again.

He cared enough for her not to worry whether she was beneath him. She had proven she was more of a lady than most women he knew.

And he cared enough to do the one thing he swore he'd never do again—marry. Only this time, it was desire—not duty—that motivated him.

"Here."

He took the glass his sister offered with a mumbled thanks.

Blythe fell into the chair opposite him and lay sprawled across the wine-colored velvet in a pose that

would have done justice to any of the ton's rakehells—
except, of course, for the fact that she was wearing an
evening gown.

"Mama will have a seizure if she sees you sitting
like that."

His younger sister lazily waved one elegant hand.
"As long as I remember to sit properly at Carlton
House, she'll be fine, and you know I always behave
myself in company."

"Yes," he replied absently staring into the depths of
the rich claret. "You always do."

Blythe thumped a hand against the arm of the
chaise and pulled herself upright. "All right, that's it."

Miles looked up in confusion at her abrupt tone.
"What?"

"What the devil is wrong with you? You've been
moping around here for the last two days. Ever since
your return from Rochester's you've been listless and
boring, and I demand to know why." She brought her
hand down on her knee with a resounding *thwap*.

Miles grimaced. "Not now, Blythe."

"Yes now, Miles," she replied, mocking his exasperated tone. "Is it Varya?"

"She's not the only person in my life, you know!" he
snapped, slamming his glass down on the pedestal
table beside his chair.

His sister grinned. "Oh? So it's Carny who's responsible for this depression? Maybe you shouldn't spend
so much time with him, Miles; I have always thought
your relationship with him to be—*unnatural*."

If he could have knocked her senseless with a glare,
he would have. "It's none of your concern, *brat*." He

used her childhood nickname as an insult rather than a term of affection.

"Stop it, Miles," Blythe ordered, unaffected by his attempted cruelty. "I'm your sister and I love you, therefore it *is* my concern. So stop behaving as if you're playing Hamlet at Drury Lane and talk to me."

He sighed, rubbing a hand over his tired eyes. "I shouldn't speak of such things in front of you."

She snorted. "When has that ever stopped you? Really, Miles, who else have you got? Papa's gone and Carny's probably drunk."

She had a point. The only other people he had ever trusted as much as her were his father and best friend, and unfortunately, neither of them was available.

"Varya and I . . ." his voice drifted off. How could he put this? "That is to say we—"

"Made love?" she suggested.

He nodded, feeling the blood rush to his cheeks. "Uh, yes. That's exactly what we did."

"And the problem would be?" Her eager gaze was disconcerting.

Miles cleared his throat. "Varya was—*inexperienced.*"

Blythe nodded, unruffled. Miles scowled, realizing that his sister knew more about what went on between men and women than he was comfortable with.

"This came as a surprise to you?" She took a drink.

He nodded. "Yes. Yes it did."

"Why?"

"I should think that would be obvious—her profession, her lifestyle, her sophistication—"

Blythe laughed, cutting him off. Shaking her head, she smiled sympathetically. "Oh, Miles. For a man who has known so many women, you really don't know very much about them."

"Just what the devil do you mean by that?" He couldn't imagine that Blythe might possibly be more knowledgeable on the subject than himself. Then again, she had the benefit of actually *being* a female, so perhaps he shouldn't discredit her opinion quite so readily.

"You know as well as I, brother dear, that a woman can present one face to the public but put on an entirely *different* one when society isn't looking." She smiled somewhat roguishly. "Your own sister, for example. Here in London I play the lady, but I'd rather be at home in a pair of breeches shoveling horse droppings."

"Yes, but that's *you*," he argued, even as the image of Bella's old comfortable nightgown came to mind. He had been wrong in his opinion of her, just as he had been wrong about Varya.

"That's *many* women," his sister corrected him with a chuckle. "So, when's the wedding?"

Miles raked his fingers through his hair and sighed. "There isn't one."

"You've ruined her; you *must* marry her." She wasn't teasing now.

"I asked Varya to marry me after it happened and she refused."

Blythe's brow wrinkled. "She refused? You must have botched it."

"I . . . me?" Miles sputtered. "Why must I be the one at fault?"

"Did you tell her you cared for her?"

He scowled. "I think she's well aware of that fact."

Rolling her eyes, his sister straightened in her chair. "Did you ask her to marry you, Miles or did you simply inform her of the upcoming ceremony?"

A uncomfortable heat crept up his cheeks. He really had made a mess of it. "I might have mentioned that it would be in her best interest to become my wife."

"You idiot! No wonder she refused you. Miles, you've been married before, didn't you learn anything about women?"

"No!" he cried, losing his temper and leaping to his feet. "I find your sex completely and absolutely baffling! I let her help search for Bella's killer despite the whole mess she got us into. I let her continue to masquerade as my mistress despite my own misgivings. And then when she finally decided she actually wanted to be my mistress, I gave in and found myself in the bed of an innocent! Then when I try to do the right thing she refuses me! I've given the woman everything she's asked for. What more can she want?"

"Oh, I don't know. Respect? Trust? Someone to tell her she's beautiful even when her nose is dripping and her throat is swollen with quinsy." Blythe's eyes were bright with a wisdom Miles had never seen before. "You sound like an authoritarian—a father figure telling her what's in her 'best interest.' "

If there was a wall nearby he would have beaten his head against it.

Father figure. Varya didn't say much about her father, but he had picked up enough to know that he had been very strict. And that he had tried to force her into a marriage she violently opposed.

Oh no. He had handled her well.

"Even if I could make it up to her, she's dead set against marriage, Blythe. You heard her yourself."

Blythe waved her hand in a dismissive gesture. "Oh pooh. I'm sure Varya truly believes that marriage is horrible and awful for a woman, but she just hasn't met the right man."

Miles cocked a disbelieving brow. "You think *I* might be the 'right man'?"

His sister shrugged her wide shoulders. "Who knows? You can't be all *that* wrong if she allowed you to—" She faltered and flushed a deep crimson. Miles could only imagine what she had been about to say. "—take liberties with her person," she finished primly.

"Yes," he agreed hesitantly, wondering why her words only served to make him feel worse about the situation with Varya instead of better.

"She's hiding something, Blythe. There's something she doesn't want me to know about her past."

"Does it matter?" his sister inquired with womanly wisdom.

"No. No, it doesn't." And it didn't.

Authoritarian, indeed.

Varya was thankful for her anger toward Miles. It almost obscured her anxiety concerning the evening.

He had ignored her for two whole days before sending a dozen roses along with a note of brief apology for his *neglect*, stating that he would still expect her to accompany him to Carlton House.

She burned the note, turned the air blue cursing

him, and had eleven of the roses destroyed to make rosewater. The remaining one sat in a slim crystal vase on the table beside her bed. *Not* because it came from him, and *not* because she wanted to forgive him, but because it was a truly beautiful blossom.

If he had genuinely meant his proposal he wouldn't have given up so easily. He would have sent flowers thrice a day, and candy. He would have come to call even though she would refuse to see him. He would pine for her.

Not ignore her as though marriage meant nothing.

Of course he didn't truly want to marry her. She knew him well enough to know he had never forgiven himself for Charlotte's death, and for Bella's as well. Miles Christian believed himself to be a harbinger of death for everything and everyone he loved. She wondered if he kept his distance from his mother and Blythe as well. He probably didn't even realize that he did it.

Well, she didn't want his love, and she'd rather put out her own eyes than be anyone's wife. As it was, Miles already had too much sway over her life. If she married him he would own her completely, and she couldn't bear it if he turned into a tyrant like her father or Ivan. Better to keep him as a beautiful fantasy than as a husband.

Oh, but she had been tempted.

Even though he had bungled it. Even though she knew he was only asking out of a sense of guilt, she had been very tempted to throw herself into his arms and shout, "Yes" at the top of her lungs.

Instead, she told him to leave. And he had.

Was she now to pretend nothing had happened?

"Have I told you how beautiful you look this evening?" he asked with a charming smile as he handed her into the coach.

He had. Three times already. Apparently the time she had spent agonizing over her wardrobe had been worth it. She told herself she hadn't chosen the snug, royal blue velvet gown for his appreciation, but she couldn't stop the thrill of pleasure at his notice.

Varya dragged a cool gaze over his face before settling herself rigidly on the cushions. "Thank you."

"I don't suppose you have forgiven me yet?" the bane of her existence asked once they were shut inside his carriage.

She flashed him a smile that felt more like a snarl than a gesture of friendliness. "Of course I have, Miles. Every woman enjoys having the loss of her virginity treated like one of Shakespeare's tragedies."

"Oh, for pity's sake, Varya! Wouldn't you have been surprised to discover that *I* was a virgin?"

She gave him what she hoped was an arch look. "I already knew that you weren't, my lord."

He surprised her by grinning. "Yes, well, you had the advantage of having read Bella's journal. That stacked the odds in your favor, did it not?"

"It is not the same," she argued, fighting the urge to smile. "Gentlemen are not expected to be virginal."

"Neither are mature women who have a profession and live alone."

She sat there, swaying back and forth as the carriage bumped along the cobblestones, her mouth gaping open. She had nothing to dispute him with; he was right. If it had been anyone other than herself, she wouldn't have thought any differently than he had.

"That doesn't excuse your behavior afterward," she admonished, attacking from another angle.

His wide shoulders flinched at the comment. "No," he admitted. "It doesn't."

Well, he had acknowledged that he had been wrong. Now what? Somehow, the past two days of practicing what she would say and obsessing over his replies seemed excessive, considering with what little ease he had agreed with her.

"I thought men preferred virgins."

He winced. "For wives, not for mistresses."

A hollow ache formed in her stomach. "And that is why you asked me to marry you."

The glow of the lamp cast his face into sharp relief as he leaned forward to take her hand. Lord, but no man should be allowed to be so beautiful. Her heart ached just to look at him.

"I asked you to marry me because I felt I treated you wrongly."

Her gaze dropped. As much as she told herself it was true, it hurt to hear him say it.

"And I asked you to marry me because I realized that spending the rest of my life with you would be a grand adventure."

Her head snapped up. "Really?"

"Really. I care for you a great deal, Varya. I had hoped that you cared for me."

"Of course I do!"

"Then say you'll consent to marry me. Be my lover as well as my wife."

He made it sound so wonderful! There was no treachery in his molten green eyes, only pleading. Ivan had seemed sincere once too.

But this was *Miles*, not Ivan. And the idea of growing old with Miles was more appealing than marriage to Ivan had been. She hadn't loved Ivan . . .

"I much prefer lover to mistress," she replied brightly, intentionally avoiding his request.

"And you prefer mistress to wife." There was a resigned slump to his shoulders as he fell back against the squabs. His voice sounded like a stranger's, it was so tired and soft.

Her smile crumbled. "Yes," she replied quietly, her entire form clenched to hold her composure. "I prefer almost anything to that."

"Why?" The pain in his voice tore at her heart. "Surely I've proven to you that not all men are animals."

Not animals, she corrected silently, *masters. In control of everything and everyone in their lives—servants, wives . . . daughters.*

"I'm not certain there will ever be enough proof of that, Miles." She wrapped her silk shawl tightly around her shoulders—not that it offered much protection against her fears and memories. "But rest assured that is not my only reason for distrusting your sex."

"Do you trust me?" His voice was hesitant.

What a question! "With my life," she answered honestly. *Just not with my heart.*

The carriage rolled to a stop before he could respond to her declaration. She wondered if he found it strange that she hadn't asked him if he trusted *her*. She honestly didn't want to know the answer. Neither the disappointment of knowing he didn't, nor the responsibility of learning that he did, was a burden she wanted to carry right now.

"We're here," he announced, peering out the window at the crowd gathering around the entrance of the prince regent's residence.

"Wonderful." Had that sounded as hollow to his ears as it had to hers? Here she was, about to be hand-delivered into certain exposure, and it would bring her quiet little existence crashing down around her. Well, perhaps it was time she stopped running and claimed her life as her own.

The hand she gave Miles as he helped her out of the carriage was remarkably steady. Was this the same sense of resignation some people experienced when facing death? She had heard drowning described as a peaceful feeling, and that was exactly how she felt as the wall of people closed in around her—strangely calm and peaceful.

"Excited?"

Varya turned to gaze up at her escort. There was a mixture of hope and anticipation in the depths of his eyes. She loved him. She knew it as surely as the beating of her heart. She had never expected it to hurt so much.

"Yes," she replied with a forced smile. "I've never seen the inside of Carlton House."

Miles shrugged, offering her his arm. "It's gaudy—just like any other house of royalty."

"Not all royal homes are vulgar and garish, Miles."

She tapped him lightly with her fan and smiled.

His mouth quirked. "Oh? Have you been inside many palaces, Varya?"

"More than you, I'll wager." She chuckled at his startled expression. "I have played in many grand homes, Miles."

"Yes, I suppose you must have." Luckily, he dropped the subject.

It was a decided crush. Everyone who was of consequence was in attendance, anxious for a glimpse of Czar Alexander and other visiting foreign dignitaries.

The evening was cool, and Carlton House large enough that the regent's guests need not fear becoming overheated. Varya glanced around the opulent ballroom; it was a little overdone, but she had seen far worse. In fact, she found the vaulted ceiling and gothic touches fit perfectly with her mood at the moment.

A few of the guests looked decidedly uncomfortable at their ruler's seemingly forced gaiety. His troubles with Princess Caroline were household talk, and quite a few guests wondered aloud if Her Highness would dare attempt to embarrass the regent as he entertained foreign royalty in his own home.

The prince was across the room, deep in conversation with a mature woman rumored to be his current mistress. While most men of his years chased much younger women, the regent had a definite preference for those long past the blush of youth—often well past his own age as well. It was uncommon behavior, but Varya was well aware that royalty bred many idiosyncrasies. The prince might inspire loathing in many of his subjects, but he was a treat when compared to historical figures such as Ivan the Terrible.

"There's the czar's sister," Miles announced, interrupting her thoughts.

Varya followed his gaze through the humming crowd. Her gaze fell upon a stern Russian woman whom she instantly recognized as Catherine, Grand Duchess of Oldenburg. Silently, she prayed that Catherine would not recognize her. With any luck, neither czar nor duchess had any idea that she was living in London—or what a spectacle she had managed to make of herself with Miles.

She could only hope that the Marquess of Wynter was beyond the reach of palace gossip.

"Yes," she said softly. "That is Alexander's sister, Catherine."

"Ah." He scanned the room. "I don't see Czar Alexander."

Thank God. But Varya knew her relief would be short-lived. "He's here," she informed him, her own gaze skipping over the features of every bejeweled guest. "If Catherine is here, so is Alexander."

Yes, Alexander was certainly there. Even if someone of Miles's height could not pick him out of the crowd, there was no doubt that her king was in that room with only a few dozen sweaty bodies between them. His sister would not attend without him and vice versa.

Her certainty must have surprised him, for Miles turned to her with an inquisitive expression. "Oh? How would you know that?"

Varya's cheeks went warm. "Because they're—that is, I've *heard* that the czar and duchess are very close."

Suspicious curiosity revealed itself in his gleaming eyes and tilted mouth. "You have a better acquaintance with the habits of your country's royal family than most English lords can claim with their own."

"Including yourself, my lord?" she teased, hoping to change the topic. Her evening was already strained enough with his second proposal, and if the entire night was to come toppling down around her, it would not be through any fault of her own.

His smile was genuine. "Indeed, Miss Ulyanova, indeed."

"Ulyanova? Don't tell me we have *another* Russian in our midst?"

Varya's heart plummeted. It was starting.

She and Miles turned to greet the florid-faced prince regent. The future monarch was dressed in white satin knee breeches and a matching waistcoat that strained across his considerable midsection. His coat was a pale blue, his cravat tied in an intricate knot. He was rumored to have been handsome in his youth, but now he reminded Varya of one of her mother's prized pugs.

"I'm afraid so, Your Majesty," Miles answered with a respectful bow. "But I believe you have already met Miss Varya Ulyanova." He smiled, and Varya knew he was pleased to have pronounced her name correctly.

With a smile frozen on her face, Varya sank into a deep and elegant curtsy. The prince seemed suitably impressed. So did Miles. Her heart hammered painfully in her chest. Soon. It would happen soon.

"Varvara Vladimirovna Ulyanova!"

Oh God. She hadn't been expecting it *this* soon.

Varya was painfully aware of the many gazes fixed upon her as she turned to face the ruler of her homeland. She didn't have to look at Miles to feel the weight of his frown. What a fright she must look! Her hands were cold and her face felt too heavy for her head. Her movements were slow and jerky. It seemed quiet—too quiet—as she heard her own blood pounding in her ears. She felt dizzy, and wondered if she might actually swoon.

Then she met the happy, yet reproachful gaze of Czar Alexander. At his side was the equally countenanced grand duchess.

"Varya? It is you!" He moved toward her, a sweet smile curving his lips.

"Hello, Alexi," she managed to greet him in a soft voice that sounded nothing like her own.

She felt Miles's strong grip on her arm, and was thankful for it. He could catch her when she fell.

"Alexi?" he inquired.

Varya raised her blurry gaze to his. It was over.

"Yes," she whispered, just before the darkness swallowed her. "My cousin."

Chapter 16

When Varya finally woke, she became aware of two things. First, where she lay was far too quiet to be the ballroom, or any room in Carlton House. Second, her head felt as if someone had kicked it repeatedly.

Probably Miles, she thought.

If she opened her eyes, would there be a crowd of people gathered around her, staring at her as though she were a freak in a traveling show? Or would there be only Miles and Alexi for her to face?

Poor Alexi, what he must think of her! He would no doubt notify her father—his first cousin—of her whereabouts. How long would it take her father to arrive in London? Would he force her to return to St. Petersburg and marry Ivan, or had Ivan found someone else to torture for the rest of his life?

She could run away, but where could she go? She could speak French fluently, but the country was in such turmoil since the war and Napoleon's abdication that moving there would be more hardship than it was worth. Perhaps she could persuade Alexi not to alert her family.

She opened her eyes, blinking rapidly against the bright sunlight that filled the room. Slowly, her vision adjusted and she was able to recognize her surroundings. She was in her own house, on her back in her own bed. She never slept on her back.

She was propped up against a mountain of cushions, practically bent in two by their support. Whoever had put her to bed had done a lousy job of it.

"Ah, the *princess* is awake," came a drawling voice from across the room. "Must have been that pea I put beneath your mattress."

Varya didn't have to see the speaker to know who it was. Closing her eyes again, she leaned back wearily against the pillows.

"What happened?"

"Well," he began, his voice coming closer, "you hit your head on the floor when you fainted last night."

Her eyes shot open. "I thought you had hold of my arm."

He smiled sardonically, leaning one shoulder against the bedframe. "I did, but the shock of finding out I had relieved a member of the Russian royal family of her maidenhead overwhelmed me and you slipped out of my grasp."

She grimaced. "I am sorry for not telling you."

His face was set, his expression as cool as granite.

"Why didn't you tell me?" He pointed a warning finger at her, his eyes flashing with anger. "And no more lies. I won't stand for it."

"I've never lied to you," she replied softly. She might have withheld the truth, but she had not lied. No doubt he believed she had made a fool of him.

"Conveniently forgetting to tell me you were a virginal princess who ran away during your engagement party five years ago, leaving your family to assume the worst, is the same as lying!" He paced the carpet angrily. "Your parents don't even know where you are."

"No doubt Alexi will inform them."

He stared at her, so closely she shrank under the scrutiny. "Do they even know you're alive?"

Varya felt her cheeks warm with guilt. "I do not know." She lifted her chin defiantly.

His lip curled with a derisive snort. "I can't even tell if you're lying or not. I don't know what to believe anymore. I don't even know whether to believe that you had nothing to do with Bella's death!"

A slap would have struck with less force than his words. "How dare you! Bella was my friend. We shared everything!"

"Yes, well, now you can add me to the list of things you've *shared* with Bella," he replied coldly.

How kind of him to remind her.

"If I'm a suspect, then you are too, Miles. And you leave Bella out of this." She pointed a trembling finger at him, as she fought to keep a rein on her temper. She had absolved herself of any guilt in making love to Bella's former lover. She would not allow him to give it back.

"Me?" he cried incredulously.

"Yes, you." She didn't really believe he was capable of killing Bella, but she wanted to show him how foolish he was to accuse her.

"I saved you from meeting the same fate as Bella, remember?" he reminded her, his tone smug.

"Yes, well, I suppose that takes me off the list of potential suspects as well, doesn't it? Unless of course I hired someone to try to murder me."

She would have gloated at the sullen expression that came over his face as he conceded her logic, were it not for the fact that she was so miserable.

"I was afraid to tell you who I was, Miles. I was afraid you'd treat me differently, that you wouldn't help me find Bella's killer." *That somehow, you would find out that my family has been searching for me for five years and would send me back to them.*

"So instead, I find out from a stranger in a crowded ballroom that the woman the whole city has believed to be my mistress is actually royalty!"

She winced at the force of his words, but did not avert her gaze.

"Is that what bothers you, Miles?" she inquired in her haughtiest tone. "Discovering that socially I am actually your superior instead of your inferior?" To think she had come to respect him.

"Yes!" he admitted. He shoved a hand through his already mussed hair. "I never would have made love to you if I had known!"

"We didn't make love, Miles," she coldly informed him, shaking with hurt and rage. "There was no pleasure, and certainly no *love* for either of us." It was a lie, but oh, if only she could hurt him as much as he had hurt her!

He couldn't have looked more shocked—or hurt—if she had stuck a dagger in his heart, but the fleeting expression quickly gave way to one of tightly reined fury.

"How right you are, Your Highness. Nevertheless, our bodies did join, and you understand what that means, don't you?"

She stared at him, not quite understanding what he was getting at.

"It means," he ground out, moving toward the chamber door, "that you will no longer be my mistress."

Her heart seized painfully. "I can accept that," she said quietly, thinking not of how this would affect her search for Bella's killer, but of how she would face each day knowing he would not be in it. Even though they despised each other at that moment, she still cared for him more than she was willing to admit.

"You'd better," he warned, wrenching the door open. "Because in two weeks' time, you and I are both going to lie in this bed we've made." His gaze bore into her. "I had asked you out of desire, now I'm telling you out of duty. You will marry me, princess. Whether you like it or not."

It was more an invitation than a summons, but when Czar Alexander's note arrived requesting his company for dinner that evening, Miles didn't once consider refusing.

Here was his chance to perhaps discover why Varya had fled Russia five years ago, without a second thought to her family. His mind came up with all manner of horrifying possibilities. After all, what could induce a princess to masquerade as a mere musician?

Clad austerely in black, Miles collected his hat and cane and alighted from his coach in front of the Pulteney Hotel, where the czar and his sister were lodging.

Alexander and Catherine had been invited to stay at Carlton House, but they had refused. Rumor had it that when the grand duchess arrived in London, Prinny had paid a social call on her at this very hotel. George had arrived early, however, and found Catherine not yet dressed to receive him. A mutual dislike had blossomed during that unfortunate first meeting, and popular opinion was that Catherine had persuaded her brother to refuse the regent's hospitality.

No matter. Miles preferred a private audience to the pomp of Carlton House.

A servant answered his knock, showing him into the czar's sitting room. The accommodations at the Pulteney were well appointed, but certainly nothing like what Alexander must be accustomed to. Miles's respect for the ruler went up a couple of notches that he would give up opulence in favor of family loyalty.

Would that same loyalty prevent him from discussing Varya?

Alexander rose from the sofa when Miles entered the room. He bowed stiffly.

"Lord Wynter," he began in his heavily accented English. "I am so happy you could join me."

"Thank you for the invitation, Your Highness."

The czar gestured for him to sit and returned to the

sofa. "Please, call me Alexander. We are to be family soon."

News traveled fast in London.

"Then you must call me by my given name as well." Settling against the thick padded back of the chair, Miles watched as Alexander poured two glasses of brandy. Thank God he didn't share Varya's penchant for vodka. Miles's stomach still hadn't recovered from his last bout with the vile stuff.

Alexander passed him a glass. "I trust Varya has happily recovered from her faint?"

"She suffers no ill effects save for a bump on her head," Miles replied before taking a sip. The brandy went down like syrup.

"Her family thought she was lost from them forever. I am glad that she is well and entering into such a good match."

Miles arched a brow. A good match? Obviously, Russian society gave as little thought to loveless marriages as the English did.

"I'm happy you approve," he replied softly, wondering how Alexander could possibly be pleased his niece was entering into a union based more on passion than love, protection than devotion. Quite frankly, Miles despised the idea of yet another "duty" marriage. However, he had decided his own fate when he took Varya's virginity. Now all he could do was make the best of it.

Alexander shrugged. "She is of age; you are wealthy, titled, and strong enough to handle her." He raised his glass. "Here is to healthy sons for you."

The brandy turned to vinegar in Miles's mouth, but he drank anyway. He would not tell the czar that Varya would never have his children, not in their marriage of convenience.

"Why did Varya leave Russia?"

Alexander stiffened, his gaze suddenly wary. "She did not tell you?"

Invisible fingers trailed down Miles's spine. "Something about the man her father had chosen for her to marry."

"Ivan." The name was said with such disgust that Miles's eyes widened at it.

"And you said something at Carlton House about her leaving the night of her engagement party."

A nod. "Yes. At first her father feared she had been abducted until we learned Piotr and Katya were missing as well."

Miles could just imagine the terror Varya's parents felt when they discovered her absence. Kidnapping was a very real fear among the aristocracy. His fiancée was going to have a lot to make up for when she saw her parents again. No wonder she acted like she didn't want to see them.

"How did Ivan react to her defection?"

"Ivan is dead."

The shock was like slamming against a brick wall.

"Dead?" Good Lord! Had Varya witnessed her fiancé's death? Had she panicked and run, thinking she might be implicated?

He cleared his throat. "How did he die?"

"It is nothing to concern yourself with, Lord Wynter," Alexander replied with a smile too bright to be genuine. "Enough of this morbid talk. What does the past matter when you and Varvara face such a happy future? Come, drink with me."

Miles drank, even though his mind whirled with unanswered questions. He would get no more answers from the czar. He could only hope the investigator he hired could supply some. If Varya was in trouble, then Miles wanted to be prepared.

It seemed fairly obvious that Alexander meant her no harm, but could the czar protect her from whatever she was running from? For that matter, could he?

He didn't care what she had done, didn't care even if she had Ivan's blood on her hands. It was too late now. He was in too deep to let her go.

My dear Lord Wynter:

I would not marry you if all of England was sinking into the ocean and you were the only man with a boat.

No, that wouldn't do.

If the fate of the entire human race depended on my agreeing to your proposal, I would still tell you to go to the devil.

There, that would tell him in no uncertain terms what she thought of his *declaration* of marriage.

What angered her even more than Miles's heavy-handedness was the knowledge that, had he fallen down on bended knee and *asked* for her hand rather than demanding it, she would have said yes. The nagging doubt that he was only asking because she was a princess mattered little. She loved the overbearing fool, that's all there was to it.

Varya scrawled her signature at the bottom of the note, sanded it, and folded it. A glob of dark blue wax fell onto the paper and she pressed her seal into it, leaving behind the impression of a single rose. Now she just had to summon the nerve to actually post it.

There was a knock at the door, and Varya looked up from the desk as Katya entered the room.

"Lord Carnover is here to see you, Excellency."

Varya's mouth tilted slightly. "I suppose it was a good thing that you never became accustomed to not using that title, Katya. Although I've never liked it."

Her maid clucked her tongue and shook her head sadly.

"Not now, Katya," she warned. "Please show Lord Carnover in." She didn't want to see anyone, let alone Carny, but even he was preferable to Katya's disapproval.

Not at all pleased with her curt dismissal, her stout employee nodded stiffly and turned her back on Varya as she exited the sitting room.

Varya smiled at the blatant act of defiance. Katya was more like a mother than a servant, but she refused to play the part of chastised child today.

A few minutes passed before Carny appeared in the doorway. He was dressed very stylishly in a pale blue coat and buff breeches. He carried a cane in one hand and his top hat in the other. Not even Brummell himself would be able to find fault with his appearance.

Varya rose, smoothing the creased skirts of her plum-colored morning dress. Despite the camaraderie she had formed with the earl, she hoped the effects of the previous night and this morning's battle with Miles did not show on her face.

She sketched a small curtsy. "Good morning, my lord. To what do I owe the honor of this visit?"

Carny bowed smartly and grinned. "I've not come to plead any case for my friend, Your Highness, so you can rest easy. I have come in hopes of going through Bella's personal items with you as we discussed last week."

"Oh yes, of course. I confess I had completely forgotten." She went back to the desk to find the set of keys she kept in the top drawer.

"Yes, well, you have been under some stress."

Varya heard the laughter in his voice and sighed. "I'm glad you find some humor in this situation, Carny. I certainly do not."

He held up his hands. "Please, do not think I am laughing at your expense, Varya, but seeing Miles's countenance when he discovered that you were a princess was probably *the* most enjoyable moment of my life!"

She had to smile at the undisguised glee in his voice. "I only wish I had remained conscious long enough to see it myself."

"I would give you a description, but I could never do it justice." He grinned broadly.

"You're not angry with me for not telling him before this?"

Carny shrugged. "What goes on between the two of

you is your own business." His smile became rueful. "I do wish, however, to apologize again for my earlier behavior toward you."

Her smile widened. "I accept your apology. Shall we go take a look at Bella's belongings?"

He extended his arm for her to precede him, and moved toward the door behind her. "I suppose that in addition to your title, you are also as rich as Croesus?"

She nodded, enjoying this banter between them.

Unfortunately, the excursion proved fruitless. Either Bella's killer had been very careful not to send her any threatening notes, or he had taken them with him the night of the murder. There was absolutely nothing among her correspondence that could possibly be construed as incriminating.

"Well, that was a waste of time," Carny remarked, peering into the empty bottom of the last trunk.

Varya, who had filled a small basket with keepsakes and trinkets from her friend's belongings, shook her head. "As much as I would like to agree with you, I cannot. Seeing her belongings, reading those old letters, it was almost like having her here again. I cannot possibly regret that."

Carny smiled. "Then I recant my earlier statement. If this exercise has given you joy I cannot regret it either." He gestured to the empty trunk. "Shall we put this one back together and call it a day?"

They were packing Bella's belongings back into the trunk when Katya found them.

"Two letters have arrived for you," she announced, thrusting the missives toward her.

"Be nice in front of company, Katya," Varya teased, accepting the letters.

She broke the seal on the top one. It was from Miles. Scrawled in his lazy hand were the words, *Will you marry me?*

"I'm surprised he even asked," she mumbled, angry at the heat that suddenly suffused her cheeks and the rapid pounding of her heart. It might not be getting down on one knee, but it was close.

She popped the seal on the second message without reading the return direction. Her heart stopped pounding—in fact, it seemed to cease beating all together.

Dear Daughter:

By the time you receive this letter we will be on our way to you. Countess Karena wrote and told me of the wonderful pianist named Varya she had seen perform in London. An investigator proved that it was indeed you. Why you left us is no longer important—only that we will soon see you again. We will arrive in London on the twenty-third of June. I cannot wait to see you, my dear. There is someone else anxious to see you as well.

Love,
Mama

"Varya, what is it?"

"What has happened?"

Katya knelt on one side of her, Carny on the other. Varya looked from one worried face to the other. She felt cold, as though she had just been thrown into an icy river and left to drown.

Her parents were coming. No time to prepare. No time to escape. Her father would make her go back. He would make her marry Ivan. Oh God, it was Ivan who was also looking forward to seeing her. Would her parents actually bring him with them? He'd kill her. Her father would force her to marry the man who would bring about her death. She couldn't fight them. She could feel her control slipping away . . .

She clutched at Katya's arm, forcing herself to be calm and *think*. There was only one solution.

"I want you to send Piotr to Miles with a message." She could hear the tremor in her voice.

"What would you have him say?" Katya's eyes were bright with worry.

"Have him tell Miles that I said yes."

Chapter 17

"What made her change her mind?" Miles demanded, pouring himself and his guest a glass of brandy. He had been imbibing more than was his regular habit as of late. The reason for that could be summed up in two words—Princess Varya.

"How the deuce should I know?" Carny replied, accepting the liquor. "She got your letter and she said yes."

"Something's happened." Miles slumped into a wing-backed chair and took a deep swallow of his drink. "There's no way she'd consent so easily." Had Alexander told her about their conversation? Did she fear being arrested? And what was her involvement in Ivan's death?

Carny sighed. "I have no idea what prompted her

to accept your proposal, and what does it matter? She consented, and the two of you will be married in two weeks. Her reasons are no doubt very similar to your own."

"No doubt." He couldn't even convince himself.

Since Varya's acceptance of his proposal earlier that day, he had been reluctant to consider the strange happiness that had struck him upon first hearing of it. Instead, he forced himself to concentrate on *her* reasons for consenting to become his wife.

She lacked neither rank nor fortune, as Blythe had so *lovingly* pointed out, and she had made her opinion of marriage quite clear several times in the past few weeks. What could have possibly happened to change her mind? He shuddered to think what other secrets his betrothed might be concealing.

"I say," Carny drawled. "I do believe I might have struck a nerve."

Miles shot him a stern glance. "The only thing you have to worry about striking you, my friend, is my fist."

Carny laughed. "There you go, threatening my person with violence again! Why can't you just admit you have feelings for Varya?"

"I cannot deny that I care for her, no." As good a friend as Carny was, Miles wasn't prepared to admit just how deep his feelings ran.

His friend grinned. "Taken away the ennui, hasn't she?"

Miles shrugged. Didn't the man ever give up? "Perhaps."

"Perhaps, my arse," Carny growled, his speech giving way to the soldier beneath his elegant veneer.

"For almost two years I watched you try to get yourself killed in Spain, remember? *I* was the one who dragged you to the surgeon after that Frenchie's bayonet convinced you that death wasn't so appealing after all."

Miles opened his mouth to argue and quickly shut it. His friend was right. All those months in Spain he had dared the Grim Reaper to come for him, and when it had . . .

He was very glad to be alive.

He hadn't felt the need for adventure since meeting Varya. Hadn't she offered him a new mystery to solve? Yet, somewhere along the way, his quest to find Bella's killer had given way to a deeper desire to solve the mystery that was Varya herself.

"Perhaps I have found something in Varya that my life was sadly lacking."

Carny's jaw dropped.

"But her acceptance of my proposal does not mean that she feels the same for me." He stood. "This marriage is taking place because it is what we are expected to do given the situation. I will have a suitable wife and Varya will have . . . whatever it is she wants." He set his jaw mulishly.

"What about an heir?" Carny inquired softly.

Miles stiffened. "Given the circumstances of our marriage, there will be no children. I killed one wife that way. I will not kill another."

* * *

She looked like a princess. She *was* a princess.

Shimmering sapphire satin draped her figure in a Grecian-styled gown. The gown was simple and elegant, with no adornment or sparkling threads in its folds. Gathered at the shoulders, it left her upper arms bare and revealed just enough of the swell of her breasts to be provocative without seeming vulgar.

Her hair was coiled and pinned high on her head but for one thick lock left loose to curl down around her shoulder. Her eyelids had been darkened, her lips and cheeks pinched to give them color.

Varya turned away from the mirror to face her houseguest, her hand going to the large tear-shaped, platinum-set diamond at her throat. She hadn't worn it for years, and it felt cool and heavy against her flesh. "Well?"

A grin as big and bold as the rest of her spread across Blythe's face. "You look beautiful. I can't wait to see the expression on Miles's face when he sees you."

Varya grimaced. "I certainly can." What *would* her fiancé think of her appearance? Would he find her as beautiful as his sister seemed to, or would her apparel remind him of her deception of him these past few weeks? At this point Varya wasn't certain which reaction would be preferable.

"I think," Blythe predicted slyly, "that Miles will fall hopelessly in love with you tonight."

Choking on a sudden intake of breath, Varya turned to her soon-to-be sister-in-law. "I highly doubt that," she croaked.

Blythe made no reply, but smiled as she gently patted her between the shoulder blades.

It had been Miles's idea to have Blythe move into Varya's townhouse. Since it would not be proper for him to stay with her before the wedding, he claimed Blythe was the most logical choice. She would provide little real protection, but her mere presence would dissuade any potential housebreakers.

Also, having her future sister-in-law in residence was a public announcement of Miles's family's acceptance of her. Not that it mattered. Varya had gone from social pariah to ton darling. She could walk down St. James's Street in breeches and no one would criticize her for it.

Varya was more amused than angered by the fickle nature of the ton, as well as Miles's sudden urge to observe the proprieties. A part of her couldn't help but wonder if he had changed his mind about staying with her simply because of her social status or because he didn't want to see her.

"Are you happy to be marrying my brother, Varya?"

Varya drew a pensive breath. "I'm not at all certain that I could be *happy* marrying anyone, Blythe." As the younger woman's face fell, she hastily added, "Your brother is a good man—once you get past his strange ways of thinking. I'm sure we'll learn to get on very well together."

That clearly was *not* the answer Blythe sought, but it was the only one Varya was prepared to give. She couldn't shake her old fears about matrimony and being under a husband's control, even if deep down she believed Miles would make a good husband. She had to believe that in time they could make the marriage work.

And if they couldn't she would run away—just as she had run away from everything else. She refused to feel ashamed of her actions. There could be no shame in self-preservation.

She hoped she wouldn't have to run away from Miles. In fact, she desperately wanted the chance to get to know him better, and perhaps regain some of his trust. And she was just so tired of running.

"What about you, Blythe?" she heard herself ask. "Do you still wish to marry someday?"

The statuesque woman nodded slowly, her auburn hair shimmering as it caught the lamplight. Her expression was sorrowful.

"I would wish to, but I have given up hope that I will ever meet a man who will accept me for who and what I am."

This moroseness was something Varya was not accustomed to in her new friend. Shocked, she could only stare. How could a woman so incredible, so beautiful and full of life, truly believe that no man could want her?

"Perhaps you have not yet met a man *you* can accept," she suggested sagely.

Blythe sighed. "He'll have to be one very *large*, very *patient* man."

Varya smiled warmly and took her hand. "Oh, Blythe, whatever he looks like, he'll find you."

Blythe shrugged. "Ready to depart for your engagement party, Your Highness?" she asked, changing the subject with just a touch of forced lightness.

Varya's smile was shaky at best. "Yes," she replied. "Time to face the wolves."

Why did she have to be so bloody beautiful?

Miles tore his gaze away from his bride-to-be and stared sullenly into his glass of champagne. Mere seconds passed before he lifted his head and sought her out again.

It wasn't hard to find her among the crowd. She was clearly the most vibrant, arousing woman present, and his gaze automatically settled on her. That gown she was wearing skimmed every delightful inch of her ripe figure, exposing enough tantalizing flesh that he wanted to uncover the rest. Their last encounter had been a disaster, and he was anxious to show her just how satisfying making love could be.

She was chattering away to Alexander. Miles was certain he was the first person in England ever to have a czar attend his engagement party. Of course, Prinny had demanded to be allowed to come also—not to be outdone by a foreigner in his own country.

"So, should I get used to calling you 'Your Majesty'?"

"No, sir," he replied dryly, turning to face his companion. "It is a good thing I don't harbor such lofty ambitions, Carny, or I would be sorely disappointed. As you well know, I cannot take Varya's title, and since she is my superior . . ." He swallowed the rest of his champagne, not needing to add that his betrothed would probably not want to lower herself by taking the title of marchioness.

Carny smiled and shifted his gaze to the bride-to-be. "You'll make a handsome couple."

Miles did not deign to reply, his gaze searching the room for a footman bearing more champagne.

"I don't suppose you've changed your mind about giving me godchildren?"

"No," Miles replied stoically. "I believe I answered that question before."

"Pity." The other man sighed. "She'd look so fetching with a child in her arms, don't you think?"

Carny's tactics were as subtle as a blow to the head, and just as effective. The image of Varya cradling a babe—his babe—to her breast brought a very hard lump to Miles's throat. It was a low blow, especially since Carny knew how devastated he'd been by the loss of his son.

"I have no idea," he lied, his voice a little shaky. He plucked another glass from a passing footman's tray and replaced it with his empty one. "But I wouldn't form too deep an attachment to the image, my friend, as it is never to become a reality."

"Never is an awfully long time," the earl observed.

Miles met Carny's gaze squarely, determinedly. "I daresay I can survive."

The blond man quirked a brow and smiled in that infuriatingly *knowing* manner of his. "I believe you can do anything you put your mind to, Miles."

"Thank you."

A warm hand clamped onto his shoulder before his

friend left him. "And that includes forgiving yourself for a tragedy you had no responsibility for."

Miles shook his head sadly as the other man walked away. How could Carny possibly understand how he felt? Carny hadn't gotten Charlotte with child, effectively killing her.

It had been his duty to impregnate his wife and produce an heir—a child to continue the line. No one had ever thought that *his* child might be too large for Charlotte to birth, or that anything might be wrong with the baby. By the time the stillborn boy had been taken from her she had lost too much blood.

Shuddering, Miles forced the memory down. He would not think of it. After all these years, he could still see the child—so motionless. Hot tears pricked the back of his eyes. He had wanted a son. He cried more for the loss of that unknown child than he had for the wife he had known for years. He hadn't deserved Charlotte.

"Having second thoughts?"

Snapped out of his melancholy, he looked up and met Varya's deep blue gaze. Part of him still felt resentful and distrustful toward her, another part of him was ridiculously happy to see her.

"Not when you're standing before me looking more beautiful than the first night I met you," he heard himself reply.

She blushed prettily. It occurred to him that he always seemed to be able to bring a flush to her cheeks, whether it be in anger, embarrassment, or passion.

"The first night you met me, I held a gun to your chest."

"Touché. I was referring to that night at the theater. I thought you were the most beautiful woman I had ever seen."

She stared up at him as though he had just told her he was Napoleon. "You did?"

"I did. What about you, Varya?" he asked pointedly. "I know how you feel about marriage. Are you having second thoughts?"

She shook her head. "No."

His brow furrowed slightly. "What made you decide to marry me?"

Her color deepened, sending a tingle of something very much like dread down Miles's spine. Perhaps he was better off not knowing.

"Would you believe it was your charming personality?" she quipped.

Miles actually laughed. "Not for an instant."

He was still smiling at her as she searched for a reason. She could hardly tell him that she had received a letter from her mother and was simply marrying him because he was the lesser of two evils, now could she?

Well, it was better than admitting she loved him. He was marrying her because he had ruined a princess, and she would do well to remember that.

"I would not wish to shame my family," she replied, using what she perceived to be his reason for proposing in the first place. "As the cousin of the czar I have a responsibility to consider not only my own reputation, but his as well."

She had said the right and honorable thing, but she swore that a glimmer of disappointment flickered across his features. The light in his eyes seemed to dim.

He had been hoping for some kind of declaration on her part, she was certain. Her heart floundered hopelessly against her ribs.

Why should she lay her feelings out in the open for him to dissect and ridicule? Had he given her an indication that he cared as deeply for her?

She remembered their lovemaking and shivered as heat raced through her veins. But even before all that, he had rushed into her room and saved her life. He had chased her all the way from the Rochesters' because she had left him. Surely that meant something?

But could she trust him with her heart, with her soul?

"Will you force me to give up performing?" she blurted, instantly wishing she could take it back. It hardly mattered.

He seemed startled by the question. "I hadn't given it much thought." He paused. "In fact, I haven't given it *any* thought." He rubbed his jaw, which was already showing a shadow of stubble. "Do you want to continue performing?"

Nonplussed, she nodded. This was not the response she had been prepared for. "I do, yes."

"Then by all means continue. Of course—"

Ah, she thought, *here it comes.*

"—I would prefer that you didn't tour, but I see no problem with you playing some of the local theaters and for various acquaintances."

Her eyes widened. "You won't stop me from playing?" Not that it made much of a difference. Now that all of the ton knew she was one of them, it would be unseemly for her to perform in public anymore.

He grinned crookedly. "I'd have to be pretty cruel to prevent you from doing something you love so much, wouldn't I?"

"Yes," she replied, a little disconcerted. "I suppose you would." Ivan would have forbidden her to continue with her music. He would have been ashamed of her performing for the general public.

The orchestra struck up the first few chords of a waltz. Couples began to gather around the dance floor.

Varya watched them without really seeing them. She was too busy trying to sort out why she was simultaneously dismayed and pleased by Miles's words.

"Would you care to dance, Varya? It is, after all, normal behavior for the betrothed."

Snapping out of her reverie, Varya nodded. "Yes. I would like that, Miles. Thank you."

He led her onto the floor with a gentle hand at the small of her back. She could feel the warmth of his palm through the thin material of her gown. A tingle raced through her body, tightening her nipples and flooding her lower body with heat. She wanted him with a sudden desperation.

Instead, she stepped into the strong circle of his arms and allowed him to guide her around the floor in graceful turns. He danced as if on a cushion of air—incredibly elegant for a man of his stature.

"Some conversation is appropriate, I believe."

She stared up at him. "What would you like to talk about?"

He thought for a moment. "You found nothing in Bella's belongings to give us any further idea who her murderer might have been?"

Varya shook her head, and her earrings swung against her throat. She was a little annoyed that he felt compelled to discuss the murder at their engagement party, and guilty for forgetting about Bella. "Nothing. Carny was quite dismayed."

Miles grinned, and Varya caught her breath. What a beautiful face he had.

"Yes, Carny would be disappointed. He loves nothing more than a good mystery that needs solving."

"Perhaps we shall find our answers at Lord Dennyson's evening party tomorrow." She tried to sound hopeful, but she had begun to despair ever finding her friend's killer.

She must have looked as disheartened as she felt, for Miles's hand tightened on her waist. She raised her questioning gaze to his.

"We will find Bella's killer, Varya."

It had been a long time since anyone had promised her anything with such conviction. She nodded, unable to voice her fears.

There was always the chance that the killer would find them first. Hadn't someone already broken into her house and tried to smother her because of her connection to Bella? She shuddered at the thought of what might have happened had Miles not barged in when he had. Odd, but they had talked very little of the attempt on her life—as if by ignoring it, they could eventually convince themselves that it hadn't happened.

But it had. A very swift attack in the privacy of her own home had almost—how did the English say it?—put a period to her existence. Varya couldn't shake the feeling that the attack had been personal, driven by more than a desire to keep her from finding the identity of Bella's murderer. But what other reason could anyone have to want her dead?

The waltz ended. As Miles escorted her off the floor, Varya caught sight of Caroline waving to her. Summoning her brightest smile, she waved back, knowing that one of her guests could very well be Bella's murderer.

And that she was next.

Chapter 18

"**D**o you think anyone saw us?"

Varya knelt behind Lord Dennyson's desk and began opening drawers. Miles felt around the surface of a globe in search of a hidden compartment.

"It's doubtful," he replied in a loud whisper, moving to the bookcase. Rifling through the volumes, he continued, "Even if we were seen, it is not considered wholly improper for an engaged couple to sneak off for a bit of privacy."

"I suppose not," she replied somewhat coolly. "It's nice to know our engagement offers such a convenient excuse. So did our earlier arrangement."

He turned to face her, his features cast into harsh relief by the pale light. "You know that's no longer feasible. Would you prefer that we *had* snuck off for a moment of passion?"

Her cheeks burned with embarrassment. "Perhaps." She lifted her chin defiantly. "Not that you deserve such sentiment."

He laughed. He actually *laughed*.

"Just what do you find so amusing?" she asked in the haughtiest tone her wounded pride could manage.

"I missed you as well." His gaze was as soft as his voice.

Varya could only stare. He had missed her? She didn't know what to say.

Miles cleared his throat and turned his attention back to the books. "Have you found anything yet?" he asked rather stiffly.

She sighed. Now she had offended him with her silence. Is this what their marriage would be like? Decades of mincing words for fear of wounding the other?

"Not yet." She stretched her arm as far as it would go into one of the desk drawers. Nothing.

Miles snapped the book in his hands shut, sending up a thick cloud of dust. Lord Dennyson needed to have a word with his housekeeper.

"I'm not having much luck here either," he rasped, choking. He leaned against the mantel to steady himself until the coughing subsided.

Wiping his eyes, he stared intently at one of the carved cherubs on the mantel. "What's this?" He pressed the angel's belly. A low grating sound filled the silence of the room.

Varya moved from behind the desk. "What is it?"

Miles stared into the small hole his fumbling had revealed. "I daresay it's a secret compartment." He reached inside.

She was at his side in seconds, clutching his arm as he withdrew a small wooden box from within the mantel.

"You know, I really think I should install one of these things," he remarked lightheartedly. "It seems I'm the only man in London without one."

Her nose wrinkled. "Smells like smoke."

He smiled. "Well, it was hidden inside a fireplace."

"Open it."

Rolling his eyes, Miles moved toward the desk. "If you'll be patient for a few moments, I shall do just that."

He set the narrow box on the polished surface of the desk. It wasn't locked. Obviously Lord Dennyson had assumed his hiding spot was sufficient to protect the tiny chest and whatever secrets it held.

"Hurry up," Varya urged, practically jumping up and down in excitement.

Miles cocked a brow and pretended to study her intently.

"You're exceedingly anxious. Are you in need of a tonic?"

He was pleased by her answering laughter.

"Just open the box, Miles."

Holding his breath, Miles did as he was bid. As much as he hoped that Dennyson *wasn't* the murderer, he wanted nothing more than to catch the madman who had not only killed Bella, but had attempted to take Varya's life.

Inside the box were various papers. Both Miles and Varya began leafing through them. There were business contracts and missives, but the bulk of the letters were from former mistresses, Bella in particular.

"It would seem our Lord Dennyson has very peculiar sexual preferences," Miles remarked derisively.

"I'm learning more than I ever wanted to know about these *gentlemen*." Obviously disgusted, she placed yet another bill for "damages" from a London brothel on top of a steadily growing pile. It seemed Lord Dennyson enjoyed a little violence with his debauchery.

"The man's a pig," Miles spat. "What I don't understand is why he would keep such incriminating records."

"A trophy, perhaps? A sign of his power?"

Her insight was both astute and troubling. Miles was of the opinion that no woman should have to know just how evil some men could be.

"And to think up until this point we believed his only fault to be an abundance of saliva."

Varya suddenly caught his arm in a tight grasp. One look at her face told him that she had found something much more enlightening and important than Dennyson's nasty secrets.

"What is it?"

"A letter from Bella," she replied, and began to read, " 'Lord Dennyson—I ask that you please refrain from further attempts to correspond with me. You will no longer be admitted to my home or granted an audience in my rooms after a performance. In exchange for your promise to pretend we have never met, I give you my solemn vow not to go to the authorities with all I know about you and your "secret." The choice is yours.' "

Miles met Varya's astounded gaze with an open-mouthed stare.

"Do you think Dennyson did it?" she whispered. "Is he the killer?"

Her excitement was contagious. The idea that they might actually be able to bring Bella's murderer to justice was more deeply meaningful than any of his experiences during the war. He truly felt as if he was doing something *important*.

"We still have to prove it," he reminded her. "First, we must find out where Dennyson was on the night Bella was killed."

"Yes, of course." It was obvious she was trying to rein in her excitement. Her eyes were bright, as if fevered, and Miles could almost see her trying to link Dennyson with the murder in their dark blue depths.

He took Bella's letter from her trembling hands and wrapped his fingers around hers.

"We need proof, Varya," he repeated. "Without it we have nothing. We can't go off half-cocked and expect Dennyson to confess. We must be careful." It would not do for either one of them to give themselves away, which Varya might do in her haste to uncover the truth.

She nodded, taking a deep breath. "Yes. I understand, Miles." She lifted her face to his. "But don't you find it stimulating that we've made such a discovery?"

Much to his chagrin, Miles realized that it wasn't the thought of catching a killer that was the basis for his "stimulation." It was a pair of sparkling dark blue eyes and slightly parted pink lips, and yes, the way her breasts rose and fell with every excited breath, that were the cause of his sudden agitation. He closed his eyes as he felt a familiar tightening in his groin. How *completely* inconvenient.

When at last he opened his eyes, it was to find Varya staring not at his face, but at his crotch.

"Oh damn," he groaned. "Pretend you don't see that."

She gazed at him, eyes dark and wide with surprise. "Why? Isn't it because of me?"

Not only did Miles's treacherous flesh jump under her scrutiny, but his whole body lurched at her softly spoken question.

"Uh . . . yes. It is." He felt a hot flush creep up his neck. "Most women would be mortified by such— demonstrations."

Her eyes glittered with amusement, and something else. Something wild and hot that only made the throbbing in his groin more acute.

"You should know by now that I am not like most women, Miles." Smiling, she wound her arms around his neck and kissed him softly on the lips. "I'm flattered."

That was all the encouragement he needed. Miles grabbed her hips through the thin silk of her gown and hauled her to him. She was soft and warm against his hardness and he pressed himself into her, wishing desperately there was less fabric between them.

Ignoring her soft gasp of surprise, he slipped his tongue into her mouth as one of his hands slid down to cup her buttocks. Oh Lord, she wasn't wearing drawers!

Miles's brain was on fire with images of Varya's naked body, of her pink and white breasts, and of shoving himself between her soft thighs. He didn't care if it happened on the floor, on the desk, or against the wall, but he was going to have her.

Now.

"If we don't stop," he said, tearing his mouth from hers, "I'm going to drive myself into you right here and to hell with the consequences." Somehow, his other hand had found its way into her bodice; her nipple was hard and puckered against his palm. The urge to pinch and tease it until she cried out was almost overwhelming. The last thing he wanted was to lose control, but his resolve was slipping . . .

And went completely out the window as Varya wiggled her alabaster shoulders, allowing the top of her gown to slip down her arms and torso, baring herself to him.

"Isn't this what we want people to believe we're doing?" Her voice was a low, husky purr.

Miles was speechless. Her breasts filled his hands, starkly white against his dark fingers. The nipples were hard and tight against his palms. He caressed them with his thumbs, pinched them with his fingers until she whimpered and squirmed against him.

Keeping a desperate grip on his control, Miles forced himself to stop long enough to ask, "When was your last monthly?"

She stared at him, her eyes dark and dazed with desire. "Just two days ago."

Then there was little risk of pregnancy. "Good."

He lowered his head, taking a hard nub of warm pink flesh into his mouth. He sucked it, nipped at it, and laved it with his tongue until her whimpers and cries of delight became desperate moans. Then he moved on to the other.

Lord, but he was mad for her! Every nerve ending in his body was acutely aware of his desire for her. Never had the need to be one with a woman made him forget his surroundings or his common sense, but it did now. His one and only thought was to lose himself inside her, with her.

He pinned her against the desk, just as on the night they first met in that tiny hovel where she had unmanned him. She still had the power to strip him of all his arrogance and control, and just as on that first night, he could do nothing to stop her.

Driven by lust, defiance, and something akin to anger, Miles bent her back over the desk, his mouth and tongue still torturing the softness of her breasts. Her flesh was rosy from his passionate attentions and glistened with moisture from his mouth. Her fingers gripped his shoulders as she arched her back, rhythmically pressing her loins against his and thrusting her breasts toward him.

"Do you want me, Varya?" he growled against her flushed throat. His fingers tangled in her skirts, bunching them until her entire leg was bare and he could slide his hand underneath the froth of fabric to stroke the soft flesh beneath.

"Yes," she panted. "I want you now. I want you here. Please, Miles, please."

The pleading hunger in her voice was the only incentive he needed. His hand moved between her splayed legs and felt the dampness there—on her thighs and on the downy lips of her sex. She was ready for him. She wanted him.

"You're so wet," he murmured, sliding a finger inside her warm, tight passage. Her muscles clenched at him, and his body throbbed in answer. He found the sensitive nub between the warm folds of her flesh with his thumb and rubbed it almost violently. Varya moaned and fell back against the desk, spreading her legs even wider for him.

He wanted to taste her, wanted to tease that little bud with his tongue until it pulsated with her release and left her sobbing in pleasure with her thighs around his shoulders. He also wanted to bury himself inside her, and it was that selfish, almost unbearable need that finally won out. Miles withdrew his hand and moved over to the sofa just a few feet away.

He was seated before she seemed to realize he was even gone. He met her surprised gaze with a lazy smile.

"Come here, Varya," he commanded softly.

She did; desire shone in her eyes as bright as the jewels around her neck. Unable to take his eyes off her, Miles fumbled with his falls.

Varya watched in sensual fascination as Miles pushed aside the fabric of his breeches. He drew out his hard shaft, stroking it with his hand and watching her as she moved toward him.

"Straddle me," he demanded hoarsely.

Varya did. She could feel the head of his sex blunt

and warm against her own as he guided it to her. Every muscle in her body quivered with anticipation. She gripped the carved wooden back of the sofa as he pushed down on her hips, filling her. She had never experienced anything like it. There was no pain like last time—only the intense sensation of his body becoming part of hers.

"Am I doing this right?" she asked, moving her body up and down on his. It felt good, so good.

"Yes," he groaned. "Ride me. I want to feel you come when I explode inside you."

That sounded good to Varya and she thrust herself down on him, only to quickly lift herself again. She kept going until the ache became too much and she had to quicken her movements.

"That's it," Miles grunted. His fingers dug into the soft flesh of her buttocks, rhythmically lifting her. His rasping breath was hot against her ear.

Varya's thighs screamed in protest, but she refused to stop. She slammed her body down onto Miles's lap feeling as if a dam had broken inside her, releasing a torrent of the most incredible spasms of pleasure. She wrapped her arms tightly around his neck and cried out against his jaw.

His cries mixed with her own as he held her firmly to him, his hips lifting and bucking as he emptied himself inside her.

They stayed that way for quite some time. Locked together, they were silent, save for their slowing breathing. Varya eventually became aware of his hand rubbing her back while the other massaged her thigh.

It had felt so good, so right to lose control with this man. The realization both pleased and frightened her.

"Are you all right?"

She raised her head and smiled at him. "I believe so. You?"

He gave her such a sweet, warm smile that her heart twisted painfully at it. Lord, how she loved him! She loved this man who claimed to be incapable of returning the emotion. Surely this was no less than what she deserved for all her lies and deceit.

"I don't believe I've ever felt this incredible," he replied, planting a small kiss on each of her breasts as he repaired her bodice. "Just think, once we're married we can do this every day."

Once they were married . . .

Varya bent her head to kiss him so he wouldn't see the tears filling her eyes. She would have a lifetime to prove how much she loved him. A lifetime to make him love her.

"I do."

From the minute the words left his lips, Miles wondered if he had truly lost his mind.

Standing at the front of St. George's, in the sight of his peers, friends, family, and the Almighty, Miles Edward Thomas Christian pledged his troth to the woman who had held him at gunpoint, accused him of murder, and turned out to be a princess. He had to be crazy, because he was happier than he had been in years. One thing was certain—life with Varya would never be boring.

Now, standing in the receiving line at his parents' home, Miles's mind wasn't on the wedding at all. The only thought he had been capable of retaining—other than that of being insane—was of his wedding night.

Ah yes, his bride might have pulled off one deception, but his body ignored her betrayal and reacted to her in a way that defied all reason. When it came to Varya, Miles feared he was ruled by an organ other than his brain—and not the one Carny would suggest either. Miles had been ruled by *that* part of his anatomy before, and knew that the only thing *more* dangerous to a man's reasoning was his heart.

"I'd like to know where your mind is."

He gazed down at the woman beside him. His wife. Clad in an elegant gown of silver silk with her thick black hair pinned high on the crown of her head, she looked every inch the princess, every inch the blushing bride. But it was the inches hidden from view that tantalized him the most.

"You'd probably slap me if I told you," he murmured close to her ear, his lips brushing the velvety flesh.

Varya shivered. "That would depend on where you wanted to be slapped," she replied, her voice low and husky.

Miles laughed, and all the guests turned at the happy sound. Some were surprised to see the marquess so pleased. Of course, it stood to reason that only the deepest affection—and the dowry of a princess—could have induced him to marry again after losing the wife he had so *obviously* adored. Some guests thought it unseemly for him to so publicly display his affection for his bride. Other guests didn't care—they had come only for the champagne.

"What did Lord Dennyson say to you?" Varya asked when there was a break in the receiving line.

"He congratulated me on my 'prize' and wished me luck on my wedding night—not that he thought I'd need it," Miles replied wryly.

"Has your investigator uncovered anything?"

"Not yet." Guilt made him avoid her hopeful gaze. No, his investigator hadn't discovered where Dennyson had spent the days surrounding Bella's death, but he had completed his investigation into Varya. He would send the information package by special messenger later that day.

"What a beautiful wedding and what a lovely bride you make, Your Highness!"

Varya rolled her eyes at her husband before turning to Lady Pennington. The older woman's smile was as false as her compliment. Miles bit the inside of his mouth to keep from chuckling.

"Thank you, Lady Pennington," Varya replied graciously. "Lady Jersey arrived just a few moments ago and is waiting for you near the punch bowl. I expect the two of you have much to discuss."

Lady Pennington had the grace to blush. No doubt she couldn't wait to discuss the wedding *and* the bride with Sally Jersey.

"Indeed. May I wish you both great happiness." Lady Pennington walked away, her back as stiff as her well wishes had been. Lord Pennington skulked silently behind her. Ever since Miles had beat him senseless, Lord P been very careful not to approach Varya again.

"I hink m' mowth ith beeing."

"I beg your pardon?" Varya stared at him quizzically.

Miles moved his tongue away from the torn flesh of his inner cheek.

"I said, I think my mouth is bleeding. I bit it so hard trying not to laugh at you and Lady Pennington that I think I broke the skin."

She shook her head in disbelief and fixed him with a smile. "Let's get you some champagne, then. It seems we've finally come to the end of the guests."

They drank and ate and danced continuously. After their first waltz, Miles didn't see much of his new bride as she danced next with Czar Alexander, and then Prinny.

Miles took advantage of his wife's popularity and sought out his former sister-in-law. Caroline was only too happy to dance and chat with him afterward.

"Are you in good health, Caroline?" he asked, handing her a glass of champagne. "You look a little peaked."

She brushed away his concern with a wave of her slender hand. He frowned at her offhandedness. "I am well, thank you, Miles." She gazed up at him with large sad eyes. "Please forgive me, but I was just remembering your last wedding."

"Of course." How stupid of him not to think that she would be upset seeing him marry another woman. She had been thinking of her sister while Miles had been completely focused on his new life.

"I still miss her, Miles," she confessed with a small sob.

"So do I, pet," he replied, offering her his handkerchief. He missed Charlotte's friendship and her kindness. He missed their son.

"No you don't! You had that French girl to console you."

Her sudden, sharp bitterness threw him. Of course it must have wounded Charlotte's family to see him run to his mistress so soon after his wife's death.

"Yes, I did, but she left me for another man soon after."

A strange expression crossed her delicate features. It was full of such foreboding that Miles almost shivered.

"You seem to have a habit of losing women, Miles," her voice was so low he had to strain to hear it. "Take care that you don't lose Varya as well."

He turned his back on the crowd, forcing her into a corner. "Are you threatening my wife?"

Caroline's laughter eased the tension that had suddenly knotted the muscles in his neck and shoulders.

"Of course not!" Her merriment faded to a friendly smile. "I just hope you don't get scared and run this time, that's all."

He raised a brow. "Since when have you ever known me to 'get scared and run'?"

Caroline's smile faded. "You've done it with every woman you've met since my sister died."

Miles felt her words as sharply as though she had stepped on his toes with the heel of her shoe. He *had* been running ever since Charlotte's death.

He cast a quick glance toward Varya before returning his attention to his sister-in-law. "I think you have to agree that I'm not running anymore."

"Miles, I—"

Whatever else she might have said was cut off as a commotion stirred near the entryway.

Standing in the door were a man and a woman. Their regal bearing and dress spoke volumes about their consequence, and one look at the older man told Miles who he was. There was no denying the black of his hair or the blue of his eyes.

His gaze shot over to Varya. She couldn't have known, could she? The guilty way she lowered her gaze from his confirmed his suspicions.

She had known. She had been *expecting* them and never told him they were coming. Even after he had asked her about them she hadn't said a word. Was that why she had agreed to marry him?

"Varvara!" the man at the door barked in heavily accented Russian as if he were commanding an army and not his child.

Miles watched as his deceiving bride stepped forward, her shoulders somewhat slumped, her face white save for two red splotches on her cheeks. He could almost see her tremble as she kissed her father on the cheek. He strained to hear her greeting, wondering what she would say.

"Papa, Mama, you're just in time to join the dancing." It wasn't much of a hello, but what was she expected to say after five years?

Varya tried to step away from her father, but he held

her tightly by the upper arms. She cringed, waiting for his censure, and when it didn't come, she glanced at him in surprise.

There were tears in Vladimir Ulyanov's eyes. Horrified, Varya turned to her mother, but Ana faired no better than her husband.

This was not what Varya had expected. She had expected ranting, raving, threats even. She hadn't expected that her father, of all people, would actually seem happy to see her.

The realization that he was pleased to see her settled in her stomach like a lead ball. She suddenly had the feeling that she had been running for nothing these past five years. Surely she couldn't have been that blind?

"We have much to discuss," her father told her in Russian. His eyes were still watery, but he kept the tears at bay. He seemed content just to study her face.

Out of the corner of her eye, Varya watched Miles approach. The expression on his face was all politeness, but his feline eyes glittered with anger. She should have told him about the letter, but she hadn't been expecting her parents to arrive so soon! She thought she'd at least have a few days to prepare before they arrived. She had just wanted to make certain she and Miles were married before she told him—so he couldn't change his mind.

Oh, she had made such a mess of things.

"We'll talk once all the guests have left, Papa," she replied in Russian, then said in English, "but may I introduce to you my husband, the Marquess of Wynter?"

"Husband?" her father exclaimed, releasing his grip on her as his shocked gaze fell on Miles.

Tentatively, Varya glanced up at her husband. His expression said that he wanted to talk to her as well, but he wouldn't accept "later" as an option.

"Yes," he said with a charming grin as he offered Vladimir his hand. "How wonderful that you arrived in time to help us celebrate."

"But this is impossible!" Varya's father blustered.

"Oh, I assure you, Your Highness," Miles replied, still smiling as he wrapped a possessive arm around Varya's shoulders, "it's entirely possible."

Chapter 19

❦❦

"I cannot wait to discover what you've got planned for me next."

Miles kept his fists clenched at his sides—probably to keep from strangling her, Varya thought. He had kept his anger in check since the arrival of her parents, but now that he had her alone in his study she could feel his restraint slipping.

"There are no more surprises, I promise."

"Well," he retorted stiffly, "that will no doubt make the *rest* of our lives together relatively boring, won't it?"

"I am sorry," she mumbled, rubbing her aching forehead with the heel of her hand. She leaned against the back of the sofa. God, she was so tired.

"Why couldn't you have told me so that I might

have prepared for their arrival? God, what a fool I must have looked! If you won't trust me, you cannot expect to be trusted in return." He smiled bitterly. "Never fear, though; I've seen many marriages survive on less."

"I cannot imagine either of us being happy with such an arrangement." She spoke with all the dignity she could muster. It wasn't much.

He crossed the room swiftly to stop directly in front of her, his eyes narrowing in distaste.

"I daresay *that* was the least of your concerns when you accepted my proposal."

"I never meant to hurt you," she whispered, and she meant it. She had been thinking only of saving herself.

Miles caught her jaw in his hand. She flinched as his fingers bit into her flesh.

"Hurt me? You sought to *manipulate* me," he seethed. "I am not your piano, Varya. You cannot press a key and have me do what you want. I am a *man*."

She tried to twist away but he cupped both hands around her head, not hurting but holding her captive.

"From the first moment we met you have sought to control me. I have tried and tried to earn your trust and yet you willfully deceive me every chance you get."

"It wasn't intentional!" she cried. "I was afraid. I never thought—"

"No, it's clear that you never thought." He released her and stepped away, as though he couldn't bear to be near her.

From where she sat, Varya could see he was shaking. She wondered if he had heard even half of what she had said.

"What more do you want from me?" His wide shoulders slumped. "You have my name, my life, my pride. I have nothing left to give."

Your heart, Varya screamed silently. Dear Lord, she wanted his heart, and she wanted to give him hers.

"I would've married you anyway, if you had only told me," he was saying. "I wouldn't let anyone hurt you. Don't you know that by now?"

The anguish in his eyes was more than she could bear.

"I know that. That's why I married you."

Obviously she had said the wrong thing. His expression hardened and he paled.

"Yes, to protect you from the parents who thus far have done nothing more evil than weep over how much they have missed you. I saw this *horrid* father of yours weep in happiness at having found you! The poor man had actually believed you were dead! Don't you think you have paid him back for all his many sins?"

"You know nothing about my father!" she shouted. Oh, but he had struck a nerve. Vladimir Ulyanov had looked so old, so tired. Varya wondered if maybe she had been wrong in believing her father would punish her . . .

Instead of arguing with her, Miles shrugged. She hated this cool indifference.

"Varya, you must tell me why you were so afraid of their arrival that you broke your vow to never marry. We have to start somewhere. Tell me about Ivan."

Varya's breath froze in her lungs. How did he know about Ivan? *Alexi.* He was the only one who could have told him. Inhaling deeply, she gathered her courage. Yes, it was time to tell him the truth. If they were going to have any future at all, she had to tell him everything.

"Five years ago," she began, noting that he seemed surprised to hear her speak, "I was betrothed to a prince. Ivan. My father had arranged the match. Something about Ivan frightened me, but I was even more fearful of disappointing my father, and so I agreed to the marriage." She drew a steadying breath.

"During our engagement party at Ivan's palace, my father sent me to find Ivan so that Papa might toast our marriage. I . . . I found Ivan upstairs in his chamber. He was raping a servant girl." She didn't want to remember this. "I believe he killed her."

The color drained from Miles's face. "He attacked me when he discovered me there. I hit him over the head and I ran. I left that night for Italy, then went to France." She smiled sadly. "I've been running ever since."

"No wonder you were terrified." Obviously disturbed by her words, he turned his back to her.

"Miles, please." She stood and moved toward him, slowly closing the gap between them physically as well as emotionally. Gingerly she placed her hand upon his sleeve.

"I didn't mean to hurt you. I was frightened. I was certain my father would force me to go back to St. Petersburg and marry Ivan." She swallowed. "He would have killed me."

"How do you know someone hasn't already killed him?"

Varya laughed—a brittle sound. "If anyone could get away with murder it is Ivan."

A strange expression flickered across his features, only to be replaced with a cool mask.

"You told me marriage robbed a woman of her independence."

She nodded. "That's what I believe, yes."

He turned to face her, shrugging off her hand. "So I'm the lesser of two evils?"

Varya felt a guilty flush creep up her cheeks. Hadn't she used those exact words to describe him?

She reached up to touch his cheek. "There is nothing evil about you, but I am more afraid of you than of my father and Ivan combined. They cannot touch me now, but you . . . you have the power to wound me with a glance."

He caught her hand in his own, pressing her cold fingers to the unyielding warmth of his lips. His eyes seemed unnaturally bright as he regarded her.

"Yet you put yourself in my hands, under my control."

She nodded. Miles would never hurt her; she knew that.

"I think I must trust you." She could scarcely hear her own voice, but the softening of Miles's expression told her that he had no trouble distinguishing her words.

He pulled her closer, so that their bodies were touching. She could feel the heat of him through the thin silk of her gown, feel the hardness of his body against the softness of her own. Her nipples tightened in response as tingling warmth blossomed in her loins.

"You drive me mad," he whispered hoarsely, his fingers toying with the hard, sensitive tips that pushed against the fabric of her bodice. "I think I must be mad, wanting you the way I do."

Varya gasped as sharp stabs of pleasure raced from her aching breasts to that equally hungry place between her thighs. His touch shattered her equilibrium and she leaned back against the mahogany desk, bracing herself against this sensual onslaught.

He advanced on her like a cat on a mouse, slowly, purposefully. His face was set, his expression intense. His eyes pinned her where she stood, mesmerizing her with the stark longing in their golden-green depths.

With the toe of his boot he nudged her feet as far apart as her narrow skirts would allow and stepped between them. His hips were solid and hard in the narrow cradle of her thighs. The thin silk of her gown and chemise were pathetic barriers against the solid ridge of his arousal.

As his deft fingers sought to release her straining breasts from her bodice, Miles pressed his lower body deeply into hers. Varya moaned at the shock of sexual pleasure that pierced her. She rocked her hips against him, seeking more of the incredible pleasure, the undeniable rhythm that could bring her to climax.

She didn't care if he trusted her, didn't care how she felt about her at that moment. The one thought in her mind was the need that set her body throbbing. Her body craved the release that only he could give her,

craved the physical love that neither had any intention
of denying the other.

Groaning like a man who knew he was lost, Miles
ground himself into her, shoving her buttocks against
the desk, arching her back until her breasts thrust
against him.

Varya felt a violent tug on the neckline of her gown,
felt the bite of seed pearls high against her skin as her
breasts were freed from the bodice of her wedding
gown. Pushed up by the stretched fabric, they were incredibly full and taut. Her nipples were tight and red,
aching for the sweet pinch of his fingers, the hot, wet
pressure of his tongue.

Delirious with desire, Varya thrust against him, reveling in the hard flesh rubbing her through his
trousers. He was fully erect and ready for her.

"God, how I want to be inside you," he growled,
meeting the rhythm of her hips. His fingers massaged
her breasts, pushing them together. Very gently he
touched the tip of his tongue to each puckered crest
before taking both nipples into his mouth.

It was more than Varya could bear. The sensation of
his mouth and tongue on both breasts at once made
her head spin.

He released her breasts and raised his head. His
gaze locked with hers as his hands lifted her skirts. His
fingers slid up her thighs to the wetness between,
sending her over the edge in just a few strokes.

Without waiting for Varya to recover, Miles laid her
on the polished surface of the desk, sweeping aside
anything that might prevent him from reaching his
goal—feeling her flesh wrapped around him.

Lord, but she owned him. All it had taken for him to forget his anger, his disappointment, was her telling him she trusted him. He hadn't quite realized until then how much he wanted her trust.

Almost frantically, he grabbed her skirts, shoving them up over her shapely legs until they bunched beneath her hips, leaving her bare before him. Her fragrance teased his nostrils; the damp curls at the juncture of her thighs parted to reveal the tantalizing pink flesh he longed to claim.

He slid his thumb along the damp cleft, delighting in the moist warmth that greeted him and the soft, panting gasps Varya issued as he gently stroked the petallike folds.

With one hand he teased her while the other struggled with the front of his trousers. A tiny bit of moisture met his fingers as he released himself. He closed his eyes and groaned with the effort of controlling himself. He was ready to explode.

He opened his eyes to find Varya staring at him from behind heavy lids. Her cheeks were flushed and her lips parted with every labored breath. Her nipples were still dark and hard. He wanted to taste them again, but the need to bury himself inside her was even stronger.

"Touch your breasts for me," he whispered, removing his hand from between her thighs.

She didn't hesitate to do as he asked. The sight of her long white hands against the fullness of her breasts brought a tortured groan to his lips. Reaching down, he hooked a hand beneath each of her knees, lifting her legs to rest her calves against each of his shoulders.

"I want you inside me," she murmured huskily, cupping her breasts. "Now, Miles. Please."

He could not deny her or himself any longer. The fingers of one hand sought the throbbing little nub within her again, while the other guided his shaft into her hot wetness. The position of her legs made her passage incredibly tight, and Miles ground his teeth as he slid deep into her. He would not last long.

The sound that escaped Varya's throat sounded like the low purr of a lioness. Miles's erection throbbed at it. Closing his eyes, he buried himself to the hilt within her.

Slowly, he withdrew and filled her, wanting to prolong the pleasure. With every languid thrust, his thumb mimicked the movement along her cleft. Varya panted with the rhythm, arching her hips against his hips and hand.

"Touch your nipples," he urged hoarsely, knowing that if she did he would ride her right off the top of the desk.

Miles watched in excruciating pleasure as she caught the rosy buds between her thumbs and forefingers, rolling them, lifting them. Varya met his gaze with dark, smoky eyes. The tension in her face told him she was close to climax again.

Muffling a curse, Miles shoved himself into her, gripping her hip with one hand to keep her tightly against him. With every fevered thrust, he jerked the pad of his thumb against her, heard her keening cries, until she convulsed around him.

Her orgasm sent him over the edge. He tore his hands away from her, curling his fingers around her ankles. Splaying her legs wide, he pulled her toward him as his hips pumped wildly into her. As he threw his head back, his mouth fell open and a guttural cry tore from his throat.

His release was intense, threatening to buckle his knees with its sheer force. He pitched forward, dropping Varya's legs and falling over her, one hand braced on either side of the desk.

Still panting, he stared at her. She stared back, neither one of them prepared to break the silence.

Lowering his head, Miles brushed his lips across hers, deepening the kiss until their mouths were fused, their tongues lazily stroking each other in languid fulfillment.

"That was incredible," Varya whispered when they finally broke apart.

"Yes," Miles agreed, reluctant to remove himself from her.

"Um, Miles?"

"Yes, love?" He nuzzled her hairline.

"I can't feel my legs."

Laughing at her rueful tone, Miles straightened and withdrew from her. He quickly tucked himself back inside and fastened his trousers before helping her into a sitting position. He watched with some disappointment as she tugged her now sagging neckline back into its original position.

As she smoothed her skirts, Miles sought to straighten her hair. Somehow a quill had gotten tangled in her coiffure and tiny grains of sand from an overturned canister had found their way into the silky strands.

"We can't have you looking like you were taken on a desk when your parents come in," Miles remarked with a humor he hadn't felt in some time. He wasn't in the least bit concerned about the meeting he had promised the prince and princess. Varya was his wife and nothing could change that.

Varya froze. Awareness washed over Miles along with a sickening feeling of dread. He glanced at the clock in the corner. It was almost five o'clock.

Her parents were going to descend upon them at any minute.

Cursing—Miles in English and Varya in Russian—the two of them frantically struggled to set themselves and the room to rights. They crawled around on the floor, searching for the objects Miles had sent flying earlier. Varya yanked open windows, hoping the faint summer breeze would distill the lingering scent of their lovemaking.

They were seated side by side on the sofa, the picture of domestic tranquillity, when a sharp tap at the door announced Vladimir and Ana not three minutes later.

They entered the room silently, seating themselves side by side. Now she was confronted with explaining her actions to them.

Miles greeted them with a relaxed air and easy smile. He looked about as pleased with himself as a tomcat with a saucer of thick cream. Varya smiled, knowing how he felt. Even her anxiety at attending her parents couldn't shatter the serenity making love to Miles had elicited in her.

Her mother was watching her strangely, almost as if she knew what Miles and her daughter had been doing just moments ago. Despite the disapproving expression on Ana's aristocratic face, Varya caught a glimmer of amusement in her mother's gaze that shocked her. Was it possible that her own mother had a warm and passionate side too?

Her father looked somewhat rested, but there was a tiredness around his eyes that Varya had never seen before. He looked years older than he actually was, and as responsible as she was for his haggard appearance, it pleased her to know he had worried about her. She hadn't believed he would.

"I would like you to now explain, Varvara," her father was saying in his heavily accented English, so that Miles could be privy to their conversation, "why I have spent the last five years believing my oldest child to be dead."

As a child, Varya had only been asked to explain something to her father when she had done something horribly wrong. Feeling very much like that same frightened child, she looked to her mother for guidance.

Ana Ulyanova sat beside her husband with that same quiet, expectant countenance she had worn for the past twenty-five years. She looked more like an angel than a mother, but her eyes were bright with love and support—and still a trace of the same amusement Varya had seen just a few moments before. She smiled faintly and nodded at her daughter to speak.

Strangely, comfort came from the least expected

source. Miles reached over and gathered one of her icy hands into his own warm, strong one.

Varya hadn't tricked herself into thinking that their lovemaking had made him forget her deception, and she hadn't expected it to change anything between them. But perhaps the same admission of trust that had sparked his passion had also warmed her husband's heart. He turned his head and smiled at her, giving her hand a gentle squeeze. From the warmth of his touch and the encouragement in his gaze, she felt his strength slowly seeping into her.

"You're right, Papa," she said evenly. "I owe you an explanation."

And so she told him. She told him about Ivan's depravity and their struggle. She told him how she had feared he would not believe her, of her escape, and of how Isabella Mancini had befriended her. She left out the parts about Bella's murder, how she had met Miles, and his reasons for marrying her. She surprised herself, however, by admitting that she had wanted to marry before their arrival so they couldn't force her to return to St. Petersburg and Ivan.

When she had finished, her father stared at her as if she were a stranger to him.

"Varenka," he began softly, using her childhood name, "how could you think I would not believe you and force you to marry such a monster?"

He sounded so hurt. "Papa, it was you who wanted the marriage. I thought you would think I was lying to avoid marrying Ivan."

Prince Vladimir's fist slammed down on the mahogany table. "You are my daughter! Of course I would have believed you!"

"So you wouldn't have forced me to marry Ivan?" Varya couldn't believe it.

Her father snorted. "If you had stayed instead of running away like a coward you would know that Ivan was arrested and hanged for the murder of that girl!"

Varya was silent. So the poor maid had died and Ivan had hanged for it? All the pain she had caused herself and her family had been for naught?

"What a fool I have been," she murmured.

Miles squeezed her hand but said nothing.

"If you had stayed with us instead of running like a coward you would be living as you should be at Alexi's court," her father rumbled. "Not married to an *Englishman!*" He spoke as if he had stepped in something foul.

"Papa!" Varya gasped, dismayed not only at her father's attitude but also by the tightening of Miles's fingers around her own.

"I don't suppose there's a chance the marriage can be annulled?" Vladimir continued as if Varya hadn't spoken.

"No," Miles answered smoothly, meeting the prince's bellicose gaze. "Your daughter is my wife in every sense of the word, Your Highness."

Vladimir's face turned a mottled red. For one sickening moment, Varya was terrified he might have a seizure. Ana tried to soothe him.

"Miles," Varya said quickly, "why don't you let me

talk to them for a little while?" She placed her free hand lightly on his thigh. "Please?" she whispered so that her parents couldn't hear. "Let me deal with Papa."

Miles nodded, some of the hardness leaving his face. "I'll go out for a bit." Desire flickered in the depth of his gaze. "I'll meet you in your chamber later this evening."

The promise in his words heated Varya's blood. "I'll be waiting."

"Your father means well."

Chin-deep in fragrant bubbles, Varya rolled her eyes at her mother. She leaned back in the tub and allowed the steaming water to soothe her aching head and knotted muscles. Dealing with her father had left her feeling as though a hundred elephants had used her body as a dance floor.

"He's a tyrant," she replied with a smile. It had been difficult, but she had finally convinced her father that Miles was worthy to be her husband. Admitting to her responsibility in bringing the marriage about earned her more than one disparaging remark from her father, but he could not fault her for her fears. In the end he allowed that if Miles still wanted her for a wife after all she had done, then his son-in-law just might be worthy after all—despite his being English.

"Seeing you has taken ten years off his face."

"Ten years that I put there in the first place," Varya reminded her.

Ana made no reply, but her full lips curved in a faint smile.

Pleased that her mother didn't pursue the subject, Varya ran a bar of rose-scented soap along her arms and shoulders.

"I will leave you to your bath," Ana announced, stifling a yawn.

For the first time Varya noticed how drawn her mother's face was. There were dark moons under her eyes, and fine lines fanned out from beneath her lashes and around her mouth. Guilt washed over Varya as she realized that the past five years had been just as difficult for her mother as for her father.

Her throat constricted painfully. "I'm sorry, Mama."

Ana nodded, her eyes glistening. "I know." She pressed a swift kiss to her daughter's forehead. "We'll talk more tomorrow. Good night."

"Good night, Mama."

With a mixture of happiness and guilt, Varya watched her mother leave. She hadn't realized how much she missed her parents until she saw them again. She hadn't realized how stupid and selfish she had been five years ago. How could she have gone all those years without letting them know she was alive and well? The pain and suffering she must have put them through was tremendous, yet they forgave her. The knowledge was lowering.

She was fortunate to have such parents. She was also fortunate to have Miles as a husband—a husband whose protection she hadn't needed after all. How different her life might be right now if she took the time to think before she acted.

She had made her bed, as Miles would put it. She

had to admit that lying in it wouldn't be punishment at all if Miles was there to share it with her.

Varya stayed in the tub until the water turned cool and her skin began to wrinkle. After drying herself with soft towels, she slipped into a silk dressing gown and padded barefoot into her bedchamber.

Removing the towel she had wrapped around her head turban-style, she glanced at the small clock in the far corner. It was almost ten o'clock.

Her heart lurched against her ribs as a knock came upon the door. Could Miles have finally returned?

"Come in," she called in a somewhat shaky voice.

But it was only Piotr, wearing his customary scowl and carrying a package.

"This just arrived," he said gruffly, holding up a flat parcel.

Varya sighed. She had spent the last week unwrapping more presents than she ever wanted to see again. She was tempted to tell Piotr to open it himself, but she supposed that wouldn't do. She would have to put it with the others and catalogue it so that all the appropriate thank-you cards were sent out.

"Thank you, Piotr. I shall take care of it."

The stocky servant brought the package to her, grumbling under his breath with every step.

"Your English husband has left you already," he growled. "I do not like it."

Varya managed a faint smile. "He has not left me, Piotr. He offered to go out while I spoke to Papa. Do you really think he would invite my parents to stay here if he wanted nothing more than to be rid of us?"

Even as she spoke the words, Varya doubted their validity. Miles told her he had asked her parents to stay so she could make amends, but part of her wondered if perhaps it was just a convenient excuse to avoid her. She pushed the foolish notion aside.

"Why don't you stop fretting and go to bed?" she suggested teasingly. "You'll want to be well rested tomorrow when you tell Papa what a hardship I've been."

He stiffened at the obvious dismissal, but did as he was told. He always did. Varya wondered at his blind obedience, but she thought it had more to do with his feelings for Katya than with loyalty to her.

Once the door clicked shut behind him, Varya opened the package. Inside was what looked like a report of some kind.

"That's odd." Shrugging, she lifted the bundle of papers and began to read.

Lord Wynter—regarding the matter you hired me to look into for you last month, the background of one Varvara Ulyanova—

Varya went numb with shock. He had hired someone to pry into her past? It couldn't be!

But it was. With growing rage she read the remainder of the report. It contained nothing that Miles did not already know by now, but that didn't stop her from wanting to stuff every page down his hypocritical throat! All his talk about her not trusting him, and now it was painfully obvious that he hadn't trusted her either!

But he cared for her. He actually did, she could feel it. The passion they shared wasn't just baseborn lust; it was rooted in deeper feeling. It had to be her own secrecy that forced him to look into her past. There had to be an explanation.

She hoped.

What was that?

Varya sat up in bed, her ears straining to listen over the faint clatter of carriages. It was late and many of the ton would be returning home.

There it was again! The subtle creaking of a floorboard, no doubt caused by a certain coward who didn't want his wife to know he was home.

Quietly she waited, her tense body coiled beneath the sheets. She strained to hear Miles's stealthy movements. He was coming closer.

She expected to hear him enter his own chamber. He didn't.

Varya's heart began to pound with anticipation as she heard the latch on her door click open. She had no idea why he was coming to her, though her traitorous body thrilled at the thought of him seducing her into forgiving him. Whatever his reasoning, she knew they were about to have a confrontation—a long-awaited one. She had let her feelings for Miles overshadow her pride. She wouldn't beg for his forgiveness anymore. Let him beg for hers.

He was as silent as death as he crossed the carpet toward the bed. Only his shadow, cast on the wall by a sliver of icy moonlight, betrayed his presence.

Varya waited until he was almost directly beside

her before tossing back the counterpane and leaping to her knees on the mattress.

"You have a lot of explaining—" She froze.

It wasn't Miles.

Chapter 20

Spending his wedding night alone was *not* what Miles had planned.

He hadn't even planned on a wedding.

And he certainly hadn't planned on arriving home as drunk as he was, but nothing could be done about it. His friends had insisted upon celebrating his marriage, and since he had promised Varya a few hours with her father, he eagerly partook of the festivities.

Now, as he wearily hauled himself up the mammoth staircase to his bedchamber, he wondered if his bride had enjoyed a pleasant evening with her parents.

Or had she spent the evening feeling as frustrated and lonely as he had?

All he had really wanted to do was come home and make love to his wife, pretending she had never lied to him—learning to trust her. Unfortunately, she had five years to make up for with her parents, and the idea of spending that much time with his new papa-in-law was even less appealing than an evening at White's.

He was incredibly fatigued by the time he reached the second floor where the family rooms were. He just wanted to crawl between the soft sheets of his enormous bed and pretend the last two months of his life had been nothing more than a strange dream.

Perversely, he also wanted Varya's lush body in bed beside him.

Forsythe met him in the hall.

"Good Lord, man, what are you doing up?" Miles demanded.

"It is my job, my lord. I sent your valet to bed hours ago, and since that odious Russian bear Piotr will take orders only from the marchioness, I've come to offer my assistance should it be required."

Miles waved him away. "I can fend for myself, thank you. You may go to bed yourself if that is all."

"There is one other thing, my lord."

Slumping against the wall, Miles closed his eyes and sighed. "Of course there is. What is it, Forsythe?"

"One of the maids thought she heard strange noises coming from the marchioness's bedroom earlier this evening. When she knocked the marchioness told her to go away, that she did not wish to be disturbed."

That the butler expected Miles to check on his wife went unsaid, but he got away with the implied impertinence. Forsythe had always been more like a father than a servant.

"Thank you, Forsythe. I will look in on the *princess* before I retire. Now, *please* go to bed."

A faint smile tilted Forsythe's thin lips. "Yes, my lord."

Miles watched the older man disappear down the corridor before lifting himself away from the wall. He half expected to see a whole circus of servants parade around the corner, barraging him with problems that no doubt could not wait until morning. He listened. There was nothing but silence.

He began undressing as soon as he entered the room. He tossed his dark green coat and sand-colored waistcoat unceremoniously onto a nearby chair. His fingers were working on the knot of his cravat when he noticed that something was not right.

Sheets of vellum covered his bed like a neatly sewn patchwork quilt. Someone had taken the effort to line them up perfectly.

With his cravat hanging limply around his neck and chest, he moved cautiously toward the bed. He lifted one of the pages by its edge, bringing it just close enough to his face to read.

Realization came on a wave of bitter guilt. The report.

There was no doubt in his mind who had laid these papers out for him to find. There was no point in trying to convince himself that she had no right to be angry. After all his lectures about trust, he had proven himself the worst kind of hypocrite.

One thing his evening of drink and reflection had made him face was that both he and Varya were to blame for the mess they now found themselves in because they could not trust each other.

For Miles, going his separate way was not an option. He wanted Varya as his wife, if only she might learn to trust him completely.

His gaze traveled over the papers. What secrets were revealed there? He only had to read them to find out all he wanted to know about Varya's past.

Quickly, without looking at the writing, he gathered the papers up into a haphazard bundle. His first demonstration of trust would be to give the report to Varya, unread and unwanted.

Miles walked swiftly through the small sitting room that separated their chambers, pausing only to knock upon Varya's door. When he received no answer, he opened it and walked in.

And stopped.

Candles still burned in the wall sconces. The bed was rumpled and tousled as if either passion or a struggle had taken place on the pristine sheets. The balcony doors were wide open, as was the wardrobe. Gowns tumbled out like a silk waterfall. Whether any were missing, he couldn't tell.

Pain and rage descended upon Miles all at once. Left him, she had *left* him.

With a roar he yanked the door open, almost tearing it off the hinges, and stepped into the corridor.

He was distantly aware of the sound of the front door knocker, but he paid no attention. From the corner of his eye, he saw Forsythe in his robe, scurrying through the downstairs foyer to answer.

Miles ran down the darkened hall, causing lamps to flicker in his wake. He didn't stop until he reached the door at the furthest end.

"Ulyanov!" he bellowed, pounding his fist against the wood so hard his entire body shook with the force. "Open the goddamn door!"

There was always the chance that the prince and his wife were gone as well. They could have taken Varya with them. The door opened, revealing a disheveled, nightshirt-clad Vladimir. Muttering in Russian, he took a few seconds before he glanced up at his son-in-law.

"Have you lost your mind?"

"Where's my wife?" Miles growled.

Vladimir scowled. "You are drunk. Go to bed. If Varya is not in her room it is because she could not stand to be near you."

The urge to pound the older man into the carpet was tempered only by the genuine ire in his tone. He didn't know where Varya was either.

Miles blinked. Where was she?

He was dimly aware of Vladimir cursing him in Russian. Several of the words were ones he had heard Varya use before—something about the devil coming to meet him. The smaller man kept trying to push him out the door, and, too stunned to put up a fight, Miles allowed himself to be shoved out into the hall.

"Miles? Whatever is the matter?"

He turned at the sound of his mother's voice. She scurried down the corridor in a flurry of silk and lace with a more sedately clad Blythe jogging at her heels.

"What's all the noise?" Blythe demanded when he did not answer their mother immediately.

He dragged his hands through his hair. "Do either of you know where Varya is?"

"She retired shortly after dinner," Blythe replied, frowning.

"Is she not in her bedchamber?" the dowager inquired.

Miles shook his head. "She's gone and I believe she took clothes with her."

"What!" Blythe looked as shocked as he felt. "That doesn't make any sense."

The bedroom door opened again and Miles braced himself for another confrontation with Vladimir.

It was Ana, looking as distressed as only a mother could. She looked first at Blythe and the dowager's worried faces and then to her son-in-law.

"Miles," she said, clutching his hand. "You say Varenka is gone?"

He nodded stiffly, giving her fingers a warm squeeze. Too bad his father-in-law wasn't as personable as his wife. "Ana, did she say anything to you tonight about leaving?"

She shook her head. "She took a bath; we talked. She was looking forward to your return."

Inwardly Miles cursed himself. If only he had returned sooner!

"Ana," Prince Vladimir bellowed, coming up behind his wife. "Come back to bed. The Englishman is drunk." He took her arm and tugged her away from the door, attempting once again to shut it in Miles's face. His face tight with anger, Miles slapped his palm against the smooth surface, preventing Vladimir from shutting him out.

"Do *not* close my own door against me, Prince." If the tone of his voice wasn't warning enough, the glare he directed at the shorter man was.

Varya's father scowled back, his thick brows drawing together to form a black caterpillar above his icy gaze.

"My lord!"

It was Forsythe. The butler panted for breath as he ran toward them. Miles had never seen the man run before.

"What is it, Forsythe?"

The butler sagged against the doorframe, effectively preventing Prince Vladimir from retreating into his bedchamber.

"A messenger just brought this. He said it had to do with the marchioness."

"Varya?" Miles ripped the folded paper from Forsythe's fingers.

"My daughter is *not* a marchioness," Vladimir reminded them with an indignation ruined by a wide yawn. "She is a *princess*."

Miles shot him a glare. "Right now I don't care if she's the goddamned Queen of Egypt as long as I find her!"

Obviously the prince was ready to take him seriously, because he stiffened. "She's really gone?"

Miles didn't reply. He was too busy reading the message. "Send for Lord Carnover."

"My lord?"

"Just do it, man! My wife's been kidnapped!"

It was dark. Rough cloth covered her eyes and forehead. The knot on her crude blindfold had caught several strands of her hair and pulled painfully on her scalp. A rag sucked the moisture out of her mouth, making it impossible for her to cry out. Her arms were bound so tightly behind her back she was beginning to lose feeling in them.

With every jostling sway of the carriage her shoulders screamed in agony, despite the softness of the cushions beneath her. She bit her lip to keep from crying out.

"Why do you suppose he wants her?"

"Who cares? He offered us more money to take her than she was paying us to protect her and that's all that concerns me."

Varya choked back a gasp of outrage. She had been abducted by the same soldiers hired to protect her.

"We're almost there."

"Anxious?" the first one asked.

"Mm. As good as the money is, I've no taste for this kind of work."

"Got to put food on the table somehow."

"You're right there, but that don't mean I have to like it."

If she could only speak! She would offer him a position, gold—anything he wanted just to take her back to Wynter Lane. But the gag made it impossible to say anything. She was scared but she also knew that this might be her only chance to discover the identity of Bella's killer. It only made sense that whoever was responsible for her kidnapping had also murdered her friend.

The only problem was that discovery of the identity of the killer might not come until she met her own death. And even if it didn't, how could she possibly escape?

The carriage rocked and bounced to a halt. Varya ground her teeth against her gag, squeezing her eyelids tightly together against the dazzling lights that danced before them.

The door opened but not even the smallest trace of moonlight could be discerned from beneath her blindfold. A cool breeze swept in, a welcome respite from the stuffy confines of the carriage.

"Help me carry her in."

"What do you need my help for? She ain't *that* big."

Varya made a mental note to horsewhip the soldier if she ever discovered his identity.

"Neither am I," came the sharp reply.

Varya frowned. Sensitive about his size, was he? Vaguely she remembered one of the men Miles had sent as being a tiny little man—about her height and very slender. No wonder he needed help. She doubted he could carry her very far on his own either.

She heard the other man sigh. "All right, but I'd better get paid extra for this."

"You take her head. I'll get her feet."

Relaxing every muscle in her body as much as she could under the circumstances, Varya went completely limp. If there were some way to turn herself into stone she would have gladly done so, just to make their job more difficult.

Their groans and curses as they lifted her sagging form filled her with grim satisfaction, and took her mind off just how much danger she might be in.

"Wish we could use a light."

"And what?" the man Varya had recognized as the short soldier demanded. "Have some of moral toffs we got as neighbors see us carrying a tied-up woman in the middle of the night? They'd have the watch on us before we even get this cow inside."

Cow? Oh would his death be slow. If she lashed out with her foot, she might be lucky enough to strike his face. Instead, Varya was quiet. She had no way of escaping them with her arms tied behind her back and blindfolded. At least now she knew that it was still night and that they hadn't left London.

From the smells and sounds surrounding her, Varya guessed that they were in a residential section of the city. It was reasonably quiet and the smell of fresh baked bread lingered on the air. They were also closer to the river than she was used to—the Thames in the summer had a very *distinctive* odor.

A door shut and she realized they were in the house. The smells of beeswax and baked apples warmed her senses. This house did not smell frightening at all, and that seeming normality terrified her.

"Ah, so our little bird has arrived. All trussed up like a Christmas goose."

That voice! She knew that voice, but it was different somehow. The low timbre, the menacing singsong lilt disguised it just enough that she could not put a face to it.

"Where do you want her, sir? She's heavy."

"Upstairs, third door on the left. I've a special chamber prepared for her."

He touched her. Cold, smooth fingers drifted across her face, like the touch of death itself. Varya stiffened in revulsion.

"Idiots!" her captor bellowed. "She's awake."

There was a cacophony of voices—one shouting accusations and insults, the others arguing ignorance. All the while, Varya felt the strength of the men holding her ebbing. She was starting to fold in half as her bottom sank toward the floor.

Suddenly, a damp cloth was pressed to her face. It smelled of something cloying and sweet. It was the same liquid they had used in her bedchamber.

"Mmf!" She struggled against it, thrashing her head from side to side in an effort to elude him.

It was pointless. With her mouth gagged, she had no choice but to breathe through her nose. Sobbing in defeat, she inhaled.

"That's it, Varya," the singing man cooed. "Breathe."

"Any news?" Carny strode into the room without being announced, tossing his coat onto a chair.

Miles looked up from the papers on his desk. "The

messager says the man who hired him wore a mask. He knows nothing."

"Damn. Have you slept?" The earl helped himself to a glass of port.

"What do you think?" Miles asked peevishly, rubbing a hand along his unshaven jaw. "Of course I haven't slept. I can't sleep knowing some maniac has the woman I—my wife."

"I know how you feel about her, Miles. Not even your bizarre sense of honor could have forced you to marry a woman you didn't care about." Carny lowered himself into the chair before Miles's desk.

"I have no idea who took her or where she might be." With a weary sigh, he slumped back in his chair. "I've half of Bow Street out looking for her and still nothing."

Carny sipped his wine. "But we know it has something to do with Bella's death. What have you found out about Dennyson?"

Rubbing his tired eyes, Miles yawned. He wiped his hand over his face and regarded his closest friend with a bleary gaze.

"Only that he's not our killer."

Carny sprang out of his chair. "What?"

Miles stood, moving to the cupboard to pour himself his own drink. Unfortunately, there wasn't anything in the cabinet that could deaden his fear.

He took a long, fortifying draught.

"Dennyson was in bed with a bad case of quinsy the days surrounding Bella's death. I have the apothecary's sworn statement that he attended the earl's bedside. Dennyson was quite delirious with fever for days and unable to even use a chamber pot by himself, let alone orchestrate or commit a murder."

He ran a hand along the glossy surface of the desk, remembering his and Varya's lusty embrace on it just the day before. What if he never got the chance to tell her how he felt?

He slammed his fist down on the wood. "I can't just wait for the bastard to send me another note!"

"You may not have to." Calmly, Cary handed him a folder. "I took the liberty of investigating another possible angle just in case we were wrong about Dennyson."

Puzzled, Miles opened the pages. "What is it?"

His friend cleared his throat. "It's a file I had prepared on you."

Miles froze. "You did what?"

Carny held up his hand. "Hear me out. For some time now I've wondered if perhaps this whole mystery didn't go a little deeper than Bella."

"How?" Miles demanded, angered that his friend had investigated him, but even more angry that he hadn't confided in him about it until now.

"You remember Maria?"

"Of course I do." She was a beautiful Spanish courtesan who used to spy for Carny and sometimes Miles. Her relationship with Miles had gone far beyond business, however.

"I trust, then, you also remember how she died?"

She had been strangled months after they'd ended their affair. Everyone assumed the French had done it. "Yes. I remember."

Carny sipped his port. "I went out on a limb and asked a few questions. The answers are in that report."

A muscle in Miles's jaw twitched. "And what are the answers?"

His friend shook his head. "I don't know. I wanted you to see them first."

What Miles saw on the first page was a list of five women's names. All the names he recognized as women he had once been involved with.

Ones that he had actually cared for.

Beside each name was the letter D and a date. All the dates fell within a year period—starting with Maria's death in Spain and ending with Bella's in England. Before Bella was Emile—a French dancer Miles had been involved with when Charlotte died. Awareness washed over Miles like thick, black oil. In the back of his head he could hear Caroline's voice, *"You had that French girl to console you."*

He handed the file back to Carny. "It can't be true." His voice sounded hollow in his own ears. This was a nightmare.

Pale-faced, Carny quickly scanned the papers. When he was done, he met Miles's gaze grimly. "It is." He sighed. "We have to get to the bottom of this quickly, my friend. If this falls into the wrong hands, you're going to find yourself as the number one suspect."

Miles chuckled bleakly. "If I didn't know the truth, I'd think I was the *only* suspect."

"It appears, however," Carny spoke meaningfully, "that you are the intended victim. And whoever is doing this is someone who knows you. Someone who was in the Peninsula with us."

Weighing the empty tumbler in his hand, Miles stared blindly at his distorted reflection in the glass. He squeezed the glass as his terror and frustration mounted.

"And now the son of a bitch has Varya!"

The tumbler cracked.

Chapter 21

~~~~~~~⌒◯⌒~~~~~~~

Groaning at the stiffness in her shoulders, Varya rolled slowly on to her side when the daylight awoke her. She was surprised to discover that she was untied and alone in the room. She hadn't expected to be given any freedom of motion or privacy at all. No doubt there was a guard outside her door. Probably the short one.

Gritting her teeth, she pushed herself up into a sitting position. She was still wearing the gown she had been forced to don the night before. It was wrinkled beyond repair.

Tossing back the blankets she swung her legs over the side of the mattress. A wave of nauseating dizziness swept over her. Gripping the edge of the bed with all her strength, she waited for it to pass before even trying to distinguish where she was. As the sickness passed, she opened her eyes.

She had been correct in assuming she was being kept in a middle-class home. While the room was large and charming, it was nowhere near as large as her chamber at Wynter Lane. Several pieces of finely crafted, yet obviously out-of-date furniture were scattered along the walls. A hand-painted screen standing discreetly in the far corner no doubt hid a chamber pot, of which she was in need.

Gingerly, she slid forward on the bed, holding on to the bedpost for support as she placed one foot, then the other on the short steps that led down to the floor.

She had to lean on furniture all the way to the painted screen as her legs threatened to give out beneath her. The drug they had given her, combined with hunger and stiff muscles, made her as weak and clumsy as an infant learning to walk.

Relieving herself took a little bit of ingenuity, but the task was soon accomplished, and by the time she made it to the washstand, her limbs were feeling decidedly stronger.

She was moving toward the barred window to try to figure out just where in London she was when the door opened.

Sure enough the short guard stood sentry outside as a squat, heavyset woman Varya could only assume to be the housekeeper bustled in carrying a tray.

Breakfast? Varya's stomach growled.

"Why am I being held here?" she asked the woman.

The servant stiffened, but continued unloading the

contents of the tray onto a small table near the wardrobe.

"I don't know, my lady," she replied without looking up. "I was told only that you were a lady and that I was to treat you as such but not to allow you out of this room."

Varya could have struck her. "He's keeping me here against my will."

The woman reddened. "I know."

Varya's stomach turned. "You *know*?" She crossed the floor as quickly as her tortured legs would carry her, her fists clenched tightly at her sides. "He has taken me away from my husband and my family and you accept it?"

The woman's frightened gaze flickered briefly to Varya's face. "I need my position, my lady."

Varya was very tempted to strike her. "I am cousin to the czar of Russia. If that means nothing to you, then perhaps the fact that I am also the wife of the Marquess of Wynter will." She stepped directly in front of the woman and stared down at her harshly. "When my husband finds me, your master is going to hang and so will all those who assisted him. Is your *position* worth dying for?"

The empty tray clattered to the floor as the housekeeper ran pale and shaking from the room. The door slammed shut behind her. Varya heard the very distinct *click* of a key being turned in the lock.

"Damn!" Not only had she lost her temper but she had also frightened off possibly the only person who might have been persuaded to help her.

Mentally berating herself, Varya sat down to breakfast. She would eat, and then find a way to escape.

Breakfast was delicious but she ate only enough to take the edge off her hunger. She did not want to stuff herself and be too lethargic to move quickly if need be.

Winding her hair up into a bun, Varya paced the carpet. What was she going to do? How was she going to get out? She couldn't just sit there and pretend she was a houseguest, not with bars on the window. There was no doubt in her mind that her abductor was the same bastard who had murdered her friend, and that he intended the same fate for her.

She couldn't rely on Miles coming to her rescue either. Even if he did by now have some idea as to who had taken her, he would have no idea where to find her. The view outside the barred window had been nothing but courtyard. She had no idea where she was.

Chewing anxiously on the side of her thumb, she willed herself to be calm. She had to think of something.

Her gaze landed on the table. The teapot wasn't overly large, but it was solid and would certainly stun someone who was struck with it.

It wasn't long before the housekeeper returned. Her eyes downcast, she didn't even look in Varya's direction as she began to clear the table. She didn't even seem to notice that the teapot was missing.

Grimly, Varya walked up behind her, gripping the pot by its handle. She would have to think fast when the guard came in to investigate the noise. Hopefully the teapot wouldn't break.

She brought the pot up and crashing down onto the housekeeper's cap. It exploded into hundreds of pieces on impact, raining lukewarm tea and porcelain all over Varya and the rest of the room. The woman grunted and crumpled to a heap at Varya's feet.

Varya stared at the remains of the pot in her hands. All that was left was the gold-rimmed handle.

The short guard burst through the door not even seconds later. Thankfully he was unarmed. He ran toward Varya with a mixture of fear and determination on his face.

Without thinking, Varya swept up the china plate containing the remnants of her breakfast and swung. It caught him full in the face, covering his features with egg and ham, and snapping in half with the force of the blow.

One broken edge caught Varya's hand, slicing the skin, but she didn't care. As the plate crashed to the floor, so did the short guard, blood spurting from his nose.

Varya hiked up her skirts and ran. Her heart hammering wildly in her chest, she flew along the corridor and down the stairs, her legs pumping so hard she almost fell several times.

She skidded on the carpet in the foyer but kept on running. The door was only a few feet away. She was going to make it.

No sooner had she felt the thrill of victory than the door opened. For one brief second, as her eyes fell upon the distinguished-looking gentleman, she thought she had been rescued. As he caught her in his arms, she almost sobbed in relief at having been rescued. Then he spoke.

"Oh, my dear Varya. You're not going anywhere."

She had been taken by men he had trusted to protect her.

Miles sat at his desk with his head in his hands. He had scarcely moved from there since Carny had left near dawn. The sun was now creeping stealthily higher in the clear blue sky and he had yet to change his clothes.

He had brought Varya men he thought he could trust, having served with them in the Peninsula, but that wasn't what disturbed Miles the most.

What disturbed him was that soldiers were, for the most part, a loyal bunch. Whether noble or common, they held themselves as a separate breed. If they had betrayed Miles it meant they had betrayed him for one of their own—someone who could afford to pay them—someone Miles knew.

A list of men with the means to hire such a group of mercenaries lay on the desk before him. It had half a dozen names on it: Pennington, Rochester, Dennyson, Phillips, Edwards, and Carnover.

Their personal history automatically removed Carny from the list. Even if Miles found Carny standing over a body with a bloody knife in his hand, he wouldn't believe him capable of cold-blooded murder.

It had been horrible enough to find out about Bella. Learning that others had died because of him was sickening. He could have believed Pennington, Rochester, even Dennyson capable of killing in a moment of passion, but he couldn't imagine anyone he knew being so insane.

Whoever it was had known he wasn't at home on his wedding night. He had to know that Varya was alone in her room and that there was no chance of Miles returning home. He tried to recall who had been with him at White's, but couldn't summon up a single face.

"Good Lord, you're still wearing the same clothes you had on when I left you."

Miles leaned back in his chair, all too aware of the smell of his own sweat and the state of his hair and clothing.

Carny's grimace turned into a concerned frown. "Have you heard from the kidnapper?" Tossing his hat and gloves onto a small table, he crossed the room.

"Not yet." Miles's frustration seemed to grow with every step his friend took. "It tears me apart knowing this monster has Varya. I feel so helpless."

Carny seated himself in a chair on the opposite side of the desk and leaned forward. "That's how he wants you to feel. Don't give him the satisfaction."

A chorus of voices outside the door announced the arrival of what sounded like a small circus.

Carny arched a brow. "The family approaches?"

"Yes." Miles sighed. "I can't have a hysterical Russian prince running about the city demanding to have his daughter back."

"Of course not," Carny agreed with a chuckle. "The less people who know about this the better."

"Mm. I'm hoping that since the kidnapper is someone we know he'll slip up—say something wrong. If no one else knows Varya has been taken"—his face hardened—"any slips will be easier to catch."

"Let's hope our boy decides to be social then."

The door opened and in walked Blythe and the dowager, followed by Vladimir and Ana.

"Have you found my daughter?" Vladimir demanded.

"No," Miles replied, sounding as tired as he felt.

"No? Why not?" Vladimir's face was red with rage. "Because you sit in here and do not look! My Varenka could be dead for all you know! She was taken because of you! Her blood will be on your hands—"

"That's *enough!*" snapped a steely voice.

Miles's mouth dropped open in shock as he realized the voice had come from his mother.

The dowager marchioness faced Vladimir with a stern expression Miles hadn't seen since childhood.

"Your daughter chose to marry my son, Your Highness," Elizabeth informed him, hands on her hips. "If there is anyone to blame, you can blame yourself for Varya's fear of you, but right now the most important thing is finding her and bringing her home. So I want you to sit and listen to what my son has to say or leave the room. This is not Russia. You don't rule under this roof. *I* do."

For once, Vladimir was speechless. He stared at Elizabeth in stunned silence. Even as Ana coaxed him onto the sofa, his wide gaze remained locked on the elegant woman who seated herself across from him.

"You wanted to see all of us, Miles?" his mother asked sweetly.

Forcing back his surprise, Miles nodded. It quickly

faded as his mind focused on why he had summoned them.

"Yes, Mama. Bow Street has all of their available men out looking for Varya. Carny and I have a few leads of our own to follow as well. What I need the rest of you to do is pretend that nothing is wrong. If anyone asks about Varya, simply tell them that she is ill. The fewer people who know she is missing, the easier I'm hoping it will be to find her." He gazed pointedly at Vladimir. "Not even the czar is to know. I don't care what you tell him, but I don't want a bunch of Cossacks running around London making matters worse by trying to find my wife."

The prince nodded stiffly.

"Good. I expect to hear from the kidnapper soon. If it is truly me he is after, he'll be anxious to get me under his thumb as soon as possible. It's imperative that we keep up the charade, especially at home. If the villain is someone we know, I suspect he might actually pay us a social call to see the effects of his work."

Both Ana and Elizabeth gasped.

"Surely you don't believe he'll come here?" Ana stared at him in horror.

"Do you truly believe it is someone we know?" The dowager wrapped her arms around her waist in a protective gesture.

"Yes, to both your questions. That's why it is so important that you tell no one what has happened. We don't know who we can trust."

"So that's it?" Blythe demanded. "We just stay quiet and wait?"

Miles raised his hand. "For you, yes. Don't think this

isn't difficult for me, Blythe. I want her back more than all of you put together, but I am not going to endanger her life by doing something rash." His voice dropped to a warning, "And you had better not either."

Blythe looked away in sullen silence.

"I have an idea," Carny interjected, his gaze drifting from Blythe to Miles and back again. "Blythe, why don't you come with me for a ride in the park while Miles puts us all out of our misery by finally performing his toilette? Perhaps we'll run into our boy there."

Blythe's face brightened and Carny rose.

Elizabeth clutched his arm. "Don't you dare put my daughter in danger, Rowan Carmichael."

Carny gave her hand a gentle pat. "I will protect her with my life, Mama."

Elizabeth smiled as she always did when Carny called her "Mama," and she pressed her lips briefly to his cheek.

"What will you do while I'm gone?" Carny asked Miles.

"Bathe, as you so subtly suggested, and wait for word from our friend."

Blythe shuddered. "I feel like we're all flies, waiting for the spider."

"Do not worry, Blythe," Carny told her, giving her hand a gentle pat. "Your brother and I are on the case."

"Be back here in a hour," he told the departing couple.

The blond man raised his hand in salute.

Miles left the room without another word. As he climbed the stairs to his bedchamber two at a time, he bellowed for his valet.

He was a bundle of nerves, of raw energy. It felt very much as it had whenever he had gone into battle—anxiety coupled with a fierce determination to succeed, to survive. This was one battle he was prepared not to lose.

Miles felt infinitely better as he drifted downstairs almost an hour later. He had bathed, shaved, and changed his clothes, but even soap and hot water couldn't scrub away the constant fear and the near panic that clung to the back of his mind.

What if Varya was already dead?

His hand tightened on the banister. She couldn't be. He would know if she were dead. Somehow, he would know.

That was the conviction he clung to as he entered the morning room in search of the company that had arrived while he was in the tub. Anticipation unfurled in the pit of his stomach as his gaze fell upon Robert and Caroline taking tea with his mother, Blythe, and Carny.

"It is so disappointing that dear Varya has taken ill," Caroline was lamenting. "I did so wish to see her."

"I'm certain she will regret not being able to receive you," Elizabeth responded.

Miles's boots didn't make a sound on the Wilton carpet as he entered the room. He was only a few steps inside when Carny seemed to sense his presence.

"I hope she is not afflicted with anything serious?" Robert asked, lifting his cup to his lips.

"Here's the man to ask," Carny announced loudly, drawing the room's attention. "Miles, how fares your lovely bride?"

All eyes were on him as he entered their circle.

"She is a little better, I believe. Good morning, Caroline, Robert."

"Good morning, Miles," Caroline chirped. "I am so glad to hear Varya is already improving. Will you be taking your wedding trip once she recovers?"

They hadn't even had a chance to discuss a wedding trip. Miles supposed if both he and Varya managed to come out of this mess alive a long trip alone would definitely be in order.

"Yes. I expect we shall."

"Don't commit yourself yet, Miles," Robert warned with a smile that didn't reach his eyes. "Women always view travel as an excuse to buy a new wardrobe."

Miles gritted his teeth. "I think I can afford a few dresses."

"Yes, and you have a wife who looks demmed lovely no matter what she wears. I particularly admire the way that yellow morning gown displays her figure. Very fetching indeed."

Pasting a false smile on his face, Miles agreed with the lecherous bastard. "Yes, Varya always looks lovely. If you'll all excuse me, I have some work to do. Carny, you said you would go over those bills of sale with me?"

His friend didn't miss a beat. "Of course."

"We should really be on our way as well," Robert announced.

Miles bid them a brief farewell and stomped off to his study with Carny at his heels.

"Cretin," Miles muttered, shutting the door.

"He is indeed." Carny lit a cigar and perched on the edge of the desk. "I wouldn't take him off your suspect list, however."

"I wasn't planning on it." Combing his fingers through his hair, Miles began to pace.

"Your sister and I had a very uneventful morning," Carny informed him after several minutes of silence. "We encountered Pennington in the park. He appeared to be more interested in Blythe than either you or Varya."

Miles rubbed his face. "I feel like we're missing something."

"Take one of these, will you?" Carny thrust a cigar into Miles's face. "It will give you something to do with those restless hands of yours."

Miles lit the cigar and inhaled deeply. The smoke warmed his lungs, and gave him something to toy with.

They smoked in silence, each preoccupied with the task of finding Varya.

After what felt like an eternity of nothing more than his mind whirling hopelessly, the door flew open.

"I'm sorry to barge in," Blythe blurted out, as she hurried into the room. "But I think I may have some information about Varya."

Miles stared at her. "What?"

She smiled tremulously. "When Robert mentioned Varya's yellow morning dress, something struck me as strange, but I couldn't think what." Her gaze locked with Miles's. "After they left I remembered that I had talked Varya into buying a yellow gown with her trousseau because I thought the color would suit her. She told me she'd never owned a yellow gown."

Miles shook his head in confusion. "So?"

Blythe drew breath. "Miles, she's never worn it! How could Robert have seen it if Varya's never worn it outside the house?"

Horror constricted Miles's heart. Slowly, as if in a dream, his head turned toward Carny. He couldn't see him clearly.

Blythe's fingers touched his shoulder. "I checked Varya's wardrobe. The yellow gown is the only one missing."

A fist of dizzying rage slammed into Miles's gut. How could he have missed it? Robert . . .

An iron band clasped his arm. It was Carny's hand.

"There will be plenty of time for both of us to feel stupid later," he growled, steering Miles toward the door.

Miles pulled free of his grasp, walking back to catch Blythe in a fierce hug.

"Thank you," he whispered. For the first time since Varya had disappeared, he felt hope.

His sister squeezed him back. "Just find her."

Stepping out of her embrace, Miles nodded curtly. "I will." He turned on his heel and strode toward the door and Carny.

"Let's go get the son of a bitch."

Caroline had just barely settled herself behind the white and gold desk in her sitting room when Miles and Carny swooped down upon her.

"Miles, Lord Carnover!" She rose. "I certainly wasn't expecting to see you both again so soon. Will you sit?"

Miles cleared his throat. "No. Thank you, Caroline. We're here to see Robert. Is he home?"

Caroline's wide gaze skipped from Miles to Carny. She paled at the sight of their stony countenances. Pressing her palm to her throat, she sank back into her chair.

"Dear God," she whispered. "What's he done?"

Carny threw a surprised glance at Miles.

"What makes you think he's done anything, Caro?" Miles dragged a chair over to her desk and lowered himself into it.

Her gaze was nervous and unsteady as it flitted back and forth between them. "That's why you're looking for him, isn't it?"

"What's he done?" Miles prodded gently.

Caroline shook her head, staring despondently at the letters in front of her. "I don't know. Something awful, I think." She lifted her gaze to his. "He didn't come home the night of your wedding. He hardly stays home for more than a few hours at a time. He's been in an awful, bizarre mood, and there are all these strange men coming around—men he served with in the war."

Miles's gut tightened. "Do you know where he goes?"

Again Caroline shook her head. "He hardly speaks to me anymore, let alone tells me where he's going."

"Damn!" Miles swore, stomping his foot in frustration. "Does he take his own carriage?"

Caroline's brow wrinkled. "Yes, of course he does. Really, Miles, you're beginning to frighten me."

Miles watched her intently, noticing the dark circles under her eyes, the drawn pallor of the face that reminded him so much of Charlotte. Her hands were trembling.

"Does Robert ever frighten you, Caro?"

She tore her gaze away from his, but not before he saw the tears glistening in her eyes.

"What did he do, Caroline?" Miles kept his voice soft and coaxing as he leaned across the desk and captured one of her cold hands in his.

She shook her head, her other hand pressed against her mouth in an obvious effort to hold the tears at bay.

Carny offered her a handkerchief.

"Thank you," she whispered, dabbing at her eyes. Sniffing, she raised her reddened gaze.

"Tell me what happened," Miles prodded, giving her hand a gentle squeeze.

Her voice was as shaky as the nod she gave. "When Robert and I were married I cared for him very much. He made no secret that I was his second choice as a wife, but I believed that in time he would come to love me. He would often call me by this other woman's name during our"—she blushed a dark rose—"*intimate* moments. Eventually it stopped. He rarely called me anything at all. He began finding his fulfillment elsewhere and has done so for several years, but a few nights ago he came to my bed again." She fell silent.

"And he called you by this woman's name again?" Miles guessed.

Caroline nodded, pressing the handkerchief to her

brimming eyes. "Yes. He said how much he loved her." She choked on a sob.

Miles patted her hand. He had always suspected Caroline's marriage to Robert to be an unhappy one, but he had never imagined to what extent.

Caroline took a deep breath. "He also swore that the man who killed her would pay. I thought he was talking drunken nonsense, but now that you are here I think he may have been quite lucid—frighteningly so."

A shivering, bitter taste pooled in the back of Miles's mouth. It was the taste of foreboding.

"Who was he talking about, Caro?" His gaze was riveted on her now blotchy face.

She shook her head sadly. "Surely you know, Miles?"

He raised an inquisitive brow. "Should I?"

"Oh, Miles!" she gasped, her eyes filling again. "It was Charlotte!"

Shock jabbed icy fingers into Miles's chest, robbing him of breath.

"Robert asked for Charlotte's hand but she refused him to marry you." Caroline's voice sounded dim through the fog surrounding his brain. "I suppose he felt that having her sister was better than not having her at all."

Slowly, everything came back into focus. Miles stared at Caroline in horror as pieces of the puzzle fell into place. "I'm the man who killed her," he whispered.

Caroline said nothing. She didn't have to—her eyes said it all.

Miles turned his gaze to Carny, whose face wore an expression of bleak triumph. They had found the killer, but the fact that he had Varya made the victory a hollow one.

"I don't wish to be here when he finally comes home," she whispered.

Miles was tempted to tell her that if he had anything to do with it, her husband *wouldn't* be coming home at all, but he thought against it.

"You are more than welcome to return to Wynter Lane. Mama and Blythe are both aware of the situation and will stay with you until our return."

Ten minutes later, as Caroline's carriage rolled out of the drive, Miles and Carny strode toward the stables.

Robert's coachman had just returned.

"We'll find her," Carny swore when Miles said nothing.

"I know. Robert wants *me* to suffer, not her." He kicked at a stone with the toe of his boot. "We have to find her before he hurts her."

"We will."

Miles stopped. "He wants me to see her dead, Carny. He wants to be there. He blames me for the death of the woman he loved and he's been killing women I cared for hoping to get his revenge."

Carny nodded grimly. "And now he has the woman you love."

"I'm hoping he'll want to savor his revenge." Miles began walking again. "That he'll want to prolong my torture for as long as possible. If he gets impatient he may kill her anyway and then just send me a note telling me where to find her. I don't think it would really matter to him just as long as I found her body." He refused to imagine Varya dead. He would find her. He had to.

"Then let us hope John Coachman will give us the information we require." Carny opened the door to the stables.

"He will," Miles promised.

They found the man alone in the backroom of the stables.

"Here now," he cried as they approached. "What do you two want?"

"I am the Marquess of Wynter, and this is the Earl of Carnover," Miles began congenially. "We'd like to ask you a few questions about your master and where he's been going the past few days."

"Why?" The man folded his thick forearms across his chest in a defiant manner.

"Not that it's any of your business, but I believe he has something of mine."

The coachman eyed them wearily, unease flickering the depths of his muddy gaze. "I don't have to tell you nothin'."

Miles reached behind him and swung the heavy door closed. The smile he gave the coachman was cold and grim.

"Oh, but I'm afraid you do."

Chapter 22

"**A**t first I thought I had been wrong, that he cared as little about you as he had about the others, but then I saw the pain in his eyes when Caroline mentioned a wedding trip."

From her seat near the window Varya watched Robert with narrowed eyes as he paced the length of her cell. His words were supposed to frighten her. Instead, they gave her hope. Miles was worried about her; that meant he would be looking for her. Robert was certainly mad, but he was no match for Miles.

She had gone numb with shock when Robert caught her at the bottom of the stairs that morning. She hadn't even struggled when he dragged her back up to her prison.

"By the way, that was quite a fight you put up this

morning," he remarked. "I'm not surprised. Miles always did like plucky women." He ran a finger down the sleeve of her gown. "I do like this dress."

She said nothing, but stared up at him with wary distaste.

"Bella put up a good struggle too." He sighed dramatically. "But we all know where that got her, don't we?"

Icy anguish ripped through Varya's soul. Darkness swam before her eyes, bringing with it the horrible vision of Bella's lifeless body. Clenching her hands into tight fists, she stared at the toes of her slippers. Let the bastard gloat; she would not give him the satisfaction of seeing her react.

"For years I've wanted to make Miles pay for Charlotte's death. I killed his women, hoping that he truly cared for at least one of them, but he didn't. He didn't even care about Charlotte." His face darkened. "I loved her, you know. I still mourn for her, but your *husband* cared more about that dead brat then he did for Charlotte."

Varya watched his boots cross the worn carpet. Even when they stopped directly before her she did not lift her head. She would not argue with him. What good would it do to tell him that Miles blamed himself for Charlotte's death?

"But he cares now." His fingers bit into the flesh of her jaw and cheek, pinching her face and forcing her to meet his triumphant gaze. He forced her head back until it felt as though her neck might snap. "Congratulations, Varya. You're the first woman Miles has ever loved."

She jerked her head against his grip, gazing at him angrily. "Miles Christian is incapable of love. He's the first to admit it." God, but it hurt to say it out loud.

Robert chuckled and released his hold on her face. Straightening, he stared at her with a mixture of pity and amusement in his gaze. "You truly believe that, don't you?" He shook his head. "He loves you, Varya. Nothing—not even his honor—could have made him marry you if he didn't. I wish I could tell you that it doesn't have to be this way, but it does. I have to kill you."

"You're insane," she growled, not caring what his reaction might be.

Again he chuckled, but this time his laughter was bitter and harsh. "I wish that were true." He took a step backward. "Perhaps then I wouldn't feel any remorse for what I've done. I took no pleasure in killing those women. My one and only thought has always been making Miles feel the same pain he inflicted on me when he took Charlotte from me forever." He pressed the heel of his palm to his forehead and rubbed.

"Killing me won't bring her back."

He smiled sadly. "I know that, Varya, but it will avenge Charlotte."

"Miles will kill you," she taunted him with more bravado than she felt.

Nodding, Robert's smile faded. "And then maybe I'll finally be with her." He turned toward the door.

Like a statue, Varya sat frozen in her chair as he left the room. As the key turned in the lock, she slowly pushed herself to her feet. She held tight to the back of the chair, willing her trembling legs to support her.

Hysteria hovered at the edges of her mind, threatening to destroy her sanity. She closed her eyes and inhaled deeply, willing herself to be calm with every breath.

As her head cleared, her fingers groped inside the sleeve of her dress for the object she had hidden there earlier. She had grabbed it while cleaning up the broken remains of her breakfast.

The knife was cold and hard against her hand as she pulled it from the sleeve. Her fingers tightened around it, turning her knuckles white with the force of her grip.

With purpose and determination, she moved toward the window, flinging back the drapes and opening the sash like a madwoman.

She had already made some progress. She attacked the rotting wood at the base of the bar with renewed vigor, stabbing at it with the knife.

Her other hand wriggled the bar, wrenching and pulling at it until her shoulder ached. Her right hand burned from wielding the knife; her knuckles were stiff and begged for mercy, but she thrust and thrust again.

The bar came loose with a loud grating sound. Varya staggered backward from the force of its release.

Shoving the bent and battered bread knife under her pillow, Varya weighed the bar in her palm. It was solid and heavy, as big around as two of her fingers and as long as her forearm.

She glanced toward the window. The opening wasn't nearly big enough for her to crawl through, but the bar . . .

The bar would do nicely.

When Robert returned that night, she would be ready.

Robert was back.

Slipping her weapon from under her pillow, Varya weighed it in her palm. There was no question in her mind that she could use it. The question was, would it be enough? Would she be able to incapacitate Robert enough to escape?

Muffled voices drifted up from the front hall. The sound of footsteps on the stairs sent her heart pounding against her ribs.

Please God, she prayed, hiding the bar behind her back. *Give me the strength to fight him.*

The key clicked in the lock and the door swung open. Robert walked in, his expression solemn. He shut the door behind him.

The silence was maddening. He stared at her as though he blamed her for his determination to kill her. There was no madness in his gaze, just apologetic sorrow. Varya had never hated anyone as she hated him at that moment.

"Have you come to kill me?" she asked, her voice flat.

He nodded and drew a vial from inside his coat. "Drink this. It will be over with quickly."

Varya laughed. Hysterical. Brittle. She actually found the situation strangely amusing.

"No."

Robert seemed surprised. "No?"

A bitter smile curved her lips. "I'm not going to help

you do this, Robert. If you want me dead, you're going to have to do it yourself—as you did with Bella." The memory of her friend renewed Varya's rage. She cupped her hand around the end of the metal bar, drawing strength from its solid circumference.

Sighing, Robert tucked the vial back into his pocket. "I didn't want to have to do it that way, Varya."

"What you want doesn't interest me. I will not make my death easy for you."

He moved toward her. Varya tensed, bracing herself for his attack. "I had hoped that the man I sent to kill you would have been able to do the job for me. I don't enjoy killing."

Varya did not reply.

His fingers closed around her throat. His dark gaze was moist as it met hers. "I wish this could be different," he murmured.

"No you don't," she rasped as the pressure increased. Her gaze locked with his.

He squeezed.

She clawed at him with her free hand but he was a man possessed. Even as her nails drew blood, he did not relent.

Gasping for breath, her back pressed against the window ledge, Varya lifted her hand that held the bar from behind her back.

And swung.

It connected with the side of his skull with a sickening *crack*. With a moan, Robert fell to the floor, clutching his head.

Varya ran. For the second time in her life she was running from a man who would see her dead.

The door crashed open just as she reached for it. She jerked back in time to avoid being flung against the wall.

The short guard raced in. Aiming for his bandaged nose, Varya struck him with the bar. His screams of anguish followed her as she raced down the stairs.

Only the housekeeper stood between Varya and freedom. Varya didn't want to hurt her again, but she would.

"Varya!"

It was Robert. The rage in his voice reverberated throughout the house. Varya's knees locked in fear, causing her to stumble and almost fall.

The housekeeper met her gaze with a look that Varya couldn't read. If she saw the desperation and fear in Varya's face, the older woman didn't show it. She simply moved to stand in front of the door.

And opened it.

With a sob Varya flew past the housekeeper, stumbling into the night air. She ran down the steps.

And was caught in an iron grip. She raised her weapon, flailing against the relentless hold, screaming at him in a mixture of Russian and broken English.

He ripped the bar from her hand. Sobbing in frustration, Varya refused to give up easily. She kicked wildly at his shins, her fists pounded the solid width of his shoulders.

"Varya. It's me!"

Miles? Dimly she became aware that the arms holding her weren't threatening or hurtful, but gentle and strong. She raised her gaze to the man's face and saw the eyes of her husband brimming with tears.

"Thank God I found you!" he cried before crushing her mouth beneath his.

Varya clung to him, elation soaring through her veins. Miles had found her. She was safe! Pressing herself against him, she returned his kiss with all the love and relief she had. Behind her she heard the subtle click of a pistol being cocked. She felt Miles stiffen. He broke their kiss.

"A touching reunion," Robert snarled from the steps. "Miles, you've arrived just in time to watch your wife die." Half of his face glistened with blood, lending a gruesome cast to the sneer on his face.

"You won't get away with this, Robert," Miles warned.

"You don't understand, Miles. I don't care as long as I know you've felt the same pain I've lived with these five years. Kill me and I'm with Charlotte, but you'll spend the rest of your life with Varya's death on your conscience." He raised the pistol and squeezed the trigger.

Varya was tossed to the ground as a second shot rang out from over Miles's shoulder. Her head struck the cobblestones, stunning her, but she remained awake. An eerie silence had descended over the courtyard.

Groggily, she struggled to lift herself up. Staggering to a standing position, she spotted Robert slumped on the steps, clutching his right arm against his chest. His sleeve was dark with blood.

A hand clutched her arm. "Varya, are you all right?"

She turned. "Carny? What happened?"

"Never mind that right now." He pulled her toward

the carriage. The coachman regarded them with a mixture of terror and confusion. "Come, we have to get you and Miles home."

"Miles?" she cried as he shoved her inside the vehicle. "What's wrong with Miles?"

As she turned, she saw Miles lying on the cobblestones. Carny knelt over him, pressing his hand against the left side of her husband's chest.

Miles had been shot.

"You must eat something."

Varya glanced up at her father's concerned face. "I'm fine, Papa."

"You are not fine, Varenka. You have not eaten since the Englishman brought you and your . . . *husband* . . . home." Vladimir was making an effort to like his son-in-law now that he had been shot saving his daughter. Apparently, his heroic deed had proven Miles worthy.

Varya smiled, turned away from the window through which she had been staring at the moon for the last two hours, and accepted the plate he shoved under her nose.

Her father beamed at her. If he patted her on the head Varya wouldn't be surprised.

"That's a good girl," he praised as she nibbled on a hard-boiled egg.

There was a moment of comfortable silence between them—something Varya had never experienced with her father before.

"Do you love him?"

"Yes," she admitted, staring at the food on her plate. "I do."

His blue gaze bright and anxious, her father inched closer, so that she alone could hear his words. "Then you must tell him, Varenka. Do not lose him because of silly pride."

Tears burned the backs of Varya's eyes as she realized her father spoke not only of her marriage, but of their own relationship as well. Reaching over, she caught his large hand in her own and squeezed.

"I will tell him, Papa."

Vladimir nodded stiffly. "Good, because he loves you too."

And Varya didn't know if he referred to Miles or himself.

The door opened and all heads turned as Forsythe walked in.

"Your Highness," he said, addressing Varya. "His Lordship is asking for you."

Varya's heart turned over in her chest. She hadn't been allowed to see Miles while the surgeon removed the bullet, and the doctor had been unable to tell her when her husband might regain consciousness. It had been two days.

"Thank you, Forsythe."

The walk from the sitting room to Miles's bedchamber seemed to go on forever. With every step, Varya's limbs felt more awkward, her heart heavier. She both dreaded and longed to see him.

Announcing her arrival with a tentative knock, she stepped into the chamber.

And stopped.

Propped up against a mountain of pillows, his russet hair shaggier than usual, was her husband. Naked save for the blankets that covered his lower body, he looked more like a disheveled god than a mere mortal. The snowy white bandage around his upper chest and shoulder was a grim reminder of his mortality.

"I was hoping you would come," he said softly and held out his hand. "Come here."

Quickly, Varya went to his side. As she placed her hand in his, he gently tugged, urging her up onto the bed beside him.

"I thought I'd never see you again," he told her, gently massaging her fingers.

Varya bit the inside of her lip to keep the tears at bay. "So did I." She raised his hand to her lips, planting feathery kisses on each knuckle. "Miles, I am so sorry you were shot."

The corners of his mouth twitched. "So am I." His expression sobered. "I'm sorry for a lot of things, Varya. I'm sorry you had to go through this."

"Shhh." She pressed a finger to his lips; the stubble above his mouth was sharp and rough. "It's not your fault, and it doesn't matter now."

Miles arched a brow. "He's dead?"

"No. Carny has arranged for him to have a private cell at the . . ." She thought for a moment. "Bethlehem Hospital?"

"Bedlam." He nodded. "A good place for him. He'll not see Charlotte again for a good many years."

"That's why Carny arranged it. He said life in prison knowing you had won would be Robert's best punishment."

"He was right." His expression softened. "I don't know what I would have done if I had lost you."

Tears filled her eyes. "I would have thought you'd be glad to be rid of me."

"Don't ever say that!" he cried, wincing as his shoulder lifted off the pillow. His eyes shut, his face twisted with pain as he eased himself back down.

"I'm sorry! Please, Miles, I'm sorry. Lie still." Releasing his hand, she adjusted the cushions so that he would be more comfortable. She smoothed the hair back from his face, running her fingers along his brow and eyelids until the agony in his features disappeared.

His lashes fluttered open. "I have something I want to tell you."

Her breath caught in her throat. "What?"

He stumbled over a string of broken Russian.

Varya stared at him, a bubble of laughter threatening to burst from her lips. "I beg your pardon?"

Miles's brow furrowed. "My heart without you was empty."

She couldn't help it—a bark of raucous laughter tore from her throat.

"Stop that!" He poked her thigh with his index finger. "I was trying to tell you how I feel about you!"

"You said . . ." A deep belly laugh sent tears streaming down her face. "You said that your *stomach* was empty without me!"

The bed shook with her mirth. Miles chuckled with her. He waited until the shaking stopped and she wiped her eyes with the hem of her gown before attempting to speak.

"What should I have said?"

She sniffed and smiled at him. His eyes glistened like slivers of gold. The love she saw there nearly took her breath away. She whispered the correct phrase with all the love she felt in her heart.

He took her hand again, stroking the sensitive flesh of her palm with his fingertips. His eyes darkened, the amusement fading as something warmer ignited in their depths.

"Say it again," he urged, his voice thick and husky.

She did.

He brought her palm to his lips, tracing the delicate lines with the tip of his tongue. She shivered beneath his touch.

"My *life* was empty without you." He pulled her closer. "*I* am empty without you." He gently hauled her toward him until their torsos were touching and their faces were mere inches apart.

Slightly dazed, Varya met his intense gaze. "I almost lost my mind when I saw you lying on the ground bleeding. I couldn't bear to live without you.'

"Show me."

She arched a brow. "How?"

"Take off your gown." He pulled on her sleeve. "Make love to me."

"Miles! Your shoulder!"

"Is of no consequence, madam." His hand traveled up her arm.

"Not even five minutes ago you almost screamed in agony when you moved too quickly. Now I'm to believe you're fine?" She shook her head in amused disbelief.

He brushed his fingers along the curve of her breast. "I want you on top of me. I want to make *you* scream. Here. Now. In this bed. I want you to show me how much you love me." His hand came up to cup her heated cheek. "I want to show my love to you."

His words sent a flood of sensual warmth through her body. Her nipples tightened in anticipation of his touch. A warm tingling stirred between her legs. Emboldened, she slid off the bed, her fingers reaching around to struggle with the buttons of her gown.

"I'll be eighty before you get that damned thing off," he growled with mock gruffness. "Get me some scissors."

Giggling, Varya lifted her skirt and began wiggling the muslin up over her shoulders and head. The neckline snagged her hair, yanking it free of its pins. By the time she tossed the gown across the room, several colorful Russian curses had escaped her lips, and her hair hung down her back in a tangled mass.

"Shall I continue?" Giving him what she hoped was a seductive glance, she ran the flat of her hands down the front of her chemise. Her hardened nipples pushed at the thin lawn.

"Leave it. I like it." Careful not to disturb his injured arm, he tossed back the blankets, revealing his naked limbs and hard erection.

Eagerly, Varya climbed back onto the bed. She wanted him with an intensity that seemed to grow stronger every time she was with him.

She straddled his hips and reached down to guide him into her. She was already wet and ready for him, and she slid down his shaft with a deep moan of pleasure.

Neither of them lasted for long. Finding a rhythm

that teased and stimulated, Varya tried to go slow and prolong their pleasure and not disturb his shoulder, but the sharp stabs of ecstasy were more than she could bear. Gripping the bed hangings above her husband's head, she lifted and plunged her body onto his until a shattering climax shook them both.

Afterward, lying in the crook of his good arm, her palm against his chest, feeling the steady beat of his heart, Varya looked up to find him watching her.

"Did I hurt you?" she asked. It had been a powerful feeling, knowing she was in control of their lovemaking, that she gave him pleasure.

"I'll live," he replied. "I'll take some laudanum in a few minutes."

She shook her head at him. "I'd like to say I'm sorry, but I'm afraid I enjoyed it too much."

A smile curved his lips as he nuzzled her hair. "I always want it to be like this with us," he murmured.

She grinned. "Sticky?"

Chuckling, he hugged her closer. "I want us to be as honest with each other as our bodies are."

"No more lies. No more secrets—for either of us." She kissed his cheek. "I like that."

"Me too." Wrapping a lock of her hair around his finger, he smiled. "Can you be honest with me now?"

Varya leaned up on her elbow and met his sparkling gaze with an earnest one. "Of course."

"Do you regret our marriage? You were once very opposed to the institution."

"I could never regret marrying the man I love. Never."

His eyes warmed like molten pools at her words. "And to think they used to call you elusive," he teased.

Smiling, Varya lowered her head to his.

"That was before you took my heart," she whispered, before silencing his mouth with her own.

Epilogue

The screams were driving him crazy.

"I can't take any more of this!" Miles raked a hand through his hair. "What are they doing to her up there?"

"I believe they are trying to bring your child into the world," Carny reminded him calmly as he lit a cigar.

The dowager marchioness shot him a reproving look before turning to her son.

"Everything is fine, dear. There's nothing to be worried about. These things take some time."

"Time! It's been twelve hours!" It took only six to kill Charlotte. "I'm going up."

"Miles, no!" his mother cried, but he was already out of the room and halfway up the stairs. She couldn't have stopped him anyway.

Miles paused, out of breath and terrified, at the door to Varya's chamber. He didn't know if he could face what was waiting for him inside.

It's your fault this is happening. If you had used protection . . .

There was no use running through the list of "what ifs" again. He had made love to his wife several times without precautions—Varya had sworn it was the wrong time in her cycle to conceive—and now, even though he knew his fears were unreasonable, he was scared he might very well be responsible for her death. After all his promises not to let anything happen to her, he owed it to her to be with her now.

He turned the knob and walked in.

"Lord Wynter!" the midwife gasped in horror. "You shouldn't be in here!"

Miles ignored the woman. He ignored the shocking amount of blood between his wife's thighs. He walked straight to the top of the bed and fell to his knees on the floor. He braced his forearms on the mattress beside Varya's head. She smiled weakly, her face and hair damp with perspiration.

"Hello," she murmured.

"What can I do?" he asked, ashamed of the tears that pricked the back of his eyes.

"Hold my hand." She held out her right arm. "It's almost over."

Almost over! A hot tear slipped down his cheek as he clutched her limp fingers. "Please don't leave me, Varya," he whispered hoarsely. "I couldn't bear to lose you."

Her smile faded as a strange expression fell across her face. Oh God, she was dying and there was nothing he could do!

"Miles, do you trust me?"

"What a ridic—of course I do!" To think at one time he wouldn't have been able to say that.

"Then just hold my hand and don't let go, no matter what."

He did, but instead of her grip growing weaker as he feared, her fingers tightened and clutched at his until they became like a band of iron around his own. Awed by the strength she exhibited, he stared at their clasped hands. Her grip was surprisingly painful.

He looked up at her face. Her jaw was taut, her lips pulled back from her teeth as she strained and pushed. Below them, he could hear the midwife's encouraging voice.

"That's it, my lady, almost done now."

A wave of excitement rolled over Miles. He forgot his fear as he leaned on the mattress and wiped the sweat from Varya's brow with his free hand.

"I trust you, Varya. I trust you," he murmured against her ear. "I love you."

And then suddenly her back arched a bit and her fingers bit into his with enough strength surely to break them. Her mouth opened and out came a keening wail—and then she fell limp.

Miles froze. "No. God, no."

Then he heard it—the lusty wail of an angry child.

"Alive," he whispered, numb with relief.

His head snapped around as the midwife plopped a

small, cloth-wrapped bundle into the crook of his free arm. "Congratulations, my lord," the old woman said. "You've a son."

A son.

Miles found it hard to tear his gaze away from the tiny red-faced infant nestled against his chest. The tiny arms with their tiny little hands waving in the air were the most amazing things he had ever seen.

"I suppose you're going to take all the credit for how perfect he is."

Miles's heart flipped over in his chest as he looked up to see his wife smiling happily at him.

"If he's perfect, it will be all because of his mama," he told her thickly.

She flushed with pleasure. "Flatterer. What shall we name him?"

Miles glanced at his son. "I'd like to name him Edward, after my father."

"Of course. Edward Vladimir Mancini Christian."

His head jerked up. "*Vladimir*? Do we have— Mancini?"

Varya nodded, lifting her proud gaze from her son to her husband.

"For Bella," she replied. "If it hadn't been for her, we never would have met."

Stroking her damp hair, Miles smiled, a multitude of emotions coursing through him.

"And I would never have known such perfect happiness existed."

Raising a brow, Varya's expression was one of weary amusement. "It hasn't always been perfect, Miles."

Casting a loving glance at his now sleeping son, Miles lowered his head to his wife's.

"But it is now, love," he murmured against her lips. "It is now."

The very best in historical romance
By the most talented authors . . .

Coming next month, two spectacular stories that will
make you believe in the timeless power of love . . .

***

THE MACKENZIES: ZACH
Ana Leigh

"One of the most exciting western
romance series of all time."
Romantic Times

He's a rugged undercover Texas ranger—and a MacKenzie
man. She's a beautiful Harvey Girl who thinks he's a dangerous
outlaw. Together, theirs is a love that defies all rules.

••

THE WARRIOR'S DAMSEL
Denise Hampton

A spectacular new series by a dynamic new author . . .

Sir Rafe Godsol, courageous warrior knight, selects as his
bride the most beautiful—and unattainable—woman he's
ever known, Lady Katherine de Fraisney. She's the daughter
of his most hated foe, but theirs is a love that can overcome
all obstacles . . .

"A wonderfully talented writer!"
Rexanne Becnel

"Enchanting, vivid . . . exciting"
Susan Wiggs

America Loves Lindsey!
The Timeless Romances
of #1 Bestselling Author